Great Things,
A Novel

K. Adrian Zonneville

ACKNOWLEDGMENTS

To those who inspire, who truly give of themselves. To those who take the stage and share their gifts, poetry and compositions. To those who labor over the word, the phrase, the note that remains long after the evening has ended. To those who fill the world, our hearts, our souls, our lives.

To Charley Bowman-Editor

Nancy Mumford-Front Cover Photo

Tom Misuraca-Ghost Designer

Steve Szabo-Back Cover Photo

Charlie Wiener-Cover Concept and Design

CHAPTER ONE

His footsteps crunched through the hard, crusty snow. Twilight filled the empty countryside and he knew it would soon be bitter cold. But that was life. There was nothing he could do about the conditions. There was nothing he could do to change his circumstances.

He should be pissed, he usually would be, but instead he was just tired. Dog tired. Maybe dead tired. Who could he be pissed at? The car? The weather? The death of his ride? Or the guy who made the decisions? Yeah, him. Dumb bastard.

He took one more look over his shoulder, at the blinking yellow hazards dimming in the distance, like the eyes of a dying animal. He knew how it felt. In short order it would be him if he didn't find someplace warm. He tried to zip up his heavy leather jacket, but it was to the bottom of his throat as it was. His black knit cap pulled down as low as it would go. There would be no more warmth.

He shifted the weight on his back. An old, worn army backpack he picked up in a second-hand store in, shit, where had that been, Cheyenne? Winnipeg? Boston? Yeah, maybe it was Boston, '88. He played that beer joint for tips and drinks. That'd been a good night.

The night hadn't started off that way. Most of them didn't. Some shaggy hippie asking if he could set up and play some tunes. Bartender stares. Drunks laugh. But what the hell, buddy, why not? If you don't suck, we'll get you a beer, OK? Yeah, that was OK.

He always started off with a couple tunes he'd written, just to warm up the fingers and get comfortable. Get the blood flowing to weary vocal cords on a cold, tired night. They'd heckled and laughed, thrown a couple quarters to see if they could get them through the sound hole in the old nicked up guitar. He was a carnival game for them. He didn't care anymore. He just needed enough to grab a sandwich and maybe a flop.

Not that night. He threw in some tunes he knew they'd like. Old Irish tunes and some hillbilly. Yeah, they liked hillbilly in Boston. Hell, they liked hillbilly damn near anywhere. A couple oldies and finish off with a bunch of shit he'd written, and he'd made a couple hundred. Yeah, it'd been a good night, clean sheets and a breakfast.

Now here he was, stuck between nowhere and nothing, about to freeze to death. He cursed his love of back roads, especially mountain back roads. Stick to the main routes, he'd told himself a thousand times. If you break down, there's traffic. Someone will give you a ride. Not here. Desolation wasn't convenient. Desolation would kill him.

The wind gusted and died, pushing the bulky guitar case in his right hand while he tried to control the computer bag hanging from his left shoulder. Bitter hadn't waited. Apparently, it had things to do and so arrived on the express train. He had paired down to as few possessions as he could. He kept his life, that was it, and these three bags represented everything in his life. His music, his writing and his clothes. And he was rapidly coming to the decision that a dead man didn't need clothes.

If it wasn't for the raw wind coming out of the northwest it would've been a beautiful night. Clear, crisp sky. Stars that, literally, went on forever. Just a sliver of moon so as not to interfere with the view. A few wispy clouds showed he would not be buried in any hard, driving snowstorm. That was little comfort.

Crunch. Crunch. Crunch. Crunch. Like the slow ticking of the clock of doom. Each step, each breath drained another ounce of life. A gust of wind whipped and twisted his guitar, banging it against his bad leg. He swore under his breath, quiet so as not to tempt God.

He almost laughed, almost, not wanting to allow any precious warmth to leave his body. A God he'd once actually believed in. In fact, had been shoved down his pre-pubescent throat until he thought he would choke on Him. He thought about praying to this entity he did not believe in, then chuckled, no, that would be the epitome of hypocrisy. No thanks. He would die honest, without a lie upon his lips.

Now, he tried to save every ounce of warmth. He pulled his coat tight around his neck to protect his vocal cords. He needed his voice, though he might survive without it. What was the use? A singer without a voice is a man without a need for breath.

He scanned the horizon seeking any insignificant glow that might indicate a town or a farm, or his death. Come into the light. Yeah, right now he was just tired enough to do so. Crunch. Crunch. Crunch. Crunch. His leg hurt, the right one, the one they broke in the brawl down in Baltimore.

How many years ago? Twenty? Twenty-five? It had never healed right because he didn't have the money to have it heal right. It cost bucks to have a Doc set it and put a cast on. He had that girl—what the hell was her name? Betty? Susan? Yeah, whatever. It didn't matter now, did it? — she was small, petite, they call it, but strong like a gymnast and had yanked on his leg—the pain so intense he'd thought he would pass out—until it looked straight enough and they'd wrapped it tight with strips of torn up sheets and broken pool cue. It'd held, long enough to heal. Not perfect but he could walk—with a slight limp, of course—but he got around just fine. Didn't need a cane, though there were times he thought it might've added to his roguish image if he'd used one.

But that had been when he was younger and cared about his image. The bad boy. The one they couldn't tie down. The hard and wizened troubadour, rakish and rough. He'd love and then be on his way to the next town, the next broken heart. It helped get the girls. They thought they could be the one. That one woman who tamed him and made him settle down. Let them think what they would. If girls came to your shows, the boys would follow. If girls dug what you did, the boys would buy your CD's and tapes to try and figure it out. Stupid. But whatever kept the wolf from his belly and clean sheets under his worn-out body was just fine in his book.

Well, the leg hurt now. The cold set up camp in the old break and settled in for the winter. It shot a twinge of pain up his thigh and into his brain with each frozen step. Why did he have such a love for back roads and small towns? He could ask that until he died—which looked more imminent with each step—and never find the answer.

He loved the cities. They were vibrant, filled with life and opportunities. Places to set up shop. Local bars and street corners, well, until the cops came asked about permits and handed out tickets like Cracker Jacks. What the fuck did you need a permit to play music for? Music brought life to the city, made people stop and listen, if just for a second. They would take a moment out of lives focused on money and non-essential spirit quests, to just bask in the notes and lyric. Was that such a horrible thing?

In the city, if times were sparse, he could find a place to park his van, either for free or for five or ten bucks for a night at a lot and hunker down for the eve. No one would bother him. Mostly because they couldn't see him sleeping in the back. In small towns the cops had nothing to do and were bored out of their minds. They'd fuck with you just out of pure nastiness and power tripping. Banging on the window of any vehicle with out-of-state tags just on the off chance you were camping.

Then things got tight, gas spiked and the van with its sixteen miles per got traded for a sedan. Back seat of a decent sedan might not be king sized comfort, but you could stretch out and cover yourself so as not to be too obvious. He missed the van. But that had been when the green was flowing a bit more regular. Those had been good days.

Crunch. Crunch. Crunch. Crunch, turn and look at the fading, dying eyes of the Buick, pull up his collar against the wind, pray to some forgotten god for a glimpse of life in the distance.

He had a small regional hit, nothing special, nothing that would end up on anybody's 'remember when' list. But it had got him in the stream of small halls and opening for some large festivals. Gigging some of the better clubs, not shot and beers. It'd been a whirlwind of music, women, drugs, parties and a marriage with a kid. Yeah, just a real good few years.

And then just as quick it went south. Some was him being unpredictable — booze and drugs combined with ego can do that to a career. Some was a change in culture. Some was the people who liked his stuff started getting old and dying. Some was just life.

Gigs dried up, well, the good ones, so the money got choked off, so the party train came to an end and his wife and kid got off up the line. He'd hardly noticed. He thought from time to time he should make an effort to find them, well, to find her—his daughter—but could never bring himself to do it. To face her. To look in her eyes. To have her tell him to go fuck himself, leave her alone. He was good at that, wasn't he?

So, he stayed away from the search.

He hadn't noticed the clouds closing in, lost in his recriminations, but the stars were gone, the moon was gone. His hope of lasting the night quickly waned. His energy was depleted, the cold sucking life from his aching bones. He had to find a place to hole up and get out of the wind and hope to make the morning light.

He pulled the ugly orange blanket that Irish chick had made him buy from the top of the knap. He hated it. Hated orange. Hated himself for allowing her to push and prod, to goad him into buying something so godawful ugly. It had been St. Patrick's '97 and they were in Savannah. Huge party, parade, crowds, liquor, and this Irish chick asked him if he was Irish. He said, yeah, yeah, he was he lied. "Well, then, why aren't ya wearing o' the green," she chided. Because he was protestant Irish, he lied again. "Then ya need something to proclaim it," she forced, and pointed at the bright orange blanket sitting in a store window.

He bought it just to shut her up. Half his last fifty bucks. Woke up in an alley with the ugly thing wrapped around him, a hangover that would kill a bull moose, two bucks hidden in his shoe, and no idea where the chick had gone. Ah well, the blanket was warm and probably would-n't leave him, so, he'd kept it all these years.

The pain is his leg was going away. Of course, it could just be that the leg was going numb with the cold. He might be limping again, he couldn't really tell, and he didn't care right now. He was numb from head to foot, inside and out, physically, mentally, spiritually. He pulled his stocking cap down again, as far as it would come. Pulled his collar up as far as it would pull and then wrapped the ugly blanket around and over him, prayed to anything that might be listening, that it would hold in enough heat to keep him alive.

He fell. His numb, bad leg gave out and folded under him. He hit his knee hard as the guitar and computer skidded off in different directions. He lay in the snow and thought about not getting up. Enough! He'd rolled the dice and they'd come up snake eyes. He was going to die. Alone. In the middle of the mountains. Him, a city boy dying in nature and no one would ever know or care.

Fuck that! He was not going to let fate or life or whatever have the last laugh. He got to his knees and crawled to collect his most precious belongings. Leaning on the hard-shell guitar case he rose. Damn, that leg hurt, but not as much as the thought of dying in such a pathetic, clichéd manner. Up, boy, up. Rise and be recognized as a man and walk, you sonofabitch, walk. Crunch. Crunch. Crunch. Crunch.

He was just so damn tired. He turned to look. The car was gone from sight. Just white greeted his eyes, a grayish white that comes from full snowfall after dark. If he hadn't been about to die from frostbite, cold and hunger, he might've thought it pretty. Ah, what the Hell, if he was dying, he should go out on a note of appreciation. He was, after all, supposed to be an artist.

And that was the rub, wasn't it? The curse he and a few others he had crossed paths with carried like a cross of iron. Artists. If he wasn't so sure he was going to need the fluid, he would've spat the word at the laughing universe. What good had that done him? Not much. A couple good years and some tours. He thought about walking away a thousand times, giving up the ghost on artistry. But you couldn't escape creativity. He'd tried.

He'd thought about turning his back on the music, the wandering, the lost soul bullshit. From satisfying the requisite starving artist stereotype. He'd had enough rejection, thank you very much. He'd lived on poverty long enough to satisfy any muse who could've or would've adopted him by now. If he was supposed to write, to play, to live this way, shouldn't some musical sprite have come along and dusted him with pixie powder and allowed him some recognition? Some success? Something more than a few years opening for more successful people? Something to hang his career on? Nope.

He would find a job that had regular paychecks, and benefits. Vacation, paid vacation, for just forty hours of misery every week. Shut down the mind, turn off the imagination, shut down the artist and live in one place. With working heat and electric. Become a regular Joe. Go to the same bars and hang out with the same folks. Get to know their lives, their wives and kids. Go to ballgames and barbecues, fish fry every Friday night down at the lodge. Maybe get married again and have a couple kids he'd actually stay with and raise. Drive a car with less than two hundred thousand miles on it and with no rips in the interior; maybe it wouldn't even leak oil. Or break down in the middle of fucking nowhere on the coldest night of the millennium. He could die in a nice soft, warm bed, surrounded by family and friends. Not out here, surrounded by wishes and lost hope, just to become a frozen dinner for some wild animals. Shit.

Well, aren't we Mr. Positive, Mr. Happy, Mr. Depression? Yeah, he'd even tried that Normalville route years ago, for a very short period of time, and it damn near drove him insane. The songs kept coming. He couldn't keep them at bay. He'd be at work, at a dinner party, a bar, alone, and they would creep into his brain. He'd be humming something no one had ever heard before because he needed to write it. But he'd push it down, push it away. He wouldn't write it. He'd ignore the damn thing.

But it wouldn't be ignored. And the next thing you knew when he wasn't working, he was jotting down lyrics and chords, staring off into the face of the pretty little Muse, promising him another chance, another round at the star bar. And soon, he would be looking for another job to hate, surrounded by people who were nothing like him and couldn't understand why he just couldn't put childish things away. Because he'd have to cut them out of his soul, that's why. He'd have to dissect what he was and surgically remove anything worthwhile. He'd rather die.

The laugh was loud, hard, filled with sorrow and brought him to his knees. Be careful what you wish for, boy. And he was done. The last of his energy, his life force, drained into the freezing, deep snow. He sat hard and wrapped the blanket around his guitar and computer, around his knapsack and himself and prepared to die.

It wouldn't be so bad. He could just close his eyes and let go. No one would know. No one would miss him. 'Hey, whatever happened to that guy, you know, the singer guy, used to come around every so often. I kind of liked him.' He leaned against the signpost, he thought it was a signpost. Did it matter? He got comfortable in his ugly orange tent and closed his eyes. He drifted. It really wasn't that bad. It didn't hurt. Death enfolded him in its loving arms. He leaned into that death; the Reaper cuddled him to its breast.

He heard others talk, call to him. He saw a dim light and knew the way to go. He could feel the arms of lost loved ones embrace him, telling him it was going to be alright. Just come with them. All the suffering would be taken away and he would be filled with love and warm foods. It was going to be alright, just let go. Just let go.

He floated in and out of a dream state. He could see his mother and father calling to him but could not hear their voices. Others from his past walked by where he stood, rooted to the ground, unable to join them.

He called back but his voice was just as silent as theirs. Old acquaintances from school, not really friends, he hadn't had friends, just folks he did drugs with or hung out with, slept with, skipped school with. But he knew them, and they should recognize him. So many, so many here, in the afterlife.

Wait, he didn't believe in any afterlife, did he? He had never ascribed to any religion, hated most of them. Why would he be in their idea of death? Shouldn't he be floating in the vacuum of nothing? In the cosmos? Part of the energy that makes up all things? He didn't believe any of this claptrap, why was he here?

How could he have been so wrong? He was shocked and astounded. Number one, if all the religious zealots had been so right, shouldn't he be in Hell? He had demeaned them, mocked them. He had railed against God and all concepts of Heaven; Christian, Muslim, Jewish, Hindu, Buddhist, Confucianism, Moonies, you name it. He had not believed with the fervor of an evangelist. And yet, here he was.

His soul basking in the warmth of somebody's pious concept of Heaven. Oh shit, he had to be in trouble with some kind of deity. He just had no idea which one. And he couldn't bring himself to care. His Earthly trials were over. He no longer would have a care about finances or love, new songs and uncomfortable back seats, being a target for the stupid and uncleansed. He was free of earthly sorrows and pain.

Well almost. Because something in his leg was killing him. And his hands were on fire. He ached from head to toe as if someone had wielded a baseball bat in an attempt to get his attention. The pounding on the inside of his skull convinced him that whoever or whatever was making a break for it would soon be free. Death was supposed to be without suffering. He was in the wrong death.

And then it was gone again and so was consciousness. All was black and empty. He was well and finally dead. He heard his mother call to him. She screamed, "I told you so, but you wouldn't listen, would you? Mister, 'I know better than all you religious bigots.' Well, what do you have to say for yourself now?"

Oh, dear God in Heaven, was this to be his eternity? Brow beat by his fanatical mother. Maybe this was Hell after all. The pain had returned with a vengeance to his old barroom injury and he thought if he had a knife, he would've cut his leg clean off. His head ached, and his fingers burned on his right hand. The hand that had held onto the guitar. He had grasped it with a death grip, pun intended, while he walked. He would not give it up. Someone would have to cut his fingers off to get that old Gibson. Maybe they had.

So, that was Hell. Momma's bitching and no fingers to satisfy the itching. Even in death he wanted to play, to sing, to write one more song. He always said he wanted to write his greatest song as he died. Ah well, another shut out on dreams not realized. It was going to be a long eternity.

This time he felt the cool on his brow and running through his veins. Did you still have working veins and arteries and such after you were dead? The black enveloped him once again. Where was god in all of this, his mind wandered off, thinking to itself. He once again lost the afterlife.

Voices surrounded him, pushed down on the fight to cognizance. He had no idea if this was how it worked in the afterlife, but it was extremely inefficient. The deceased could never seem to get their feet firmly placed on the Heavenly soil before it was pulled out from under them again. Somehow it felt wrong for those in charge of bringing the dead across the River Styx to mess with a newly dead soul this way. Jeez, let a guy get his bearings!

Whatever happened to RIP? Where was the peace? It was bad enough his leg was being pounded by a nine-pound sledge and each stroke shot excruciating pain spiking through his brain. This was surely not the happy, bliss filled, angel singing, cherubs flying, joyous afterlife he'd had dangled in front of his sinning face for a lifetime. At least it was warm. You had to count your blessings, even in Heaven.

The pain was gone. Maybe God had amputated the damn leg. Whoops, should he say damned here? And where was here? He still didn't know if it was Heaven or Hell, purgatory or a train station in limbo. Shouldn't there be a welcoming committee? Somebody to direct him hither and yon? An angel, a demon, a Walmart greeter, a front desk clerk or a cop on the street? He was hanging here with no clue as to where he would spend eternity.

The voices returned. His mother told his dad that he was not getting any better. No shit, woman! He was dead! You didn't get better from dead. Yet, she sounded so concerned, as if she expected him to. Why would she think he was going to get better from the hereafter?

And yet…What the hell was that screeching, pinging noise? OK, he was in Hell, that was now a given. The high-pitched squalor assaulted every nerve. Nails on a chalkboard, an ice pick to both ears and meeting in the middle of his abused brain. What kind of place was this?

He would've been fine until the shock, like a million volts of electricity though his body. Like the time he'd opened that festival in England and the rain came just as his lips touched the mic and his hands grabbed the neck of the guitar completing a very disturbing electrical circuit. He'd thought he was going to die that day. Now, he was dead and still could feel the pain.

It stopped. Followed quickly by another jolt and then a pounding where his heart used to be. This was just getting better by leaps and bounds. And no peace. If he had known death was going to be this traumatic, he would have kept on living.

He believed he finally had been moved to Heaven. A light that burned through his eyelids bright enough to pierce his eyes straight through to his brain lay testament to that fact. Divine illumination flooded the landscape. He could feel the warmth, the blinding love, the healing bliss, filling him, his soul basked in the holy...he jerked awake. Not in Heaven or Hell or wherever the next incarnation might have him, but in a softly lit, comfortably attired, homey, hospital room. If your ninety-year-old grandmother ran a hospital from her home, that was where he lay. Well, that was a different perspective of life after death.

A gentle insistent beep reassured from somewhere to his right. Breath flowed in to and out of lungs, lungs that were very much of this world; not the next. He was awake. Awake. Not dead, not floating across the river, taking that last train, meeting with the family in the great beyond. He was still here, wherever here might be, and, most important, apparently still very much alive. Though weak as a kitten, every joint ached and he had a hard time focusing, but alive.

The swish of a door being carefully opened and closed caught at his attention. With all the effort he could summon he turned his head slightly to the left and watched the blurred, grey figure tiptoe, gently across the room to check the machines that surrounded his bed and make note on her –yes, it was a she—handheld pad. They didn't have technology in the hereafter, did they?

He tried to speak. Nothing. Not even a croak or a heavy sigh. His throat was parched, probably that big frigging tube shoved down there. He hadn't noticed that. Maybe he could raise a hand and get her attention. Nothing. What the hell was going on? He couldn't talk, make a sound, couldn't move a muscle, lift a finger, twitch a toe. Nothing. The light from her small flashlight flared in his right eye. His left shot open, startling the woman. She shrieked, stood straight up and scurried from the room. Well, that ought to get some attention, he thought.

Seconds later a doctor, he assumed, and the nurse were standing by his bedside. "Can you hear me?" asked the doctor. He tried but could not utter a sound or raise a finger to acknowledge.

"Blink your eyes, or an eye, if you can understand me," came the instruction from the doctor, now recognizing the problem. He concentrated with all his will, every ounce of energy he could summon, and blinked once. He was exhausted.

"Excellent," she whispered, "you just might live through this after all." She checked the machines for, who knew what. He didn't, and she seemed satisfied for now. "Rest. I'll be back to check on you in a little while," she gave his arm a squeeze, "just rest for now. Sleep."

The dreams came immediately, just as sleep overcame his tired and drained psyche.

He was back playing the open mic downtown Buffalo. What the hell was that place called? They had really good wings and cold beer. But what place didn't in Buffalo. He was third up and nervous as hell. He'd only been playing for a couple years and had just started writing his own songs. He knew they were immature love songs. Songs of hurt, infatuation, longing, betrayal, all the feelings and insecurities of being nineteen and in and out of love. But there were a few good turns of phrases and some interesting chord progressions; or so he thought when he wrote them. He was not so confident now that he had to play them in front of people he didn't know. He wanted to run. Tail between his legs, hide his head, throw his stupid guitar away, and keep running. But he couldn't. He'd told her he was going to do this, and she'd said she might show up. Though she hadn't, yet.

He drank the beer his fake I.D. had bought him. It would settle his nerves, stop the shaking in his hands. Why in all fuck was he doing this? His folks had told him how stupid this was. Stop screwing around with that guitar and concentrate on life. He would be an adult soon. It was time to act like one. The shop where his dad worked was hiring. He could get a job, with benefits, and be set for life. Why did he always have to take the hard road? Why couldn't he be like everyone else?

That was the question for the ages, wasn't it? Because he wasn't like everyone else. He didn't think like them. He couldn't just hang out and smoke cigarettes, drink beer, watch the game, try to get laid and not care about the rest of the world. He saw things different. He could feel what others felt when they hurt. When they were hungry. When they were down and at the end of it all. He couldn't just say 'fine' when asked how he was. He had to tell them how he was, and he wanted to know how they were too. He was a freak, an oddball. That kid.

And now he was about to get laughed off the stage by people he didn't even know. What the fuck was wrong with him? Indeed.

But they hadn't laughed. They'd critiqued, complimented, shared ideas. After the mic everyone, well, most everyone, players and audience alike, had stuck around for another beer and talked. They didn't just say what they liked or didn't, they knew why. The more seasoned pickers and writers could tell you why a line worked, what might work better. Find that word, that phrase. Switch that to a minor chord or hold the root just a beat longer. They got it, they understood. They listened, and they encouraged.

There wasn't good or bad, there was just a work in progress. Always in progress, art was never done, never a finished project. It stopped when you moved on to something else and whatever you had would have to do. Or you would only ever write one song, and then spend the rest of your life polishing it until it was worn down to nothing.

She hadn't shown up. He had been disappointed but only until he walked on the stage. They clapped, tentatively, but they'd clapped to encourage. They'd clapped with appreciation after his first song. Not because they felt sorry, not because they had to, but because they liked it. And they'd liked the next two as well. He was filled with joy. He forgot she hadn't come. And he would come back, over and over, and he would learn what they knew and work harder to earn their respect. He knew what he was supposed to do in life; he would never question it again.

He struggled, pulled at air and fog. The surface had to be up, right? Maybe if he just quit fighting and let go, he would float to freedom. He wasn't drowning but he wasn't breathing. He had to break free of this haze. He needed to think, to let his mind work, to…there it was. Sound. He could sense someone was in the room. Maybe he could get them to help him break free. He cracked his right eye open, mind over muscle. Now, how to get that to translate to a signal. How can you blink to get the attention of another in a semi-dark room? She padded over to the machines on his right. Well, that was good, she was on his good side. Wait, he thought, wait for it. She watched the numbers for several seconds before she turned her attention to him. Just before she flicked her pen light on, he blinked. He had been ready, and it caught her attention.

"Ah, so you're still with us," she whispered conspiratorially, "and awake and aware. Can you hear me?" She waited. He blinked. Once, twice. It was like lifting a three-hundred-pound weight with his head.

"Excellent," she smiled, "we'll try a couple simple questions first. Blink once for yes and twice for no. Do you understand?" He fought back the swirling dizziness threatening to pull him back under. Blink.

"Do you know where you are?" Easy, start off very easy.

Blink. Eternity. Blink.

"You are in a hospital," there was a slight hesitation on the word as if it were not exactly true, "about twenty miles from where you were found," she answered what she assumed would be his question. "They thought you were dead but brought you here anyway."

He had no idea who 'they' were, and he didn't care, 'they' had saved his life. He thought he should be grateful, but he was holding judgement on that for the time being.

Now for the harder question, "Do you know who you are?" She waited.

Blink. A day passes. Blink. Into night. Blink.

"Hmm," says she, rocking back on her heels and considering, "I am going to give you something to help you sleep. We'll talk tomorrow."

He watched her as she inserted the hypodermic needle into the IV line. He wanted to yell for her to stop. To tell her he needed to come out of this drug induced stupor. He opened his eyes as wide as he could, signaling now, with a left and right movement of eyes, but she failed to note. He tried to get her attention and raised his finger, maybe two. Or did he imagine it? He was exhausted from the effort and the drugs kick in. The darkness of space surrounded him.

They had shown up, not all of them, but enough. Those who weren't working or gigging. They had shown up to support him in the biggest gig of his life. Five thousand people, not to see or hear him, They had come to hear the headlining act. It didn't matter. He was going to open the show. He would play the songs he had been sculpting and honing for the past three months. And some would listen. If only ten percent heard him, that was five hundred. Maybe they would buy his record when it came out. Maybe they would come to the local tavern and listen to him play. Maybe they would pay attention to his music. And maybe pigs would shit gold bullion. But if you didn't believe it was possible, why bother to take the stage? To write the songs? To buy the damn guitar.

And his family was there to show support. Not his parents or siblings, no aunts, uncles, cousins, no, but his music family. Those who loved him and supported the dream. Those who rode the wave, sitting on his shoulders, living vicariously through this night. These were the people he cared about, not those who tried to squash his dreams. No! This was for those who shared them.

They would go out after the concert and either drink to celebrate or to commiserate. They would be there for him. He prayed they would celebrate.

The promoter met him as he walked off the stage to a nice round of applause. They weren't standing and cheering. There would be no encore. But they weren't booing, they were supporting and giving him some love. It was all he could ask for. When you're the opener, you do your job and hope to be invited back. The guy handed him a hundred bucks. He would be. They would celebrate. It would be a good night.

Soft rubber soles on linoleum floors. Swish, swish, squeak. Someone was back. He had to summon all the strength he had in reserve to stop this train. They would check his vitals, the machines, the numbers, then push the drug into the IV to stop him from functioning. It had to stop. He could sense her to his right, she was getting close. He dug in his mental heels and concentrated every ounce of will to his right hand. It moved, ever so slightly, but it moved. It hadn't been a hallucination; he was certain of it. As certain as a drugged up dead person could be. He had moved his hand, he just had to moved it more.

If he could push through the drug induced coma. That was it. He wasn't paralyzed. He wasn't helpless or disabled. They had him so drugged up he couldn't function. He couldn't make his muscles respond to anything he begged of them. He had to fight his way past the opiates. He had to be stronger than he'd ever been. She was asking him questions; he kept his eyes closed. No waste of energy. Consolidate everything into this one desperate move. She tired of no response. He could feel it in the air, the movement as she took the IV line in her hand. Now!

His hand flopped toward where she was pushing the drug into the vein. He missed contact. But she stopped. He didn't have to make physical contact. "So, you would like to get my attention," she leaned over his face. He could feel her breath soft on his skin.

He forced his eyes open and pushed the 'please' until it shone like a billboard across his pupils. Would she see it? Would she read the message? Would she understand? Would she care?

She leaned back, took a step away from him. He heard the scrape of a chair on hard floor. She settled down next to him, contemplating. He knew. It was as if he hovered just north of his body. He could 'see' everything. The look on her face. Her setting the needle on the tray and pushing the mobile table away from his bed. She understood. "No more drugs?" she asked.

Blink. Sigh.

"OK, we'll try it your way for a little while and see how life goes." She stood and patted him on the shoulder, "I'll be back in a few hours, I have to eat, and have other patients, but there will be a nurse on duty to check on you. If the nurse thinks you are in too much pain, she will have my order to give you this." Even though he couldn't see her he knew she held up the syringe. It wasn't a threat; it was reassurance they would not let him suffer unnecessarily.

He slipped back to the comfort of oblivion, drained from the exertion of the last ten minutes. He would sleep, but he would not be drugged, he could rest.

And hope.

CHAPTER TWO

Morning came slow. The swim to consciousness was less of an effort—more than waking, less than a brawl. He swore he could sense, if not fully feel, his extremities. He couldn't tell you where they were, but he could tell you they were there. Just as he couldn't tell you it was actual morning, just his morning.

He was waking. The nightmare remained but now he was aware it was nightmare not reality. He was pretty sure he took a breath that was his own, not the machine's. It didn't really matter the relief was real. Pain filled his old wounds and, apparently, some new ones. His shoulders ached. His head felt like mush packed tightly into burlap, and he still couldn't feel his fingers or toes. It was the fingers that worried him the most. You didn't need toes to play a major seventh chord. Silently he prayed to a god he didn't believe in for salvation he didn't deserve. He could live without his feet or legs, but he needed his arms, hands and vocal cords for life. Time — he threw the word carelessly around the inside of head. Time. That was all he would need; he had to believe. Time to heal. Time to come back to the land of the living. If he could've clapped his hands to save his own personal Tinker Bell, he would've given her a standing O.

Feet shuffled. The scent of a light, ocean scented cologne. The shift of air as a body busied itself around his prone frame. He was losing his mind. Human beings were not meant to be trapped in their own bodies. Blind, unable to move, imprisoned, it was torture and he would go insane if he couldn't rouse himself from this stupor.

She, he assumed by the scent, checked what needed to be checked, tucked and straightened sheets and bedding for optimal comfort and left, without going near the IV. That had to be a good sign, didn't it?

Maybe this is what the drugs held at bay. The claustrophobia, the constraint of his own body. The restrictions and limitations of the human form. It was a prison cell. A tiny, cramped, closed in box, filled with stale air and hopelessness. He couldn't breathe, couldn't fill his lungs, couldn't move a muscle, wrapped tight in his own insecurities and fears. He was lost. Maybe he needed the drugs to survive this hell. And maybe not.

Panic could be controlled. Even if he couldn't overcome the mechanical rhythm imposed by the breathing machine, he could control his response. What was required was acceptance, not his strong point. Don't try to change the rhythm. Don't attempt to slow it down. He couldn't. But he could allow himself to relinquish that control, so his body could flow comfortably on the groove. He could seek peace in the constant of the machine.

Breathing exercises had been a part of meditation. He'd been a practitioner for years. It was how he calmed his nerves before performing. It was an integral element of his rehab while kicking chemicals. He would use the technique now. No drugs. Breathe. Calm, regular as clockwork. The machine forced breaths in time with his heartbeat, in time with the music, in time with the universe. He would survive, heal and grow strong enough to rid himself of these infernal machines. He only needed one machine and he hoped they had not left it by the side of the road when they picked his carcass up. He would need the Gibson if he was to live.

Seek a place of joy within. Allow the breath, the rhythm, to take him somewhere calm. A place of peace.

He had been on tour for months and was tired, cranky, and wanted to be away from humanity, if only for a couple hours. The price of even modest fame is the loss of anonymity and privacy. People didn't necessarily know who he was, but they knew he was somebody. They'd seen him on TV or his picture in the paper or a display in the record shop; or he was a friend of their kid's. It didn't matter, they knew him from somewhere, therefore they could approach him any time. While he was eating, drinking, walking, talking to a friend, trying to pick up a girl, pissing, anytime. To talk. To ask for his signature on a piece of scrap paper they would throw out a week down the line, take a picture. It was thrilling and a goddamn nightmare of imposition all at the same moment. He wanted to go somewhere where no one would care.

He found the ancient music store in the ancient part of an ancient town on the east coast. He couldn't guarantee it, but he was quite certain the ancient man who looked up, as he walked into the store, was probably the original owner. He didn't say anything, no welcome, no, 'can I help you?' He looked up, took stock of the young man entering his store, and turned to the next page of the paper laying on the counter. The walls were not lined with gleaming, sparkling new guitars, as they would've been in a music store in any large city. A few old beaters here, a few more hanging from pegs, some carelessly leaning against the walls or over in a corner. They were old, they were very used, they had been neglected for a good portion of their lives. They were beautiful. He didn't ask, he guessed he really didn't have to. He found a stool under a dis-

carded box and set himself in the midst of this musical convalescent home.

Where to start? He pulled a Martin off the wall and began to tune as he eased back onto his perch. The tone was warm and mellow, the strings old and corroded, yet he could tell there was a lot of life left in this old girl. But the more he strummed and picked out chords the more he knew she was not for him. She just didn't feel right. Just didn't fit his hand, she wouldn't rest on his lap, moving and sliding as if wanting to be somewhere else.

The Guild didn't fit his build. His arms were too short for the large body of the instrument. He felt like he was reaching for every note. Too bad, it was beautiful, but she was not for him either.

He'd been through this ritual a thousand times before. He didn't expect to find anything here except a respite from life for an hour or two. He played guitars in music stores from coast to coast, small stores, super stores, even the chains. He liked his current flame, but he couldn't calm the niggling feeling that there was 'that guitar' somewhere out here that was perfect for him., He just had to find that needle, even if it took the rest of his life.

And that looked to be a long time from where he stood. He had only just turned thirty, he had modest success, a wife and a baby girl waiting for him at home. He would ride this wave for as long as he could stand it and then, yeah, right, and then what? He'd never really thought past the next show, the next town, the next song. What did he want? He wanted to find 'his' guitar. He laughed a chortle under the breath, tilting at windmills and guitar stores in search of the elusive instrument that would allow the magic to flow. The songs would pour forth, the Muse's laughter would tinkle like tiny bells in his ear and he would jot down what she stirred inside his brain. It would be joy and love all held to-gether by six strings.

He thanked the man standing behind the counter as he made his way towards the door. A grunt caused him to turn just as his hand grabbed the door handle. Behind the counter, behind the man, behind a box, the scratched, worn, chipped neck of an old guitar leaned against the counter. He asked the man to see it. Just some old beater, says he, a kid brought it in yesterday. Said it was his grandpa's, but the old man was dead, and the kid needed some cash. Not even any strings on it.

"Can I see it?" He insisted.

Somewhere under the layers of dirt, grime and dust was a deep sunburst finish. It would need a new pick guard, it was scratched and scored in a hundred places, and the finish worn off where someone had continued to play it hard without the plastic protection. It had been rid-den hard and put away soaked and without a rub down far too many times. It was beat up and needed more work than it would ever be worth. He loved it! "How much," he asked, refusing to let go this piece, this rel-ic of a far simpler time. Though he would wager, not a simpler nor easier life.

"Hundred bucks, I guess," finally looking up from his paper. "Whaddaya gonna do with it? Bust it up on the stage or something?"

"Or something." Of course, there was no case and the store did-n't have one that would fit it. Looked like he was going to have to go on another hunting expedition. He didn't mind. He'd clean this thing up, see what needed fixing, what could be repaired and what could not, then he'd decide if it got the case.

This was his peace. This was where he came to center himself. This guitar. Cleaning off decades of abuse. Disassembling, cleaning, oil-

ing and forcing the tuning machines back into operation. The neck was surprisingly straight, a minor adjustment to the truss rod. He'd have to replace most of the frets, as they'd been worn down by years of play. This guitar had seen some things, been some places and lived one Helluva life. The question was, would she tell him her secrets?

It had taken him almost two years to bring this wonderful gift back to life. Time was not something he had in spades and with touring he could only work on the instrument when he was home. Can't take pieces parts on the road and chance losing something that might be needed later on. But it was done. Time to see what she had to say. His memory smiled. He could hear the tone, the crisp, clean highs and mellow, balancing mids and lows. My God, this thing was just effortless. As if it had been designed a half century earlier for his hands. He played until time stopped and the music flowed. Gentle, whispering, rushing towards the rapids, pooling and swirling, eddying only to break free and ride the wild torrents, careening hundreds of feet into an endless lake. Energy emanated and wrapped him, shaking him and tossing him in the air like a toy. He couldn't stop himself, the guitar had him by the scruff of the neck and would squeeze him dry. Words sprang to life on the legal pad that lay on the table at his right hand. Chordings came he would never have attempted, but they worked, they fit like tailored clothes. Made just for him.

People hated them. They wanted the songs of puppy love he'd been known for, not these deep, explorative epics. Where were the silly sing-a-longs? The songs of drinking and loving? Where were the hits? He was forced from his peace. They wouldn't listen to the beauty he was creating. They hated it and his crowds diminished quickly. He would be out of the business by spring.

He would return to vapid, innocuous, mindless drivel they so desired. But the 'It' was gone. They had stolen his love and it would never return. He tried playing the things they liked, weaving in the tunes he loved. They'd booed and turned on him. So, he turned on them. And now here he was.

She was back. She fiddled with the machines, his sheets, busy work. Almost as if she hung around waiting for him to… to what? Did she think he was going to awaken and hop out of the bed and do a little jig? Or maybe she just thought someone should be near in case he finally woke. His eyes opened. Both of them! At the same time! They were not focused. They were more like two blue pools of cloudy water stirred up by something living in the deep. He tried to find something to focus on. Some point in the room, a cup, a machine, a picture, shit, a bed pan, anything. Her face came into view. She was a blur. She could have been black or Hispanic, tanned from the mountain sun or Native. She wasn't real white or she would've blended into the walls. Her hair was dark, he thought, and she kept coming closer and moving farther away, closer, farther, closer…until he was certain he would vomit into his breathing tube.

"Shhhtoooobbb" he begged.

"What?!" it was exclamation more than an actual question.

Had he spoken? Or attempted to do so? Could he do it again? He concentrated. Formed the word in his head, thought about the muscles needed to push the air past his vocal cords and…nothing. Damn it! He was sure he'd just done it! He'd heard it with his own ears, hadn't he? And where had she gone? He was this close to communication, to saying — a word. The doctor rushed in, penlight in hand. She forced open his right eye, then his left, blinding him with the powerful little light. It hadn't been necessary, as he'd watched her, through mostly opened eyes, as she'd entered, rushed to his side and stuck her fingers in his eyes. One would think she might have noticed his open eyes.

"Janet said you talked. Did you talk?" The words rushed like a stream over rapids, fast, commanding. It was like an interrogation. The light in his eyes, the insistence in her voice, the pressure for him to answer.

He blinked.

"Can you do it again?" She leaned back to give him room in case he exploded in expression. He didn't think that was going to happen. He closed his eyes. If nothing else, it would show he was trying. What was different between when he had expelled a word and when he couldn't? He thought, considered. He'd been pissed. He hadn't thought. He'd just spit the word. The nurse made him nauseas and he wanted her to stop. He needed to find the anger and push. He thought of himself, walking in the frozen tundra, the wind whipping about, banging his guitar case against his leg, the leg that had been snapped years before. It hurt, Goddamn it, and the wind wouldn't let up. He was pissed at himself for getting off the main road, for not keeping an eye on the gauges, for allowing himself to die in such a moronic, plebeian way. Frozen to death, walking in the middle of nowhere, instead of camping in the car, with a coffee can and a candle. That would have kept him alive, but he'd gotten rid of it a few years ago, tossed it, meaning to get another. Now he was going to die because of procrastination. He was an idiot, stupid, worthless. Just like his old man told him!

"Shhttooobb!" he tried to scream, he didn't have near enough force to fill the room, but it was enough to be heard as a whisper. Had she heard it?

"Nurse, give me a hand in here, we're going to see if our friend can breathe on his own," she turned her head and smiled, "we may have turned a very important corner."

The room became a hive of activity. Though he was fairly certain there was only the two of them, they scurried so quickly it seemed a team. The nurse suctioned out the tube and the doctor gave instructions of how this was going to go; in case he couldn't breathe on his own. This would be a process. First, they had to sit him up in bed and then slowly reduce the assistance of the ventilator. Once they hit minimal standards, they would give him a few minutes to see if he could breathe on his own. Once satisfied they would suction the tube once again, then suction the inside of his mouth. If all went well, yeah, he thought, if all went well.

They pulled the tube slowly but steadily out of his mouth. He coughed, once, twice, mid-third cough it was out. Quickly the doctor pushed an oxygen mask over his mouth and nose. He could taste the purity of the flow as it entered his body. He tried to take a deep gulp of that freedom and began coughing profusely. The doctor leaned him forward, removed the mask and slapped him hard on the back.

"Not too much at once," she cautioned, "your body hasn't been operating on its own in quite some time. Slow, shallow breaths for now. We'll work on building up to the big gulps soon enough." She replaced the mask and he began to take short, ragged breaths. Within a few moments they had evened out and he felt something akin to normal. Light-headed, but close enough.

"This is going to take a few days, but I think, now, you just might live," she grinned as did the only other person present. Apparently, no matter how long one was a nurse or doctor, or a floor sweeper in this business, you never got tired of people living.

CHAPTER THREE

It was evening before he was breathing shallowly but regularly and able to speak a few words. The Doctor had warned him not to get despondent if it took some time before he could get his breathing under control and strong enough to work the vocals chords.

She didn't know the will of the folk singer. He didn't have full voice, not much more than a whisper, but they could understand him, and he was able to sip warm fluids. Could solids be far behind?

He still had no concrete idea where he had landed. Somewhere in the mountains bordered by Colorado, Wyoming and Utah, near as he remembered. The weather was supposed to hold for a few days and he had no gigs — surprise — for the week. So, why not get off the highway, the US Routes, the State routes and see where life would take him. Here. But where was here? He'd died to get here. He sure would like to know where death had brought him.

And this hospital. His first waking memory reminded him of his grandma's house if her bedroom had been an infirmary. He thought he had imagined the whole thing. His mind had taken a stroll down a very old and not real memory. Grams had died in her house, that part was true. But not surrounded by machines and doctors and nurses, just by the minister, family, a few friends and God. When you're ninety-seven, there ain't much left. He had apparently allowed his drugged mind to fill in the blanks.

And yet. This did resemble her room with the aforementioned technology. Who would turn an old woman's bedroom into a clinic? Questions. He had nothing but questions and limited conscious time to ask. He was weak as an orphaned pup. He couldn't keep his eyes open for more than an hour or two at the best of times. And he wasn't the sharpest chisel when he was awake. He had no stamina, his thoughts scattered like leaves in a hurricane and his grasp on reality was tentative. He needed to get to his phone and get hold of somebody. But who?

Who was missing him right now? His ex? If he could've he would've laughed. His daughter? About as likely as her mother. He had no other family at this point. They were all dead and cold in the earth. His friends were acquaintances he'd bump into on the road. There was no one close, no one who would wonder why they hadn't heard a peep in weeks; or months, he admitted to reality. So, mayhap he should just relax, accept the hospitality, find out where he was, find a way to repay the kindness, and try to keep living.

The nurse returned — Janet, if he remembered correctly — to check on him and see if he'd like something to drink. Whiskey, he thought but did not say. He motioned for her to sit for a minute in the overstuffed chair to his left. She sat and picked uncomfortably at the doilies on the arms. She was unaccustomed to just sitting, it would seem, and preferred motion. He focused on her perfect chocolate face. Smooth as a teen's yet the eyes showed she had lived. Crinkles around the corners of her mouth showed she had laughed. A few creases above her eyes showed she knew worry. She was beautiful in a human sort of way. She had the face of a woman you could not help but love. She was a mother, friend, nurse, comforter and his connection to life.

"Where am I?" Yes, it was the most hackish question he could ask but, also, the most important right now.

"You're at Doctor Caldwell's home," she replied.

"Not in a hospital?" he continued in a slow whispered tone. "I thought someone said I was in a hospital."

"We don't have a hospital here, just the Doctor," she replied in the same hushed tone as if they were sharing the most intimate secrets. "We kind of refer to this as a hospital as it's the closest thing we got up here to anything resembling one."

"Where is here?" Let's try this again.

"Rock Ridge," she stated and seemed genuinely surprised by his guffaw and snort of derision.

"You're shitting me, right?" he pushed past dry lips on a bark of rasped laugh. She leaned over, lifting a glass of water in her hand, holding it to his lips. He sipped.

"Why would you find that...? Oh, I always forget. We're kind of used to the name up here, we forget the reference," she smiled, and her eyes danced. She was pretty in a middle-aged, kindly, motherly way. She had seen life, she lived, and still found the joy one was supposed to find. No bitterness, no cynicism, no regrets. She wasn't twenty-one and she had no desire to be. He always found that to be unbelievably attractive in a woman; really, any person. Comfort with who you were. "One of the folks who founded the town was a huge Mel Brooks fan," she shrugged as if that would explain anything more he might wonder about this place.

"So, I am a guest of the good Doctor?" Back to basics.

"Yes, she'll tell you whatever you need to know about your condition when she gets back, I'm sure. She's doing rounds right now," She made to stand up from the chair, he waved her back, just for a second, he seemed to be saying.

"What rounds?" Curiosity once pricked will flow until staunched even through a whisper.

"She will explain it all when she comes back. Sleep," she commanded.

"How long have I been here? How long have I been asleep? It feels like, I don't know, a while since you were last here?" Too many questions, too little breath, far too little strength. He was done in.

"Sleep," the command soft and gentle and very effective.

A soft, low light from the tiffany lamp was the only illumination in the converted bed/hospital room as he woke. It gave off warm, cozy, embracing comfort. One could believe all was right with the world while cuddled under the blankets. Until the incessant beep counting his pulse or heartbeat intruded. Somewhere a pneumatic pump shoved pure oxygen through the tubes and into his nose and apparently, the room. He closed his eyes against the intrusion.

There was a chill pushing through the warmth of the atmosphere, a chill that seemed to permeate every hospital room in the world. You always felt the need for a jacket or sweater in a hospital even in the middle of summer. People must heal more rapidly in a cooler environment, he mused under his shuttered eyelids.

He heard the footfall on floor and knew he should open his eyes, but he was too comfortable. Reality was waiting patiently on the other side of those lids and he was in no hurry to stare it in the eye. A deep breath in through the mouth and out through the nose. Slowly, methodically, calming. The worst thing about reality, it had far more patience and time than did he.

"Evening," he whispered, and was slightly taken aback by the strength of his voice. He had assumed it would be dry and weak upon waking. But there was timbre and depth in his murmur.

"How are you feeling?" she enquired.

"Don't know yet, but I don't think too bad," was his slight upbeat assessment.

"How were your rounds?" he asked, not really knowing how he knew it was the Doctor not Janet, but he did, "and where were your rounds? Are there more people, more rooms, patients, here?"

She laughed. "Rounds from which day?" she asked herself in such a way he knew he'd been out again for a couple days since their last interaction. Her laugh had been tired but not sad, just weary from another long day added to an already long life. "No, I check on folks at their homes or where they work. We got some old folks who live here, but they have no intention to stop living just 'cause they hurt or don't feel quite up to par." He heard her take the few steps over to the side of his bed and manners forced his eyes open. She gently pushed his eyelids up and looked, without the bright penlight, into each of his eyes. She took hold of his wrist, her touch soft and warm, to check his pulse and heart rate. He liked that she didn't quite trust the machines to give her information. She wanted human contact to assess.

"You want to try something a bit more substantial than broth, juice and IV fluids?" She smiled.

"Dear God, yes," he enthused.

"Janet," she called, though not loud, "our guest would prefer something to eat, not drink, if you wouldn't mind." Again, she smiled as if pleased he still breathed. "I have to admit, I didn't think we were going to have the pleasure of conversation. At least, not on this side of life," she sighed and sat on the edge of his bed. "and I have many questions."

"As do I," he stated flatly. "Number one, where in all hell am I?"

"Rock…" she began.

"Yes, I know, Rock Ridge, named after the Town in Blazing Saddles," he grinned, "I love it, but where is Rock Ridge?"

"Well, a couple hours southwest of Bozeman, about and two hours west, northwest of Yellowstone. Mostly North of Idaho Falls and just in the Nez Pierce-Clearwater National Forest." She stared at the ceiling as if reading it like a map, then nodded in satisfaction.

"So, 'bout in the middle of nowhere," he concluded.

"Near as anybody's ever got, I guess," she confirmed. "We don't get a lot of folks up here this time of year. Weather doesn't really draw them in. Of course, we don't get a lot of people here any time of year. Not much to bring them here." She spoke with a certain satisfaction. "Oh, we get a few who come to fly fish, go hiking in the mountains and forest, and need a base. Some folks just want quiet, some looking for a little peace and some get lost and almost die. Them we take in and try to heal." She tapped his arm and gave it a squeeze.

"Well, I don't know how I am going to repay you for all you've done," he confided, "I'm guessing you noticed I ain't exactly flush with cash. All I got is…"

"Yeah, I know, an old beat to hell guitar, an out-of-date computer and the clothes on your back," she finished. "Oh, and that broke down car. Bobby towed it in last week, doesn't think much can be done with it. Shoot it maybe," she chuckled and stood. "You get some rest. When you're stronger and feeling more yourself we'll worry about things then. Right now, there ain't much can be done about anything except healing and getting better." She walked out the door just as Janet entered with a tray of Jell-O, cut up chicken pieces and a bit more soup. It wasn't much but right now it was a banquet.

He ate, deep in contemplation. What was he going to do? His car was beached, he had no money to speak of, no way to repay these people and no idea what he was going to do. And what had she said, Bobby towed the car in last week? How long had he been here?

Sleep would not come easy this night. Worry and wonder plagued all attempts. He had almost died. That he knew and had come to accept. The Doctor and Janet had pretty much told him so. He must have been damn near froze to death by the time someone—and who was that someone? —brought him to this town. It had to be someone from here or they never would have known the damn town was here. The questions floated around his brain avoiding any answers that might be squeezed from them like greased pigs in a county fair. Sleep was hard coming but come it did.

Morning broke a little less foggy and with a slight uptick in energy. He actually pushed himself up into a sitting position in the bed. It felt good not to be completely horizontal. Doctor Caldwell carried the tray in and set it down on his lap. Oatmeal! Real oatmeal, with brown sugar and speck of butter, not much, but it would be heaven. A small OJ and a cup of lukewarm coffee. Life was turning around. And he had more questions. He hoped she had brought answers.

"You said Bobby brought me here a week ago. I need to thank him and see what I owe him. Guess that's going to be my mission, to find out what I owe people," he grinned around a spoonful of oatmeal.

"I wouldn't lose sleep over that right now, we don't really care that much about the almighty dollar around here," she sipped her own coffee, which, unless he was much mistaken, was much darker than his own. "And, I said Bobby brought your car here a week or so back, you been here a little over a month." She sipped.

The spoon had froze about an inch from his lips. He stared and waited. Was she joking? She certainly didn't sound like it, and when she turned to look at him, he could see she was deadly serious. "A month?" Shock had turned his complexion pure white and his hand shook as he set the spoon back in the bowl.

"A little over," she replied calm, calm as a mid-summer evening without a breeze to be felt. "Jeannie found you on the side of the road. Good thing you have such horrible taste in colors and blankets. She saw the orange and pulled over to see what the wind had blown down the road. She found you. She dragged you to her truck—she's pretty strong for such a small girl—and somehow got you loaded in the front seat. Must have been a bear trying to drive with this stiff corpse in the way," she shook her head and smirked his way, "but she is not one to give up or be denied. Brought you straight here. I act as the town coroner as well as doctor, she figured you needed one or the other. I found a pulse.

"Gotta say, I honestly didn't think you had a chance. Figured you'd be dead by morning, next day at best, but you're a lot stronger than I gave credit. So, we got your temperature slowly up, warmed fingers, toes, extremities, slow, easy, so you wouldn't lose any more than necessary. Once I was sure we had you strong enough, kind of, I put you in a coma. You know, with drugs, to give you time." She gazed out the window and looked at something he would never see, "Have to admit, I'd never done that before. Had to call down to Denver and find a Doctor to walk me through it."

She took a cautious glance at his startled, shocked expression. "Why didn't you take me somewhere, you know, somewhere where they knew what the fuck they were doing?" he was aghast.

"Well, it would appear that a huge storm followed you up these old two lanes and refused to leave town while you were here." She raised her eyebrows and shrugged as if to say, 'what can you do?' "We were socked in for weeks. Happens here. But we were prepared. When you live in the middle of nowhere you prepare to be stuck in the middle of nowhere for long periods of time. Comes with the turf. You hunker down and wait it out. You were comatose, so you were really no trouble. As long as the generator would keep the machines running then you'd be fine. We kept an eye on the generator. And you is," she opened her arms to indicate all was well in god's little garden.

He sat back in the bed and stared out the window. "And I is," he wept quietly.

She allowed him his moment, cleaned up the morning dishes and took them down the hall. Men did not, as a rule, care for women to witness them display emotions. She didn't know if he was like that, but best to err on the side of caution.

He had regained his composure by the time she returned and appeared deep in thought.

"So, what's next," he asked. "I mean, where do I go from here?" He sat up straighter in bed, "I feel as though I am getting stronger but certainly not strong enough to leave, to get back on the road. And I couldn't leave without, at the very least, attempting to repay what I owe you, whoever found me, this town, this...kindness. I can't just walk away. 'Thanks for everything but I got nothing to give back', kind of thing. I have to make this right." He was adamant, there was no use arguing with him, she realized. She would have to come up with some way for him to feel he was repaying his debt.

"Then we need to build up your strength if you're going to work off your debt," she said, "and that means we start some physical therapy today."

Physical exertion is good for the soul. That she knew for a fact, and he had been bedridden for over a month. His muscles would have atrophied, and his co-ordination would be sketchy at best. They would have to begin with simple exercises, small weights, things he could accomplish while laying in bed or sitting in a chair. She didn't want him standing, walking —even with a walker or cane — for the time being. He had to understand this would be a process, a slow, steady process, and he could not rush the healing. He would require every ounce of patience he could summon.

"As far as where you are to stay, well," she rubbed her chin in thought, considering all options, "you can stay here," she indicated his room at her place, "or we could put you up down at Del's Motor Inn. It's clean, comfy, though he doesn't have the room service you get here, and PT would be more convenient here," she finished.

"I guess I am at the mercy of your hospitality," was his sheepish reply, though he didn't seem to mind the arrangement.

CHAPTER FOUR

By week's end he was able to stand. Not for long periods of time, but he could come fully vertical with a minimum of assistance and take several steps before folding into the overstuffed chair. He was lifting three to four hundred-page books, up from the empty fists and children's books earlier in the week. And rolling over and back by himself. It was a good week.

He was eating solids, with larger portions, by the meal. Not what he had consumed previously but incrementally, step by step, he improved. He could feel the strength returning to his arms and legs. It would be a while before he was back, but he could see a pinprick of light on the horizon.

Hell, he might even be able to strum a few chords — as long as the guitar would sit in his lap without tipping and falling, and he didn't try anything too raucous. It would be pretty love songs to start. He could do anger in a few weeks, he snickered.

It was a week to the day of his awakening that he first stepped into the cold gray dawn. He was bundled head to toe in layers from t-shirt to long johns, jeans, sweater, coat, overcoat, stocking cap, gloves, scarf. He was quite certain if the lovely doctor could have wrapped him in bubble wrap, she would have. He didn't care. His first breath of cold, crisp, fresh air was intoxicating. He swooned, ever so slightly, as he took in the scene, watched his breath escape his body, denoting life. The small town was covered in a deep coat of pure white snow. Everything pure, even the streets. Usually by now the streets and sidewalks of any city, USA, would be black and puddling, but not here. The cold kept the puddles away and, apparently, they didn't use salt or sand, just a shovel. There was not enough traffic to turn the snow of the avenues dark with exhaust and ground in dirt. It was breathtaking.

It was a beautiful small mountain town. Single story homes dotted with two story Victorian houses. Businesses lined the few blocks of downtown he could see. It had everything just a few hundred people could need. A small grocery, a gas station, with a bay and mechanic, a saloon and a caféé across the street from each other, some knick-knack shops, antiques and such, and a soda shop—an actual soda shop. He almost fell over from the pure joy of it. Here was a town pulled from the memory of a book reader who wanted to recreate a town out of a past only slightly in touch with reality. And there was a small bookstore with another bar around the corner from it. Perfect!

Doctor Caldwell and Janet had given him the brief history of Rock Ridge. A former mining town of the late 1800's, that had been just successful enough to become a real town, but not big enough to attract the railroad. They had been content with who they were and wanted nothing more. They dug for silver and survived on a small copper mine. After a few decades, the mine went dry, and soon the town had as well. Some folks had done their level best to keep it on life support through the forties and the war, but it soon succumbed as well. The few folks that remained had moved to larger more prosperous towns and cities.

It sat and decayed for the next thirty years until George Hendrickson had seen enough of California to last him the rest of his life. Too many people, too many cars, too many new roads, buildings, problems and crime. He just wanted out. He sold his home for a very large profit, took his savings and investments, and went in search of somewhere filled with peace and beauty in the mountains. He didn't want the pristine Vail experience, the 'new, hip and rich' Colorado. He didn't want Tahoe and gambling. He wanted someplace he remembered from movies and books. That was when he'd found Deer Cross. A ghost town that had been abandoned so long even the ghosts had, well, 'given up the ghost' and moved on. It was perfect. He bought the whole damn town for next to nothing and began renovating.

And by renovate, they meant he began tearing down what hadn't fallen down but soon would and to recreate a town. He built himself a nice compact single-story ranch with three bedrooms, kitchen, bathroom—indoors—fireplace and large living area. It screamed mountain home.

There was water up here. Fresh, running cold, pure snow melt. He only needed to get permits and such to build a small water purifying station, to keep the state folks happy and a septic system. Some things you just got to have. The electric company, at the time, was willing to run power to his new town believing he meant for it to grow and with its growth would come profits. He didn't correct them.

Then he hunkered down and lived. He read. He walked. He got a couple dogs and three cats, all of whom provided security for the homestead. He lived simply. And soon became quite bored and lonely.

There were all these abandoned buildings, at least a dozen with promise, and him. He had the energy, just enough knowledge to make him dangerous and enough gumption to make him useful. He started small. He'd renovate the Victorian house down the street, so he would have a neighborhood.

He made trips into Bozeman once a month for paint, nails, lumber, pipe, supplies, whatever was needed, and then haul them up to his hideaway and work on the house. After a few months, a fella from town followed him, curious to see what this crazy man was building. He picked up hammer and saw, lent two good hands and a little more knowledge and within another month they had two homes off the range. They were the beginning of a town.

And so, it went, for five, ten years until they really did have a town. A town of good folks who just wanted what he'd sought: peace, quiet, contentment. They came. They retired. They lived. They were happy. Now there were almost a thousand folks here and the surrounding area. They didn't want for anything. They had enough to share. People found them by accident and stayed to bathe in the quiet of the mountains. There wasn't much to do. Fish, walk, hike, read, stay a night or two at Del's, and move on. They came with tension, worry, frenzy and they left with time and lower blood pressure. No one promoted the place because, well, because why would they?

That was what he looked out at standing on the porch of the Doctor's cozy two story Victorian. He took several cautious steps on the snow covered walk. The snow crunched under foot. His mind roared back to walking along the frozen desolate two lane right before he'd almost died. Maybe he had died. Maybe this was his own kind of heaven. Maybe he just wanted it to be. His head swam, and he stopped and closed his eyes for a moment to orient himself. He wasn't there, he was here. He had to hang on to here.

He snail paced it to the sidewalk and turned right. It was the shortest distance between here and the next corner—about a half a block. He would be back inside the toasty comfort of Doc Caldwell's in just under half an hour. That was how time and expenditure of energy went. A five-minute walk done well by a healing man times the number of breaths between steps came to just under half an hour. Simple math. He knew what it was to stand atop Everest.

Warmth wrapped him as he entered the snug front room and removed his hat, scarf, gloves and outer coat. The oversized chair beckoned him, and he succumbed. He eased his tired frame into the soft comfort expelling pain on a whoosh of breath. Eyes closed against the intrusion of reality. He just wanted to relax and not think. Not think about the pain in his right leg. Not think about the lack of a future — a thought he had avoided for many years but now seemed to have ample time to consider. Not think about the woman — the last in a very long line — who had thrown him and all his belongings out just last month, so she could find life without the baggage. And what a month it had become, he chuckled. Not think about a life lived aimlessly and filled with narcissism and self-indulgence. Not think about him. Just not think.

He opened his eyes gradually to the accusation from across the room. Leaning in a corner of the living room hidden by a table and a large lamp, stood the abused, scratched, ripped and torn guitar case. Inside rested his only friend, companion and trusted collaborator. The only entity never to turn its back on him. Never left him hang, no matter how he abused or treated it. Never let him down. Not once. And he didn't deserve that loyalty. He might have saved the guitar, or maybe it had saved him, it was a toss-up, but it didn't deserve the life that had befallen it.

He should open the case, check on his friend, take it out, let it breathe. But he just couldn't, not yet. He was afraid his hands wouldn't work. His fingers wouldn't do what he ordered them. His hand wouldn't hold the pick, or it would constantly hit the wrong strings. It would not strum the way he told his hand to strum. It would be clumsy, and it would hurt. Just like it did forty some years ago when he first tried to play. If he couldn't play what good was he? He hadn't spoken much more than a harsh whisper, what if that was gone as well? What was he? What other skills did he possess? None.

He would be a beggar, trading memories for favors, washing dishes in places he used to fill with his music. Could he live that way? People feeling sorry for him? Pity, his new currency. 'Hey, didn't you used to play guitar and sing? What happened?' Life. Life happened. You done with your lunch? I gotta sweep up and get ready for the dinner hour.

Maybe he could stay here. These folks seemed to like him alright. They wouldn't know about him or his music. He was just some dope who almost got hisself dead by freezing on the side of the road. They were nice folks. They'd kid him and make him tell again how he got lost and his car broke down and he walked until he almost died. They'd laugh and punch him in the arm, all in good fun. Because he didn't die. That was the funny and good part. It was OK to mock the living.

Yeah, maybe he could learn to swing a hammer instead of a pick. Build a home or a garage instead of a song, at least whoever he made it for could use the new garage; and it would last. Maybe he could bus tables at the caféé or bartend a couple nights a week, he knew about those jobs. He'd seen them done a thousand times.

No, he'd let the Gibson rest for now. It was as beat up and tired as he. Maybe they both needed a little time away from each other. Isn't that what every woman always told him? She just needed a little time away, to think, to consider, to run as fast as she could from his insanity. Maybe the Gibson needed a little time. He'd pick it up tomorrow.

Doctor Caldwell entered her house to find the mystery man —
she should probably query him as to who he was, soon — asleep in the
large chair sitting between fireplace and front window. She closed the
door quietly, so as not to disturb, and watched him sleep. It was an interesting case. She hadn't believed it possible he would be asleep, peacefully, in her drawing room. By all rights he should be dead, froze and buried, but there he sat, sleeping. That was one tough, old, weathered bird.
Something was keeping him going. Something burned inside. He was
either too hard or too stupid to give up. This was not a fella who would
roll over and die.

He was a musician of some sort, that was evident from the condition of the guitar. It had been 'played' and used. It had traveled as hard
as the player, seen too much, been dragged from one end of eternity to
the other. She knew people who played. They'd sit down at the saloon
and strum their shiny, polished, delicate looking instruments while singing songs so pretty you wanted to put them in an envelope and send them
to your mom. You wouldn't send this man's songs to your mom, unless
she was in prison.

Yet, he didn't seem evil or criminal in any way, just hard lived.
He was a searcher. She'd known her share before coming here to get
away from the rest of humanity. It wasn't that she didn't like people, she
was a doctor, for heavens' sake, but they could just be so cruel; to each
other and to all God's creatures. It saddened her. It was why she found
herself standing in the foyer of a renovated Victorian home in the middle
of a forest, in the middle of the mountains, in the middle of nowhere
USA, staring at this man ten years, OK maybe fifteen years, her junior,
and not afraid now. She knew in her bones he wouldn't hurt her, Janet or
anyone in this town. Somehow, he fit here, though neither she nor he

might ever find out how.

And maybe she was just a foolish old woman who required a little excitement in her ordered existence. He stirred and opened his eyes. He startled awake, rubbed sleep filled eyes and half smiled his embarrassment at having fallen asleep in her chair.

"Hungry?" she asked as she took off her coat and hung it by the door. "I think there's some chicken, gravy and potatoes in the fridge. I can heat up some for both of us if you'd like."

"Famished," he grinned. "Can I help?"

"Yeah, I guess you're probably strong enough to set a few plates on the table and get the silver." She turned down the hall in the direction of the kitchen, him shambling on her heels.

Microwaves are wonderful inventions, especially if cooking is not your forte but you know someone who can. The Doctor was a doctor, and not a chef, for a reason. But she could operate the microwave. And he was a musician, so he appreciated anything that would fill his belly. His mouth had given up on finding anything truly worthy of entering it years ago. So, it was with delight it welcomed the warmed, home cooked meal. Glasses of ice-cold milk completed the homey part.

"I assume by the condition of you and your friend," she nodded towards the parlor, "you play professionally." She carefully opened the tightly sealed can, hoping she didn't set off anything volatile.

"Yeah," he admitted around a drumstick, "I guess you could say that. Though these days it's kind of hard to tell. Gigs been a bit scarce. People don't dig live so much anymore, at least not enough to want to pay for it."

"You any good?" She snorted, knowing how it sounded but thought she would see how he was feeling.

"Middlin'" he grinned back. "I did alright for a while, back in the late seventies/early eighties, before disco came and gored the music biz. But I made a living." The words left unsaid of whether that was good or bad.

"That what brought you up this way?" Curiosity can be held in check but never imprisoned.

"Nah, boredom and time brought me up here," he confessed. "Guess I was looking for a place to get lost," he grunted. "Looks like I did that right, though hadn't planned on dying. Or didn't think I had," quiet so only he would hear.

"Have you tried playing?" She would not be denied.

"Nah, just haven't had the energy, I guess, maybe tomorrow. Or the next day," he shied away from the challenge. The fear too real of what the result would be.

"Maybe after lunch you could regale me with a tune or two," she pushed. She was not going to let go of this bone. She'd known a few per- formers and artists in her time. She recognized his aversion, his fear that somehow near-death had stolen his talent. She knew enough psychology, and enough artists in her life, to also know that was all artists lived for - the art. Take that away and they had no reason to fight for life. He had to see, to know, there would be life. That he would still have the ability to play, to perform. The sooner the better. "You can consider it a down payment for the medical treatments," she smiled her best winning smile and hoped it would suffice.

"Maybe," he picked at the chicken bones.

CHAPTER FIVE

The ticking of the grandfather clock in the hallway—something he had barely noticed—was now almost deafening. The wind had kicked up outside the front windows and the chimes hung there and danced to their own tune— like an omen in a bad horror flick that something terrible was about to happen. She sat on the couch patient as time and waited for him to come and rescue the ancient guitar from its well-worn prison.

He unconsciously washed his hands and stared at the case. He sat frozen by doubt. He owed her this, but could he make the payment? Fear, like a red-hot rock, burned his belly. He just needed to stand, walk over, pull it from behind the table and lamp, open the damn thing and play. Like he'd done a thousand times a thousand times before. His legs shook as he stood. What the hell was he so afraid of? That his hands wouldn't work, his fingers would cramp or forget how to make chords he'd been making since he was twelve? That the lyrics would stick in his throat? She didn't know and wouldn't be able to tell the difference. Just get the damn thing and play it, pussy.

He opened the case and he swore the Gibson smiled. He stroked it lovingly, the neck, the frets, he patted and rubbed the body. She felt cold. She needed this attention as much as he needed to give it to her. He had always thought of his guitars as female, but this one was special. She was whom he'd chosen to spend his life with. He'd sold off all the others over the years out of need, or to fulfill his wants, but not her. Come hell or high water, or cold as death winds and almost dead in frozen hell, she was by his side. He loved this guitar. Would she love him? He rubbed his hands together to get the blood flowing, warm the fingers, buy some time. He pulled her from the case. She felt heavy, heavier than he remembered, or maybe he was just weaker. He'd need to sit to play, that was a given. He sat on the ottoman and lay her in his lap.

He stretched out his fingers, start slow, he scolded, quiet in his head. Just a C chord. Don't go for barre chords, keep it elementary. Make the chord and strum it, see how it feels. He pressed on the neck, the strings biting into the soft tips of his fingers. It hurt, just enough, like a lover's kiss, with affection and memory. It felt, not good, but not bad, like shaking hands with an old friend from high school, familiar but slightly uncomfortable.

How about an F? Well, that wasn't so bad. Could G be far behind? You know, he kidded himself, if you put those in the right order it would be simple, sweet song; like this.

His voice was rough and raspy, but the notes were within reach and the chords fit, just like they used to. As he finished the last verse and let the chord ring out, he smiled. That wasn't so bad, was it? There were a few fumbles and a dead string here and there, and some of the words got lost on their way to the song, but he'd go find them, so they'd be ready next time.

She sat, eyes closed, a crooked smile resting on her lips. As the quiet returned to fill the room she slowly opened her eyes and seemed to assess him, the lighting different, shades and colors now full, she could see his character plain as day. As if the one song, sad and sweet, had opened him before her.

"That was nice,' she spoke softly so as not to disrupt the mood.

"Well, it was a little rough," he laughed, "but it felt good." He rubbed the tips of the fingers on his left hand. Yeah, the callouses would need to be reborn and grown. It would hurt, but not as much as not playing. It did feel good. He would need to practice, a lot, but what else was there to occupy his time.

She watched him and saw the worry, the fear that had filled his features slowly melt, transform, morph into satisfaction. Not joy. No, he was not happy with what he had played, but he had played and for now that would have to do. It would help him heal; she knew that. People needed a rope tied to an anchor of hope tied by a frayed thread to life. It gave them something to work towards. They would not give up if there was just a glimmer, just a spark, an ember to blow on.

"How do you feel?" She wanted to hear him say something positive to reaffirm her prognosis. No answer. "Are you alright? What are you thinking? Do you want to play another?" Her questions patient, calm, plodding. No answer.

He could see her sitting across from him. From her perch on the couch he could see her lips move, she was talking. Probably asking him something. He couldn't hear her. He had slipped into artist mode. Every woman he had ever dated, married, slept with or had attempted a conversation with hated artist mode. It was an innate ability he possessed where he could shut out all sound, all distractions, and just concentrate on himself. His music, his writing, his creative demons. A defense mechanism to shut out the world when the Muse came to visit. Nothing could interfere, nothing could enter, when the solid steel door came down.

He began to pluck another song and she sat back. It was not one of the nice, happy love songs. It was darker. Not one of his deeply introspective, depressing ballads that would require three or four upbeat tunes to revive a crowd, but it had some depth and darker colors. A song about a man who kills his girl because he loves her too much and is afraid of losing her, so he destroys her before that can happen. It was written from a painter's point of view. He destroys her like a painting. Not a crowd favorite.

She listened intently. The song was beautiful in a dark, death inspired kind of way. Not one she would be humming later on. But then again…one never knew. She wondered what he was like before death almost claimed him. Physically he was rail thin. He obviously hadn't been heavy before, but he was skin, bone and muscle now. His clothes hung on him like a homeless scarecrow's. He would need a few pounds to bring him back to normal. It would take some time. And that was another question: how long would he stay? He certainly didn't seem in any hurry to leave. He hadn't mentioned it once! He gave no indication there was anything, or anyone, pulling him back to his life. Time would walk at its own pace, apparently.

He finished the song and let the notes fly away on their own. He was content. It wasn't perfect, chords missed, words mumbled, a complete bridge that had fallen in the abyss, but it was passable and showed hope. Though it didn't 'fit'. Neither of the songs did, now that he thought about it. They were his, he'd written them, they were a part of him. And yet, they weren't. It was like playing someone else's tunes. They were familiar, and he knew the songs, but they didn't feel as if they were him anymore.

Near-death had changed him. Changed his perspective on life. Death passed so close it seemed to have changed the life that remained. This was a journey he hadn't planned.

The front room came back into focus. She spoke to him, "…two very different kinds," she, obviously, was making some kind of point of the two songs.

"Yeah, I'm kind of all over the globe when it comes to songwriting," he picked up the thread and followed to its logical point of origin. "I had reviewers write incessantly that was the reason I would never be anything, because people wanted consistency. They wanted to know this album would sound like the last and would have the same songs, just written differently. People wanted you to play the same thing over and over, not go off on very thin limbs and dark, scary places." He set the guitar down next to him, its neck resting on the arm of the chair, close, within easy reach. "I sometimes think I started writing the heavier stuff just to shove it in their faces. I guess I've never done well with any kind of authority figures and I've always hated reviewers the most. They never played a note, never walked on a stage sick or in bereavement, hurt, tired from the road. Never knew what it was like to pour your soul into a crowd only the have it splash at their feet in indifference. And they have the balls to say, 'you seemed distracted at the show. Not one of your better performances.' No shit, asshole, my marriage just disintegrated. and she left with my kid ten minutes before I walked up here. I was slightly distracted by the collapse of my fucking life!" He glared out the window. "Sorry." It was all he had.

"What's your name?" They both laughed hard. The tension melted, his mood had returned to hope and satisfaction.

"You never looked at my license?" He was shocked. He would've thought that would be the first thing they would check.

"Eh, we got a little busy trying to save you and then everybody just forgot about that aspect," she shrugged at the lack of curiosity of all involved. "We live a little different kind of life here." As if that would explain all.

"Padon," the brogue thick as maple syrup and just as sweet, "Pa-don McKenzie."

"Folks were proud of their Scottish roots?" She jibed.

"Just a wee," he returned the serve, he bowed. "Grandfolks came over back in the aughts of the last century and brought their hard, Scottish pride with them. We were to never forget that our family can trace its' roots back to the time of Robert the Bruce. It's a good conversation starter," he shrugged with the familiarity of explanation.

"Good for picking up the lasses, eh?" she chided. She just couldn't help herself; it was truly a wonderful name and it fit him like a hand tooled, fine leather coat. Yeah, Padon McKenzie, just perfect.

"Yeah," sheepish and a slight discoloring of the face and neck, "for a minute and then...the personality kicks in and, well, they see you for what you are. The ones you really want to spend time with, that is, the smart ones, they see right through an old fake like me." He smiled, but there was no trace of joy.

"Lonely at the top?" she pushed.

"At the top, in the middle and on the floor of the ocean," he shrugged and reached for, but stopped short of his guitar. "It's funny but broke tends to be less lonely than doing well. People sense when you got nothing but yourself. They know when your only stock and trade is honesty since it's all you got left. Bullshit comes easy when you're flush. It's easier to pull off. You can make anybody believe anything when you got some jack and are surrounded by those who already believe. It just feeds on itself. It feeds like a glutton until you believe it yourself. Lies come easy when you start to believe them yourself.

"Poverty, living on the bottom rung, well, you can't hide nothing from nobody, 'cause you can't hide from yourself. When you're playing tunes for nickels, dimes, quarters and a beer, well, who you foolin' then? Sleeping in some flop with everything worth anything wrapped in your arms so you have a small chance it'll be there in the morning. Yeah, and the hunger gnaws at your chest 'cause it already ate your gut. Well, keeps you humble." And this time he barked a huge guffaw, staring at his one friend, his hand itching to pick it up again.

They had shared a life, these two. She was beginning to think of the guitar as a living, breathing entity just as he did. She could almost see the threads connecting the two. He might want to walk away from this life, but she wouldn't let him. They were a team. She couldn't play herself and he couldn't breathe without her near. It was the most symbiotic relationship Doc Caldwell had ever witnessed. "So, now what?" It wasn't a change of subject, more jump starting something gone dead.

"I guess I don't know," he admitted. "Rely on the kindness of others for a little while. Try to find a way to repay that kindness and figure it all out as I feel my way through." He stopped. He might've said more but choose a different path. This time he did grab his guitar. "I'd like to remain here, if it's not too much of an imposition, for a little while longer. I mean, I don't know anybody else, except Janet, around here. As I get stronger, I can help with chores, if you'd like, and I can ease my way into the rest."

His fingers picked and plucked a few notes before joining in a dance between left and right and he began to sing a thoughtful song about trying to come home, but never quite finding the right road to take him there. It was a lovely tale with a few japes and jaunts that made you smile and helped hide the fact it really was a very sad song.

"I have to wash the dishes," she said and rose from the couch, "before Janet shows up or she'll have my head for leaving her a mess."

"Let me," he set the guitar back to the side of the chair, "surely I am strong enough to wash a few dishes and containers. I'm sure you have rounds and folks to check on. Lives to save. Please..." he let the word lift him from his own chair and she nodded. Yes, let him help. Let him begin to heal.

Bundled against the frigid temperatures, she peeked around the doorjamb to check on him before she left. He stood at the sink methodically washing and rising each plate, glass, container and piece of silverware. He was meticulous, examining each article before it made its way to the drying rack. She smiled; it was probably how he wrote as well. If only she was fifteen, maybe a little more, years younger. She chastised herself for the dreams of the ancient woman. 'Sometimes,' that young girl in the back of her head chided her. 'Foolish old woman,' it said, 'still thinking you're going to find some man to warm your bed in your decline, yes?' No, she sighed and closed the door behind her and felt the hard slap of the freeze.

He heard the door close as she left the house. His shoulders slumped, and he leaned against the large farm sink. He knew she'd been watching him, to see if he would be fine until she returned. It had taken all the effort, all the strength he could muster, to stand erect at the sink. It amazed him how quickly he tired. But the walk to the corner had worn him out enough he'd needed a nap. Why should he be surprised that playing a couple tunes and washing a few dishes would require less effort to wear him down.

He'd finish the dishes, but now he could do it at his own pace. This weariness wore on him. He'd always been a high energy person. He could go until the sun came up and went back down. Now, he wore himself out taking a pee. Shit! Health couldn't come soon enough.

The sound of the door opening once again startled him from his reverie. Damn, she must have forgotten something. Suck it up, kid, stand straight and look like a man.

"Don't worry, I won't tell her you were slacking off." He was good with voices, once he heard someone speak, he never forgot the voice or who it belonged to. He hadn't a clue. He turned to find out.

She leaned casually against the doorjamb, arms crossed just under her breasts, legs crossed at the ankles. Her jeans were tucked into well-worn black chukka boots, fur lining the tops —though whether it was real or not he couldn't tell from where he stood — a knit fedora tilted jauntily on her head, down coat unzipped to the waist revealing a wool seater over a black turtleneck. It was laidback, didn't quite match and unbelievably attractive. She pulled the hat off and scrubbed her short-cropped hair back to life. Mousy brown with pockets of grey and few white ones signaling surrender. She didn't seem to care about any of it. She was as comfortable as you could possibly be in your own skin. And screw anybody who expected more. She looked to be late forties by the crow's feet and laugh lines and cared not a whit to appear younger. She had earned what she was and wouldn't be cheated out of one day. He couldn't help but return her crooked grin and nod a hello.

"You must be the dead guy," she looked him up and down as if assessing, "don't look that dead to me." He was cute, endearing, in an unkempt sort of way. His clothes hung on him, mismatched like a child's concept of a hipster scarecrow. He could use a shave and a haircut, and a couple pounds but not a bad looking guy for being near dead, wore out and broke.

"You should've been here a few days or weeks ago, and looking out from the inside," he touched his chest and then his left temple. "You might have a different opinion."

"Hope you've been enjoying the chow, it ain't fancy but it should stick to the ribs." She reached down to pick up the small, insulated cooler by her feet. "This must be for you, I guess." She set it on the counter next to where he stood, but not in his way.

"You been cooking my food?" he asked, a little taken aback. He thought either Janet or the Doctor had prepared his meals.

"Yeah, I own the Café up the road," she jerked her thumb over her right shoulder to indicate general direction. "Trust me, you don't want whatever these two come up with." Pointing at the empty space behind her and the ghosts of those who lived here. "Janet and Doc mean well — and are damn good at healing folks — but neither can boil water or open a cookie box. I've been cooking for them since I opened almost twenty years ago." She glanced at the past and cracked a quick hello smile to a favorite memory.

"Vittles have been fantastic!" He grimaced as he over enthused.

"Yeah, well, I ain't no chef but I can do comfort." she kindly ignored his teen angst, "People dig comfort food. Might not be healthy for the body, but it sure is for the soul," she made to grab her hat from where she'd tossed on the counter by the door out.

"Stay," it was more of a plea than he intended, "I mean if you, unless you, you know, have something pressing." He wiped his hands on the dish towel. God, when was the last time he'd been this nervous talking to a woman? Tenth grade? What the hell? Had the bitter cold of the mountain and near death taken every ounce of confidence? He was like a prepubescent kid. She wasn't that freaking stunning! Or was she?

"I got a few before I gotta get back for the early birders," she smirked enjoying the affect she was obviously having on this guy. When had been the last time she made a guy stammer? Wow! OK, it felt good, what about it? So, leave me alone, willya? I'm in my mid-forties! Well, just past. Shut up and enjoy.

"Mind if we sit in the other room? Guess I'm a bit more tired than I thought," he shuffled towards the dining room. He could've walked just fine but he wanted a few moments to collect himself.

She sat at the corner of the table, so he could sit kitty-cornered to her. She played with her hat, spinning it in both hands and looking any-where but at him.

"Is this place for real?" His eyes darted to the door, as if afraid the Doctor would return before he had his answer. "It's like a movie set or something out of the past, but not the real past. You know what I'm trying to say?" he stumbled along.

"Yeah, it took me a while to figure it out," she leaned back in her chair and half smiled, "I came here after my old man beat the shit out of me for the last time. Packed up my two kids, whatever cash was in the house and split. Somehow or other I wound up here. Not really sure how. I'd been driving through the day and into the night, and just running as fast as the wheels would turn. Got off the highway in case he was trying to find me. Thought I'd just follow the back roads for a little and then find another highway and follow whatever direction it headed. I didn't care, I was trying to save my life. And my kids," she added gazing out the window.

"The road brought me here. Middle of the night, chilly and rain-ing, and I find a town with no hotel. I started banging on doors, willing to beg, hand over what cash was left, anything just for a warm bed for the kids. Hell, I'd sleep in the car. I didn't care." She wiped a stray memory from where it had leaked out of her right eye. "Wouldn't you know it, Del comes to the door, all bleary eyed and in his bathrobe, squinting 'cause he forgot his glasses upstairs. Doesn't even ask who we are. Just looks at my face and the rain dripping from all of us and ushers us inside. Right into the living room. Rekindles his fire until it's blazing like all hell and asks us if we'd like something to eat. Can you beat that?" She shook her head in amazement, still astounded by the kindness.

"He fixed up a plate of leftovers, and while we're eating and warming up by the fire, he turns down the beds in his guest room and brings us some dry jammies. Who does that? Even back then. Nobody. That's who. Nobody." She pulled her hat on and stood. "Yes, that's who these people are. I don't know why, I don't care. They gave me a home - a real home, somewhere I don't have to run from. And then they helped set me up in business. My own damn caféé! That's who they are. And they like the food. I hope you do as well." She double-timed her way to the door. "I got people to feed, enjoy the dinner." And with that she disappeared in the glare of the sun.

Now, what in the hell had he done to piss her off? He just asked. He hadn't meant anything by it. He just wanted to know where he was.

And he didn't even get her name.

CHAPTER SIX

What the hell had just happened? She went from — what he was quite certain was — flirtatious to school marm, to defensive to downright pissed, so fast, his head was spinning. Was it because she'd had to remember the reason she'd shown up here years ago? He hadn't forced that. Just asked a question. What had set her off? He'd probably never know. Normally he'd blow off a chick like that. She obviously had too many issues, no matter what her demeanor — baggage enough for a month-long vacation through Africa—and a shortage of manners where questions were involved. Wow! He didn't need this right now. And yet…

He would just avoid her when she brought lunch or dinner or stopped by. There was no necessity to go anywhere near the diner. He could avoid this woman. And yet, he didn't really want to.

Was it the challenge? The chase? To see if he could still chase down a pretty woman at his age and health? Even a crazy one? Was the charm still hiding somewhere deep in his soul? A little brogue, his famous grin, cocksure and jaunty. Could he woo her into bed? And did he want to? He had to sit for a moment and consider. That was his normal M.O.: woo them, seduce them, bed them and run like hell. But it wasn't there. Not in his loins or in his conniving head, he just wanted to talk to her. Apologize and ask what he'd done. Have a cup of coffee. Talk, fer chrissakes! What was wrong with him?

He shuffled to the back bedroom and lay down on the makeshift hospital bed. He required some rest, some sleep, perchance to dream. To wake up himself.

The dream came almost as quickly as exhausted sleep over-whelmed him. It was that gig in Baltimore. Hotter than hell outside. Had been for weeks and people had come not so much for him, but because of the air conditioning. They wanted cold air and hot music.

The AC had broken down. Inside was a nightmare of heat, humidity and rank humanity. People were getting testy by the time he took the stage. They were hot, and they were not getting drinks fast enough to satisfy them, but too fast to process them before the next hit harder. They were turning drunk ugly. He had better pull out some charm to sooth the savage inebriated beast.

They clapped hard and rhythmically when he took the stage, half-hearted and challenging, as if daring him to try and tame the building dreadfulness of the crowd. He threw aside the set list and drove hard into a reel about a hard-loving woman who couldn't be satisfied. It was fun, funny, engaging, had a chorus people loved to sing along, arms wrapped around each other. A boisterous kind of nonsensical thing that fell like a three-thousand-pound turd right in the middle of this malevolent crush of humanity. This was going to get unpleasant and there were no exits close by.

He tried telling a story, to bring them to him but they wanted none of it. PLAY! Came the demand. Where in the hell was security? He gave an old rocker he'd written years ago a swing around the unwashed masses and got a smatter of appreciation. OK, it was a start. Find another. Something with a good beat, raucous lyric and a bridge he could show off some slick guitar work. Maybe, just maybe.

Four songs in and the wheels fell completely off. He'd never had that happen before. There had never been a time he couldn't control a crowd. Whether it was ten or ten thousand, he'd prided himself on his knack to pull a crowd anywhere he wanted to take them. They would come willingly, like the pied piper, dancing as they went, singing and loving everything he threw their way. Not tonight. And he began to freak. Fear filled him, and his brain froze with his fingers. C'mon he prayed to them, then commanded, but his hands were as confused as his brain at this point.

They began to throw things: lit cigarettes, quarters, cans. It rapidly escalated and spread throughout the crowd. Soon they were throwing punches, chairs and people. It was time to save himself.

He hugged the Gibson close to his body to protect it from the incoming missiles. He would gladly take the hit if it protected the old guitar. Turning to grab his capo, picks, tuner and such, immediately he changed his mind. If he lived, he could buy more. Right now, he had to move, fast, in any direction that would get him the hell out of here.

He grabbed his guitar case and stopped by the rear door of the club to shove the Gibson in the case and hope it provided enough protection. Kicking the door open he emerged into the rear alley. Clear. Not a soul. Maybe he could get to the van before they spilled out of the club and the riot took over the sweltering streets of Baltimore.

Timing, it's all about timing. And his lack of it. As he stepped out onto the main drag, he was accosted by people pushing through the fire door escape that had been located halfway down the wall of the concert hall. As they saw him it reignited the anger they felt for the club, the heat, the drinks, their mothers, their pissy girlfriends or boyfriends, their shitty jobs and life in general. He was now the focus of their horrible lives and they were going to have their kilo of flesh.

As they surrounded him, throwing punches and kicks, but landing few with any force, he lost his mind. Fear, the lack of flight options and self-preservation all inflamed his muscles and sinew. He began to swing the hard-shell case with reckless abandon. They might win by numbers, but he was going to take as many of them with him as he could.

Numbers would win. It was obvious, and his strength was dwindling. They were grabbing for the case, screaming they would crush the guitar to splinters and then him. He pulled it in close, hugging it to his chest. They might destroy the Gibson, but by that time he wouldn't care. He'd be dead.

Two guys hit him in the head with large rocks and he went down in a heap, still clutching the guitar. The same two big SOBs jumped on his right leg, again, and again. He heard the snap. The pain threatened to pull him under. Still, he clutched the case. He closed his eyes and prepared himself to die. He was tired anyway.

The air cleared. They weren't piling on top of him. He could breathe. He looked up from the filthy sidewalk and saw a hundred people pushing the rioters back, back away from him. Protecting him. And the Gibson.

And there was that pretty little girl, saying something to him, but his head rang, and the shouting was loud — and she was just so cute. She motioned for him to hold his guitar as tightly as he could. What the hell did she think he was doing right now? She grabbed his leg, just below the knee and just above the ankle and pulled hard, then twisted and twisted again.

His scream seared his throat, he burst several capillaries in each eye and his head almost exploded. He was quite certain the darkness that surrounded him would finally pull him under and this would all be over. Another woman was now holding his leg as straight as she could get it, while the first was wrapping several strips of torn clothing and a broken pool cue to hold the leg in place.

"We need to go before the cops come," someone screamed, and it echoed over and over in his head. Someone lifting. A van, a ride and a lot of booze and pills. And a lifelong limp.

He was soaked from head to toe. The sheets, blankets, pillows — all sopping wet. His breathing was hard, raspy and hurt his chest. His leg ached something awful and he wasn't certain where he lay. It wasn't the van; he could tell by the drapes. It wasn't any house he knew…no that wasn't true. He knew this place. And he relaxed into the cold, wet sheets. He was safe. He was going to need a shower; and soon.

He dried off. Slow, easy. Just as the shower had been. He had time. There was no need to hurry. The last thing he wanted was to slip and fall, crack his head, a shoulder, the leg, his brain, anything that might come is useful later in life.

The shower had been more than in order. It was a tasteful tile with no door, no curtain, just the shower. Good water pressure smacked him in the center of his back, and he could feel the muscles begin to loosen. Was there anything that felt as good as a shower? Yeah, maybe that, but the shower after was the climax.

He was weak, tired and confused. What was happening to him? He was not one for nightmares, night sweats or night terrors, and yet they visited themselves upon his place of residence. He was supposed to rest, convalesce, heal, not run from his past. That was not part of the deal. Then again, maybe death brought life into focus. Well, he certainly hoped he was not going to have to live the whole thing again. That would kill him.

And thus far he was only visited by ghosts of shitty days past. Would the great days come as well? Did he get to relive his glory days? Would all the women come back for one more round? Would the hangers-on return for one more party? Was this place some kind of midway on the road to death? His own personal purgatory? No, he refused to believe in something he had denied, he had completely disregarded for most of his fifty-seven years.

His truth. Something he knew in every cell of his being. Something that defined his very being. He had never believed the superstition of his parents and society. He would not now. Near Death, real death, fear would not force him to forsake truth. Whatever happened when you died, this was not it. It might be black, empty space, or energy flowing through the cosmos on to the next go round, or it just might be nothing, but there was no 'life' after death. Just death. He would hang on to that as his rock in this bizarre town of nicety.

He dressed in sweats, mismatched, the pant lost in some town with some girl, shirt thrown from a balcony in Lauderdale. Show over, the money counted. Ticket sales had been good if not great. He'd sold a respectable number of CDs, and some folks had come back to the hotel to party. A few tokes, swigs from the open bottle of Jack, and beers. Someone had a bottle of wine. Somebody else had some pills and, of course, there was line to do lines. It had been the late eighties; early nineties and he was riding a gilded wagon.

The world was going to end in ten years when Y2K destroyed the machines. Yeah, and he'd lived like it. Ask his daughter, if you could find her. He really did hope she was doing well. He hoped her mom had remarried, maybe a decent guy. Somebody with a job, a regular paycheck, retirement, a future. Someone who could give both of them something he couldn't. A guy who could give them himself. Padon could never give anybody that, as he wasn't his to give.

He'd never thought of it that way, but it was true, wasn't it? How can you give what you never really possess? And he'd never really owned any part of himself. Oh, he'd beat on himself as if he did, but when you stopped to think about it, he'd really beat on himself like a rental, not like he was making the payments. Well, that hadn't been true now, had it? Nope, because he had certainly been making the payments for years. Payments on an old clunker that barely ran, needed a ring job, a new transmission and overhaul of his heart and brain. Shit. Morbidity, you are my path and I shall ride you to the great depression at the end of the road.

He needed a drink.

Wow! When was the last time he'd thought that! He'd had drinks, sat around the bar after a show with some folks who'd dug the music, but he hadn't thought, I need a drink, since, yeah, since she left. He didn't blame her, he understood, but it had cut him deep, through to the marrow. He remembered as sharp as a second ago. He needed a drink.

He laughed at his shadow. Such a fool. And then he caught his reflection in the full-length mirror. Who the hell was that stick figure? He had never been heavy, always lean. Not that he worried about weight. It had just never been a problem for him. He was high energy in moccasins, always on the move, not one to lounge or sit for long periods of time. Except when he wrote, and that was a form of exercise, wasn't it? If he used the brain, paced to jumble thoughts free, banged on his guitar, some part of his body in motion at all times. Yeah, fat didn't stick to him.

But this, this was ridiculous. There was no meat on the bone at all. Just skin, muscle and skeleton. His skin hung like an ill-fitting suit. His face gaunt and haggard, eyes shallow and haunted. He needed to add a few pounds. No wonder he was so tired. There were no reserves. He was hungry all of a sudden and walked towards the kitchen where dinner awaited.

Doc Caldwell, as he'd begun to think of her, busied herself in the kitchen, putting the bounty that the café woman had brought into the fridge. "I thought you might be napping," she said as he entered the kitchen, "I didn't hear anything from the back room and didn't see anything in between."

"Took a nap, then took a shower," a succinct review of the afternoon. "Thought I might see if there was something to munch on," he indicated the, now empty, Styrofoam cooler.

"You met Maggie, I see," she put the empty container back on the counter. "She keeps us fed and fit."

"She seems nice," he said. "Anything we might gnaw on? I seem to have lost what little insulation I had." He lifted the bottom of the sweatshirt to expose his concave midsection.

"I'm sure we can find something to tide you over until dinner," the words returning her to the refrigerator. She found it curious that he blew by the fact he and Maggie had interacted. Something was there he didn't want to talk about which, of course, made her want to pick that scab until it bled pure, fresh blood. But she was a patient woman. You had to be when you were a physician. You couldn't rush things. Healing would come at its' own pace. But she sure wanted to rip that band-aid off.

Dinner passed with convivial conversation, some laughter and him avoiding anything to do with Maggie, his former life — except the barest of fact — and what he was doing so far from anything remotely resembling a town that might have a show. He was a man of mystery and hidden truth. But, really, wasn't everybody.

Did you really know anyone? Everyone hid secrets, desires and deeds. Love lost, found, veiled and concealed from all. Did you want your best friend to find out you'd had a brief affair with his wife, even if it was long before they met? Or that you'd lost a bundle on a guaranteed business deal, that turned into a scam? That you'd lived homeless for a while? Done drugs, drank too much? Had an abortion when you were fifteen? There was a reason for Doctor/patient, lawyer/client privilege. There were reasons no one should ever know who you truly were. And this man had secrets like Fort Knox had empty gold bins. She thought that was what made him so interesting to her. She had none of her own, or none that were exciting, forbidden pleasures — just the run-of-the-mill secrets. Nothing to shake the foundations of the world. She sighed.

"Something wrong"? he asked, putting the sandwich back on the plate.

"Nah, just wishing my life was a lot more interesting than it has been," she laughed.

CHAPTER SEVEN

Most people think time is a constant. Those who perform, who write, who live moment to moment know it is anything but. It crawls when you beg for it to run. It stops when you most desire motion. As you age, it moves with a rapidity that seems impossible. As season crashes into season, holidays mean less when you have no time to anticipate. Healing happens overnight while taking months. It creeps along. Seconds become hours becoming months. Pain forces time to slow, to stop, to reverse and suffering is infinite.

Each day he walked a little further, his pace increased though he could hardly tell. The café beckoned from the far side of town. Someday, before he died, he would enter of his own free will, but not today. Today he was going to visit his mighty steed. She was closer, only a couple blocks up the main drag.

The '94 LeSabre was scratched, dented, had rust around the left rear wheel well. Even after sitting this long, she still had a puddle of trannie fluid under her. It looked like she'd bled to death right here. He wished he'd replaced that burned out headlamp and fixed the passenger mirror. She deserved better. She had carried him for more than three hundred thousand miles. She should be buried in Arlington. She served, without complaint, brave, through snowstorms, ice, thunderstorms that would've killed an ordinary vehicle, but she wasn't ordinary. She had heart. His hand stroked her fender as he walked to the driver side door.

"She yours?" The gruffness in his voice betrayed the sentiment he obviously felt for all things mechanical. He was a car guy. Automobiles were in his soul.

"Yes." The word held all the love and respect one man can hold, feel for an inanimate object that has moved on to the great beyond.

"Bobby," he held out his hand.

"Padon," he took the offered hand and shook it gratefully.

"She was a good one, yes?" Bobby grinned knowing the answer. "They made 'em good. Made 'em to last. Bet it was comfortable. It was a cruiser, a highway car." Again, he showed his respect. "I was going to tow it to the junk yard, just south of Boseman, but thought you might like to see her before I did. That is, if ya came back from the dead," he snorted. "Heard you'd kicked it. Guess they was wrong about that." He shook his head in wonder, but his eyes were on the car. "Anything in her you need? I got the keys from where you left 'em —in the ignition." He opened the driver's door for Padon.

"If you don't mind," Padon eased himself onto the seat, touching the wheel, the dash, running his fingers across the cloth of the seat. He opened the glovebox, papers fell to the floor, the mess liberated. He dug through what remained. He searched through the pile of songs started and saved, phone numbers to clubs, agents and girls. Things he would do, someday, but the day kept outrunning him. He searched for something far more important. He found it near the bottom. An old, torn and tattered, faded picture of a young girl smiling. She wore a dress of pink satin, a white bow at her neck, dark curls flowed past her tiny shoulders and her smile was shy and knowing. She was as pure a beauty as God had ever created. Wiping a piece of dust from his eye, he shoved the photo into his inside breast pocket.

"I didn't touch nothing. Not after hearing you wasn't as dead as originally thought. Didn't want to invade your privacy," his honor shone through the grease and oil covered uniform.

"Appreciate it, though I don't think there's much here worth invading," Padon smiled his appreciation.

He popped the trunk and stared at the boxes of CDs and empty string packages. There was nothing here, but he had to make a show of going through the mess, so Bobby wouldn't think he was just throwing his old life away that quick and easy. And then he remembered. How could he have forgotten? It was his life preserver. His emergency do-not-touch-unless-death-was-imminent-disaster-loomed-large-and-self-preservation-last hope-only-option-back-up-safety hoard. It was under the spare. He'd shoved it there years ago when he'd bought the car. It might've wound up in the junk yard, if he hadn't just remembered. He remembered putting it there but couldn't remember how much. Had he been flush back then? How long had he had this car? Eight years? Six? Well, the lottery was under the tire, let's see if it's a scratch-off or the big pay-out.

The envelope was dirty, stained and just beautiful. He hoped as he slid it open. It was stuffed with some twenties. Well, that was good. A decent number of tens and, oh my, some fifties! Had to be more than a few hundred here. Maybe five or six, if he was lucky. He counted it out. Damn, almost two grand. When had he had that kind of cash to shove in his trunk? And how had he forgotten it was there? Must have been during that hard-drinking period when he'd had a bit of a resurgence in interest in his tunes and was playing a few larger venues, and partying like a small-time rock star. He had been flush, apparently, and for once didn't just throw it out the window. He'd won the lottery.

"Can I give you something for the trouble of towing it here?" He asked feeling quite charitable all of sudden.

Bobby thought for a moment, glancing at the envelope in Padon's hand. "I shouldn't, what with you being dead and all, but I guess I wouldn't turn it down if you're in a giving mood." He started to put his hand out and just as quick dropped it back to his side. His innate decency chased the little greed in his heart away. "Maybe just buy me a drink or something, sometime, when you're feeling better."

"I'm feeling pretty damn good right now and you shouldn't turn a gift horse down," he shoved two fifties in Bobby's shirt pocket. "Look at it this way, you are worth more than I gave you. It was colder than all get out. You had to pull it off the side of the road and you do this for a living. I'll still buy you a drink as soon as I am up to hanging out in bars again. Thank you." Sincerity filled his grip as he shook Bobby's hand. "You're a good man, and that my friend, is a rarity in this world."

He folded his fortune, shoved it in his pocket and walked with a little spring in his step as he headed back in the direction of the doctor's house. Maybe he could help make it right by her as well. He had never worshipped the almighty dollar and he wouldn't start now. He was alive. He had his Gibson — and now he knew he maintained the ability to use it — his voice and that was all someone like him needed in life.

The air didn't feel as cold. His leg still ached but now was more an annoyance than pain. He felt good. No, he had not worshipped money, but you always felt just a skoosh better with some jack in your pants. Like maybe you weren't a complete drain on society in general and your friends in particular. No one enjoyed being broke. No matter the myth of the starving artist — that was bullshit. Most artists didn't really dream of the big time, they considered that a sign you had lost your artistic integrity. But they liked food on the table, a smile and greeting from the bartender when you entered their place of business, rather than a scowl and anger, combined with the tab from the last few months. Friends avoided broke and girls did not find it sexy in the least. Oh, maybe right at the beginning when they saw you as a project they could fix but broke wore hard. Quick.

Hell, he might even try to make it as far as that café this week. He was feeling chipper as he walked up the path to the front door of Doc's house. He couldn't care less about money until it came time to help someone else or pay someone back, then, it was a good thing. He knew Doctor Caldwell didn't seem to have an affection for it either, but you can always use supplies to serve others and a few extra hundred might help her.

She was sitting and reading in the front parlor as he entered. "You look like the cat who ate the bird," she observed, noting the gleam in his eye and the smirk on his lips.

"I feel pretty good today," he grinned. "A nice walk, not too tired and I might actually be getting sturdier. Hell, I might live!" he barked a cackle and sat down across from her. "How do you pay for all you do? You aren't concerned about my imposition. You make rounds to those who can't come here. You take care of the town and don't seem to get much, except lunch and dinner, in return. How do you do it?" He settled into serious as easy as changing a tie.

"Oh, some folks chip in a few dollars here and there," she shrugged, "and I had savings from when I retired, and investments. I'm not rich, by any means, but I did OK. I am a doctor, you know. But I want for nothing. Everything here is paid for and everyone here helps everyone else. It's a symbiotic relationship. We feed off of each other," she chuckled.

"Well, I think it is time for me to contribute something to the trough," he beamed. Leaning back, he shoved his hand deep into his right jeans pocket. It felt so good to find something besides empty. He pulled out the folded paper and handed it to her. He'd counted it on the way down. It was most, but not all, of his emergency stash. He didn't need it and these people had given him life

She looked at him and then at the wad of cash in her hand. She didn't count it, though she could tell by the few bills sticking out and the heft of it, it was substantial. It was his fortune and he was giving it to her. She wanted to hand it right back. It was probably every nickel he had in the world, but could she? Wouldn't that be spitting in his face, slapping his hand? No, she couldn't give it back.

"I know it's not enough to cover all the costs of keeping me here, taking care of me, keeping me alive, but I wanted you to have that. I'd forgotten it was even in the trunk of the car. It was my emergency buffer. I guess this would be the definition of an emergency," he leaned in towards her. "I want you to know how much I appreciate all you've done. All this town has done. Life," tears filled his eyes, "I had forgotten how much I missed it. Put that in whatever fund you keep going for medications, supplies, whatever. It is the very least I can do." He held her hand with both of his for the briefest of moments and then sat back into the couch.

"Thank you," it was all she could say. He had given her, if not all he had in this world, then, most of it. Not out of indebtedness but out of gratitude, pure and simple gratitude, she had to accept that with the same. "Maybe I can find us a little whiskey to seal the deal," she wiped an eye as she rose and made her way to the kitchen.

"You been holding out on me?" He accused.

"It is for medicinal purposes only." She pointed a finger at him as she returned with the bottle and a couple small glasses, "and some-times just because." She seemed to consider for just a moment, then add-ed "Let's sit out here." She pointed to the dining room, "I don't know why but I always feel more comfortable having a snort at the table rather than out here." She threw him a cockeyed grin and a bob of her head to-wards the dining room table.

"When in Rome, drink like the Romans do," he allowed the words to lift him from the couch and make his way to a dining room chair.

The Kilbeggan bottle had been hardly dented when she twisted off the cap. She poured just a three count in each of the two small glass-es. They clinked in salute and sipped. She swallowed slow, allowing the liquid to saunter down her throat. She allowed the aroma of the fine whiskey to envelope her nose and slightly parted lips. She smiled and took another slow sip. "Heaven."

An easy smile welcomed his second sip and they sat back in their chairs at the corner of the dining room table, taking in the silence. "You know, this is what a good doctor does," he grinned. "Here's to alternative medicine." The clinking of glasses was interrupted by a door opening, a vocal "brrr" and a door closing. Footsteps, a coat removed and hung, footsteps, and silence.

"Hrumpf," said the exasperated female voice. "Little early in the day for a snoot, ain't?" She asked indignant. "Couldn't even wait a few minutes for the serfs to show up and share in the bounty, could you?" They turned to see a scowling Janet standing in the doorway staring ac-cusations at the open bottle.

"I'll get you a glass," Doc Caldwell said and rose from the chair.

"No, let me," Padon pushed her back down and strolled to the kitchen. "She has done more than her share of waiting on me. Allow me to return a small measure of kindness." He returned with a small glass and set it on the table. He carefully poured and passed it over to Janet with a flourish and a slight bow.

The three glasses met just above the center of the table with a clink and a silent toast. Padon had always preferred silence as a toast as it allowed each to salute whom or what they marked. He always drank to fallen friends and times only he knew. He assumed all did the same. They sat in silence allowing the fine whiskey time to enjoy its new home.

"Oh, Janet, this is Padon." Doc introduced Janet to the man she'd helped keep alive for the past month or so.

"And a musician," said Janet tipping her glass to him in salute. "Maybe I'll get to hear you play sometime," she shot the doctor a glare indicating Janet's knowledge that Doc has already had the pleasure. Another thing, like the whiskey, not shared with Janet. "We don't have any of those in this town, trust me," said she with a giggle.

"That's a fact," added the doctor, "they tried a Karaoke night down at Merle's Bar and it was the most horrendous thing you've ever had to suffer. I don't know where people get the idea they can carry a tune, but I am certain it would've preferred to be left laying by the side of the road to die." She grimaced at her phraseology, "There is no talent in this town. Nice people — folks you would give your life for, but," she paused for a sip, "you'd have to love them a whole lot, to sit and listen to them sing." She drained the glass and set it on the table.

"Well, once you ladies get me back to myself again, maybe we'll play some tunes and see if I can pay back a little that way as well." He stared at his empty glass, considering, but decided a nap might be the better part of valor. Excusing himself with a slight bow, an apology for being no fun, he made his way to the back bedroom.

The dreams came immediately. This was becoming the norm, so he sat back in his head to enjoy the show. He knew he would be starring in this production and it would probably be unpleasant but didn't feel like waking to change the program.

Of course, memories come to dreams, to taunt, to remind, to torture what is left of the soul. Here he was, thinking he could maybe settle into this town. They would accept him for what he was, not what he might or might not have been. He had allowed himself to envision himself living here. Playing music up the road and doing odd jobs to make his living. He wouldn't need much, not here. Everybody pulled their own weight, not by money earned but by what they brought to the town. He could give them something they didn't have. Music.

His dream found him onstage, that night. The one night of all nights he wished he could erase from his life. Instead, it was the turd in the punchbowl. The knife between his fifth and sixth rib.

She'd gone. He didn't think it would affect him. She'd been gone for a couple years. She just hadn't left yet. Now she had. He thought he might be relieved to have that pressure out of his life. He just wasn't good with people. He could entertain the shit out of them when he was of a mind to, but he couldn't relate. He couldn't be in a rational relationship with another human being. Not one on one, only as an audience to his own ego. His own one man show. It was how he was put together. It was him.

He'd tried with her. She bore him a child — a child he loved dearly from the moment he'd first held her tiny little body and felt her breath on his face. But he could no more give them himself than he could separate himself from the stage. That was always the problem, wasn't it? He only existed on the stage. When he sang. When he played. And they wanted him to be a real person when he was home.

But there was nothing left to give by the time he got home. He'd given it away already. To them. To the ticket buying public. They loved him as well. There just wasn't enough of him to satisfy everyone. So, he'd made his choice without even thinking about it. It wasn't a conscious decision. It was innate and made for him the day he was born. Nature or nurture. It was his nature. He had his audience. His wife had their child and the child her mother. He'd stopped trying.

He wasn't an asshole about it. He wasn't mean. He wasn't abusive. He wasn't horrible to them. He just wasn't...anything. He was an empty place in their lives and hearts. There was nothing there for any of them and she'd had the courage to realize it and call a spade a spade and walk away. He hadn't tried to stop her. She took whatever she wanted: the money, the car, even a couple guitars. Everything she wanted but him. She couldn't have that as it wasn't there anymore. He watched them drive away and then picked up his guitar, the only one that mattered, and went to the gig that night.

And every gig he could find every night he could fill. It was his life. Not his livelihood, his life. He breathed it, ate of it and took succor from it. He missed them from time to time, but he would just write another song and they would go away. It was easy. Until that night. He'd done something he hadn't in over a year. He'd let them back in. Not physically — that would never happen — but in his head. The little girl and her mother waiting in line to buy an ice cream earlier in the day had spurred his memories. He'd run up to them — he didn't know why; he'd not done that when they left — and scared the shit out of these complete strangers.

It wasn't them. How could it have been them? Why would they be a thousand miles away from the door they'd walked out, standing here, buying ice cream? He was losing his mind. He required a drink. Just a quick shot to steady the nerves. Something to stop his hands from shaking. Something to chase them away from his mind.

If one is good, two will send them further away. And three and four reinforced the battlements. He was drunk when he took the stage. He was drunk when he picked up his Gibson. He was drunk when he fumbled with the microphone. He could get it together, just give him a minute, he could do this.

The chords wouldn't fit. He was trying to shove major 7ths into 7th holes, and minors into majors into 9ths. It might have been passable if only he knew some lyrics to fit but he couldn't seem to find them. And when he finally did find a word or two, he couldn't get his lips, tongue and teeth on the same train. It was a wreck. An embarrassment and then, an end of trust.

People will forgive much of an entertainer. They will not forgive being taken for granted. They hold a grudge and word spreads fast. The cancellations outnumbered the bookings and the spiral picked up speed. He should have become an alcoholic by all accounts, but he couldn't manage it. He preferred the purity of self-pity and wallowing in self-destructive thoughts and actions. Drugs came and went. Playing places that were degrading and abusive. Living the life of the hermit pauper. He couldn't forgive himself his life and that show had knocked all of his confidence, his self-worth, right out of him. The dream wouldn't end, and he couldn't get it to end until he had lived every second of the abomination.

Until he had experienced every second of shame and the downfall. Until all hope had been seared from his mind.

He was shattered and sapped as he lay awake in the early afternoon light, gasping for breath and crying. He hated himself and hated that he had allowed himself to believe. Jeannie, whoever she was, should have driven by, let him freeze, left him on the roadside like the garbage he was. She should have let him die.

Grabbing hold of his emotions he calmed his breathing and the sobs that wracked his body. Control, he had to gain control over himself. Laying on the bed he stared at the ceiling. White, featureless, begging introspection. Allow the thoughts to flow. Allow life to wash over him like ocean waves, battering, rolling, pushing and prodding. Breathe deep, cleansing breaths. Picture yourself in a boat on a river, he smiled, or beside a deep forest pond. Quiet, peace filled. Breathe. Shit.

His depression took seed and germinated, sprouting deep within his insecure psyche, sending out feeder roots to suck into his will and spirit. Oh good, now flourishing and establishing itself deep within his insecurities and blossoming into a full-blown anxiety attack with a side of despair. He should leave this place. The was nothing for him here. These were not his people. He had no people. Just himself. What could he do except be a parasite, living off good intentions? He would suck them dry and then move on. It was his M.O. Not this time!

But how was he to leave? He had given the bulk of his fortune to the doctor. He could hardly ask for it back. He could steal it back and run like hell, but could he really? No, not even he would sink that low. Plus, it was minus degrees outside, so, there would be no hitch-hiking or walking away. He would die unless someone found him and brought him back here. A vicious cycle of life if there ever was one. He was weak and wouldn't survive an hour. He had to stay. He was left with no choice but to rehab, build up his strength and stamina until the spring and then find a way to leave these good folks without having done too much damage. He would keep a low profile and try not to involve himself in the day-to-day or any innocent lives. It was the best he could do for now.

The room closed in around him. Just as his own life closed in, condemning him, denouncing him, forcing him to face his true self. He was his music and that was all. He had forsaken all others. Relationships, family, friends, his own daughter, and for what? For songs, applause, the lights and adoration. Fleeting adoration. A few minutes in the limelight and then loneliness or surrounded by those who only wanted to be here because of the songs. That was the coin of the realm.

How shallow. How devoid of anything of value. Words, music, chords didn't keep one warm on a cold night. They didn't fill an evening with quiet conversation, laughter or companionship. You couldn't watch them grow and learn, smile with accomplishment and approval. They didn't hug you back. They didn't hold you when you were down and comfort you when you'd lost it all. They were your cold, heartless creations. Fool's gold.

The ceiling stared back, emotionless, indifferent. He'd almost died. Maybe he had died and come back, and the doctor didn't want him to know. What did it matter? It was time for change. He wasn't dead now, and he didn't have to be. He could come out of this, couldn't he? It wasn't too late for him to grab a little happiness, was it? Yeah, yeah it was. He had nothing. Some songs, a guitar and no saleable skills. Who was looking for a guy in his late fifties that had spent his life fucking around and avoiding responsibility? What did he have to offer? The scent of coffee and the sound of his name whispered through a slightly opened door roused him from his stupor. He could pretend sleep or face the evening, another empty evening.

The coffee was hot and strong. You had to appreciate the restorative powers of a good cup of coffee and how hard it could be to find one. People actually served a brown, lukewarm, water you could see through and called it coffee. Not this, this would stick to your ribs and stiffen the spine. Yeah, he'd live, though what he would do with that life was a blank canvass. But he knew he had to work his way out of this funk. And quit hating himself and his music. It may not be much, but it was what had defined him for most of his life. He could hardly throw it in the trash heap. He just had to redefine it and prioritize. Yeah, and see if he could get the world to spin backwards. Aiy-yai-yee.

"Care for a game of cards?" asked Janet.

"I'm not much of a card player. Luck doesn't seem to care for my company," he groused.

"Perfect!" chorused both doctor and assistant, giddy with the prospect of a fleecing. "Penny a point, I'll get the cards." Janet went to the buffet and pulled a well-worn deck from the top drawer while the doctor cleared a space at the table.

"Something tells me…," he began.

"And you should've listened, but too late now," said Doctor Caldwell shuffling. "You still have any cash, or do we have to run you a tab?" shot the loaded question.

"I still have a few bucks, and maybe I'll get lucky," he jibed right back.

"Tell you what," doc says, sharing a conspiratorial glance with her assistant, "you win, and I'll buy down at Merle's. I win, and you play me another tune. Janet wins and you play two."

His eyes jumped from one face to the other. Were they mocking him? Or forcing his hand somehow to make him play and give him more reason to continue therapy? Or was there more afoot than he could glom? Well, there was only one way to find out, "Deal them," and Padon put his whole leg in the pool.

"Shall we play Texas Hold'em?" asked Janet with such mock innocence none could contain their laughter. "Well, it is the most popular game right now. Everyone knows how. Do you?" she directed the question at Padon, who ignored her taunt.

Poker is a game of concentration and math, observation and cunning, and played in silence. Professional poker that is. Poker played around a dining room table, in the late afternoon, with folks you know is a game of gibes, heckles, dares, teasing and much laughter — especially penny ante. Hell, with these stakes you could possibly win a dollar all in the course of one evening. It was not a serious game. It was a time passer and a way to get to know people better.

You could tell a lot about a person by how they played games. Any games. Whether there was betting involved or if it was just to win, a person's true self would come out sooner or later. Were you a good winner? Loser? Did you really care about the score or the money? If you could destroy an opponent with one move, would you? Or did you prefer the companionship and so would allow the game to continue just to lengthen the evening? There were so many traits that would emerge during a game it was like an X-ray into the soul.

Padon was not a competitive person, not by nature. He didn't mind winning but losing didn't make him crazy and he preferred the camaraderie of an evening shared. It was why he was such a lousy card player. He was more concentrated on the conversation than the cards.

While Doctor — he has got to find out what the hell her name was — Caldwell shuffled, he went to the kitchen and retrieved three glasses and a bottle of bourbon from the cabinet. He wasn't going to grab her good whiskey for a friendly game of poker. He poured each of them a dram or two, as his grandpa used to call it, and saluted both with a tip of the glass. Sips taken, cards dealt, another round of losing for the guest.

After the next hour he threw up his hands in surrender. These two were sharks and had cleaned him out of two bucks. Damn! He couldn't keep this up 'til spring! Well, he owed them more than the cash and a deal was a deal, though after his soul-searching and crash of depression earlier he hardly felt like pulling the Gibson out of its case. But he'd made the bargain with these two devils and whether they had taken him for a ride or not, he'd pay up.

He grabbed the guitar from its resting place behind the end table in the parlor and came back to find his glass had been replenished and the two ladies sitting on one side of the table with his chair on the other. A concert, eh? He tweaked the tuning just a bit, to buy some time while he decided what to play.

At first, he thought to play something known, something written by someone else, some simple thing everybody knew and would fulfill his promise. He didn't feel like playing and it would fulfill the bet. He wasn't sure he would ever 'feel' like playing again. But these two had saved his life. He owed them big time. He owed them something special.

Hmmm, while he'd been traipsing back from the garage today a song had presented itself, almost in its entirety. He wondered — should he chance that? After all, it wasn't a concert. It's just playing for some friends. He smiled to himself. When was the last time he'd just played to play, sang for some folks he liked? No money, no lights, no stage, no glory. Just music and a little love. He monkeyed around with the tune in his head, his hands riding along, maybe change that Em to an E, oh, and slip in a Bm on the chorus. Slow to medium tempo and the lyric. He'd always had a gift of memory and words. And even if he screwed them up a bit, he could fudge them, and Doc and Janet would never know. Sure, what the hell.

It was a pretty tune, almost a love song, about those who heal. He would call it *Healing Hands*. He got most of the words corralled and rolling in the right direction and for a first time through he was satisfied. It would need some work but, OK. He looked up from where his eyes had rested on the top of the guitar, a practice he had adopted years before to block out distraction and concentrate, to the astonished expressions on the two women's faces. Both had tears filling their eyes and great big, ear to ear smiles that filled their entire bodies.

"Oh my," flatly stated Doctor Caldwell.

"Oh, dear, oh my," responded Janet.

"Like it?" unnecessary but asked just the same.

"I would almost, and please forgive my presumption, but I would almost think it was about us." Janet and Doc shared a glance and then an embarrassed silence.

"You'd be right. I wrote it today while I walked thinking about all you had done for me," he grinned ear to ear as well. So pleased they had liked the song. How long had it been that he'd felt like this when he'd played a song for someone he cared about? And he truly cared about these two women. Not just because they'd saved him, but because they did that for everyone. Without, he was quite certain, ever really thinking of themselves. He was almost giddy with pleasure. "Want to hear another one?"

"About us?" they gushed, and then, "Forgive two old women, we are just so besides ourselves, just so astounded and so, so very happy. Yes, please, we would love a little more." And they all three barked a quick laugh at the Oliver Twist, twist.

Another dram to warm the vocals and lubricate the fingers and he was off on a lively tale of love and betrayal and a horse race to win. You could feel the hooves as they pounded on the hard-packed dirt, kicking clods into the faces of those who would dare try to catch her. The tempo increased with the passion and intensity of the story until it all collapsed into a comedy of errors and misgivings. It was always a crowd pleaser and he knew they would love it. He hadn't been wrong. It was his attempt at Shakespeare in song. It wasn't perfect, but it was fun.

And then his goodnight song. A sing-along, drink in hand, arms around each other, slightly drunk and filled with love, kind of tune that made people remember what a wonderful time they'd had. And precluded anyone asking for an encore. When he was done, he was done. He had given the crowd all he had and was not one for milking want from them. Tonight, he wanted the true feel of the song to come through. The feel of companionship, love, friends, shared time and thanks. It was how he had envisioned the song when he'd written it. It was a thank you, love you, to the crowd. It had lost that meaning over the years. It had found it again here, in a dining room, in a town no one had ever heard of, to two women whom he adored. Perfect.

He set the guitar against the wall. They did not ask for another. They would enjoy the remainder of the evening in conversation and camaraderie. And that was all they would ever be, — friends, and it was more than enough. And if that was his last concert, his last show, it would be alright as well.

The thought struck him like a kidney punch. He had not expected it, as he had never truly thought it before. Not in his life. Oh, there had been times, a bad show, tired, too many in a row or just pissy at that particular moment, where he swore, he would walk away tomorrow. But tomorrow becomes today and the morning light changes everything. He knew he had never seriously considered hanging up the guitar and getting a real job. He was now. Though, again, the problem was that he hadn't worked for anyone but himself for thirty-five, almost, forty years. The real job might prove difficult.

His mental meandering was snapped back to the dining room by the end of a question, "...from?" asked Janet.

"I'm sorry, what was the question?" he focused.

The Doctor and Janet shared a knowing glance. They had years of experience when relating to recuperating patients. Concentration slipped like tires on ice and the direction of any conversation could ping-pong around a room.

"I was asking where you're from," she repeated.

"All over, really," he puzzled, not wanting them to think he was avoiding the answer but attempting honesty. "You see, it's been so long since I had a home, besides the Buick, that to answer truthfully is hard. I was born outside of Buffalo, so, I guess that is where I am 'from'. But then again, not really. It is where I was born and spent my childhood, yet it doesn't define me."

And this is where he had always had trouble with conversation. He wanted precision in his answers, not washed-out blotches of half remembered facts. To Padon, 'where he was from' denoted a place or region that defined who he was, not just a town where he happened to be born. So, to say he was from Buffalo was as succinct as saying he was from Earth. It didn't tell the story.

"I'm from the northeast, as that is the region that birthed my style, the nature, of my music. And music is what always defined me. It is who I am. Therefore, I am from the northeast. I guess, if I had to pick a town, it would be Burlington, Vermont.'

"I first showed up in Burlington in the early eighties. I'd heard they had a pretty good original music scene and I had to get away from the creative destruction that was Buffalo and my family. Two hundred and twenty-seven dollars, an old VW microbus, a very used Epiphone six string and freedom. That's where I was born," he sighed and hugged the visual close. He could smell it, fresh as a newborn child, soft as a lover's caress and warm as morning. He hadn't held this memory in a long time, he wondered how he had forgotten. It felt like home. "Found a farm outside of town where the fella didn't mind if I parked it at night as long as nothing funny was going on. Had to be in his nineties and spry as a sixty-year-old. Wasn't very big, that farm, but it gave him purpose, a reason to get out of bed and walk into the sunshine every morning. Had a couple of maple trees, I used to help him tap them in the spring and harvest the sap. It was pretty cool," he smiled, and his hand gripped an imaginary hammer in response.

"They were good days. I was just a kid, just turning twenty, with a fistful of half written songs, some chords with minors and, of course, like any lovesick kid, Major 7ths, and a head and heart full of dreams. Dumb, too dumb to know how dumb I was. Too stupid to fail. That's the beauty of youth. You're just too dumb to know you've failed, so you keep banging your head on the rock. Something will give, the rock, your head, your will, something. I got lucky; the rock crumbled. I had some songs they started playing on radio stations throughout the Northeast. And I started in motion. I began moving so constant and so fast, I just never could get it to slow down." Now the melancholy made an entrance onto the stage.

"That's the biggest trouble with this kind of life. You start to believe it's true." His gazed found the front window and followed the road to places he didn't want to return. "And now I'm here." He drank the last sip of bourbon and set the glass, slow and easy, on the table.

Well, that was as concise a synopsis as either woman would have believed. Ask a question, get an answer. And the surface had only been scratched. It would be a long winter.

"Well, we're damn glad you are," replied Doc Caldwell, "no matter how it came about. You have a home here for as long as you need." She gathered the glasses to take them into the kitchen.

"I have a question for you," said Padon McKenzie.

"And what might that be," the Doctor turned to look him in the eye, Janet grabbed the glasses with a 'look' as she passed to the kitchen.

"What is your name?" he grinned, "if we're going to be friends and sharing our lives for a time, I can't keep calling you Doctor or Doc or Mrs. Caldwell."

Mrs. Caldwell. No one had called her that in such a long time; and never in this town. It sounded old. A name from a very long time ago. Not a young woman's name. A widow's name, a spinster, a dried up, shriveled, old...stop it, woman. She screamed it loud inside her empty head. You have lived a blessed existence. A long and blessed existence. You have helped many and asked for nothing and now, you have this gift of a new friend. Do not get lost in your stupid 'old' insecurities. "JoAnn."

"JoAnn, I like it. It fits you. Like a young girl from Northern Cali in the sixties. Perfect." And he grabbed his guitar and headed to his room.

"Well," JoAnn remarked.

"How come I didn't know your name?" A little hurt, Janet finished washing the glasses.

"You never asked."

CHAPTER EIGHT

Padon had never been one for naps. He preferred to write or practice during the afternoon and early evening. People were at work or shopping or taking care of children midday or preparing the evening meal, so it always seemed the best time to hole up and work. It came down to his aversion to the human race. Friends had asked, if he didn't particularly care for people why did he subject himself to working in places filled with them? And he had, in his meticulous and precise way, explained that when he was on stage, he was not with them, he was separate. Away. He was not surrounded by them. He was not a part of them. He was not 'of the crowd', but alone on the stage. He was, most of the time, Baltimore excluded, in control of the show, the tempo, the music, the mood. He was the conductor with his back to the audience ruling all. It was his dominion. He was comfortable.

Now, having attempted the nap earlier, and seen its results, he wasn't sure he wanted to close his eyes to slumber just yet. Maybe he should jot down the lyrics and chords for *Healing Hand*s, then he could read for a while, tire himself out. Mayhap sleep without dream.

He'd had more than enough of his Dickensian Christmas Carol nightmares. He had no want to relive a life previously lived. He knew intimately every minute detail of every shitty thing he'd ever done or said. It was his own personal hell. He had relived them every time he was alone, and his mind wasn't occupied. His wife, his daughter, girls, contemporaries, sidemen, roadies, producers, people. He had treated people like shit at times. Not always. He wasn't a complete asshole but enough—enough to know there would be a reckoning. He had some Karma hard on his tail and it would not be denied.

Words to paper, notations of chords riding shotgun atop, sleep continued to run ahead of him. Reading should slow it down enough to catch up. He found a Heinlein amongst the scattered books in his room, Stranger in a Strange Land. He hadn't read that since he was a teen. That should help him drift off to never-never land.

His sleep was restful, dreamless and he woke refreshed and ready for whatever life might throw his way. The scent of dark, rich coffee found its way to his room and he followed the beacon. It was early to him, very early, to be honest — well before noon. He had never been an early riser and his life on the stage had only cemented the habit. Now, here he was up with the sun. It was ten o'clock.

"Sleep well?" asked an obviously ready-for-the-day, fully dressed, dirty plate and empty coffee cup resting in front of her, JoAnn Caldwell. She set the folded morning paper down next to his cup.

"Yes, I did," he replied gratefully. "Thank you, and I do mean, thank you. I cannot remember the last time I slept so peacefully and, actually, rested. I don't know if it's the company or the bed or the locale, and I don't care. I feel good. Think I might try some exercises before I take my walk," he poured his coffee and sat down. "Is there anything I can do for you today?" He continued, refusing the paper.

"Well, I don't know," she thought out loud. "If you eat something to put a little meat on those bones, I might let you shovel the walk. We had a couple inches last night, light, fluffy stuff, and I don't think anyone will be around 'til this afternoon. We are not high on the list." She made the decision last night as she readied for bed to allow him more activity. It was time to begin building up strength and endurance and shoveling snow might provide just the right PT. It was a light snow and shouldn't tax him. Plus, he would feel as though he were contributing.

"Think I can?" Surprise tinged the tone of the question.

"One way to find out." she smiled, "but first, you need some eggs and sausage. Something healthy." She got up, turned and stepped toward the stovetop in one fluid motion. She might be in her golden years, but she still could move smooth and easy. And she may not be a chef, but she could scramble eggs.

The shoveling was just enough to work the muscles in his arms, legs and back. He could feel the strain as he lifted the light snow and tossed it to the side. He was glad it was not the heavy snow of Vermont, where each shovel full weighed thirty pounds — or so it felt. The exertion was good. The physical action. The expending of energy. Manual labor brought a smile of satisfaction. He knew it was busy work, but he required movement. There was a wonderful freedom in manual labor that most never took the time to enjoy. The repetition of motion. The rhythm of the job and seeing what one had accomplished. And in his weakened state a clean sidewalk was just such an accomplishment.

He hung his leather coat on the peg and put his gloves and scarf on the hall table. He was worn out. Shit, when he was a boy, he could shovel snow all day for a dollar a drive and not be tired when he was done. He and his buddies would have snowball fights, then take their earnings up to the Red and White and buy a ton of candy to celebrate the spoils of a job well done. Now, he just wanted a cup of tea and a set.

The house was still, as if sleeping. He removed his boots and on cat's paws made his way to the kitchen. He filled the tea kettle with fresh water from the spigot, he turned on the gas and lit a match. He found it so endearing that JoAnn had this old-fashioned stove — the kind you lit with a wood match and set the kettle on the flame. Of course, she had a wood tea box where she kept a half dozen flavors of tea. He went with the Earl Grey, an old favorite from his coffeehouse days. He loved to order tea in a coffeehouse, it went directly to his sense of absurd.

The quiet of the house was reassuring. He could hear it settling here and there, the wind pushing a branch against the window, the soft whistle of the kettle. Tea was almost ready. He could think.

He had always thought about writing a book. Maybe fantasy, or sci-fi, or maybe the great American novel. He snorted his derision at the arrogance of the thought. But maybe here, in this quiet reflective town he could write. Write something worthwhile. Away from the performing, the distractions, the people who wanted a piece. He could concentrate here. Hell, he didn't think the Doc had a TV. Funny, how he hadn't even noticed that fact until now. Did anyone in this town? They had to.

But, maybe, just maybe, he could settle here for just a while, just long enough to think, to write, to collect what was left of him and, and, yeah, do what? Go back to fighting for scraps of respect at hole-in-the-wall bars and rundown coffeehouses? Begging for a gig from people he had filled rooms for years before, but now couldn't seem to remember what he did? Playing for nickels and dimes and a few beers while people who couldn't put a proper sentence together criticized his songs? Is that all that was left for him? He'd kill himself first. Hadn't he already tried that?

Had his breakdown and subsequent near death been intentional? He should take a few days, weeks and months to try and answer that universal truth before deciding on anything else related to life.

The aroma of the tea wafted on steam to please the olfactory senses. He could feel the calm fill his head and slowly relax his muscles. He had to find a way out of his own self-destruct mode.

Muscles tired but happy and thinking they might still enjoy a walk, whispered their want. Was he overtaxing the system? Wouldn't be the first time. He had a habit of pushing too hard. Whether in performance, driving too many hours and miles, healing — hence the pain in his right leg. Living or dying, he always had to see how far he could drive on empty. He'd tried to slow down so many times, but it just wasn't in his genes. Today would be different. He would read, try to write something, drink tea and relax. He'd done his physical therapy on the sidewalk. Maybe he'd play the Gibson for a while, toughen up the fingers. Yeah, a nice tranquil day.

The book held no interest. His head was an empty vessel floating on a sea of confusion. The tea made him pee and he'd played for an hour. He was bored and in need of motion. Damn him for what he was! He could no more change than he could fly to Venus on wings of love and satin. Where had he left his coat?

The bitter air bit everywhere his skin was exposed. He'd pull on this sleeve, raise his collar, pull down on the bottom, each time covering one body part and exposing another. He was annoyed, and it was cold. Was it always this raw up here? Probably, the altitude and the thin air combined with the vast loneliness and a dash of wrong clothes for the weather and he wanted a hot cup of coffee. Tea was pleasant when one wished civilized comfort but for living, breathing and existence one needed a hot cup of strong black coffee. He was pretty sure that was in the Bible somewhere, or the Constitution. He wandered aimlessly. Trying to focus on anything but the cold, it was impossible.

It was amazing the amount of energy expended trying to get the mind to detour from something it found uncomfortable. Once the mind zeroed in on discomfort it became a five-year-old wanting a toy — and only that toy — to the point of holding its' breath until it got it. His brain would not allow him to think of what he wanted, it wanted to contemplate the freeze. His feet moved. His breath fogged in and out. He hunkered down as far as the leather would allow, discomfort his only companion. The scent of fresh brewed coffee roused him from his frigid stupor. He needed coffee and he needed it now!

He opened the door where coffee could be had and stopped just as the door closed behind him. An uncomfortable realization slapped him hard as he saw her turn at the sound of the closing door. It had closed quietly behind him but sounded, in his ears, like the slamming of a prison cell. If his body would've responded he would've turned and walked back out. But he was frozen in her gaze like a deer about to get splattered all over a very busy highway. Shit.

The slip of a twenty something with her blond hair in braids, sporting a red flannel over black T and jeans handed him a single page menu and told him he could sit anywhere. He slunk to the empty counter and sat, hiding himself in the very skimpy menu.

"Coffee?" asked a familiar voice.

"Please," he said, setting down the piece of paper. She set the cup in front of him and made no move for the creamer and sugar, daring him to ask.

"Look, I don't know what I did or said or implied, or whatever the other day," he began, warming his hands on the porcelain cup, "but I'm sorry. We seem to have gotten off on the wrong foot, or leg..." He shrugged, and waited, took a sip and waited some more. He was not used to apologizing to a woman. This was virgin territory. He would have to tread carefully.

She considered him for several long--there's that time thing again—minutes or hours. Was he sweating? It was chilly in here—in more ways than one. He shouldn't be sweating. Should he take off his coat or would that be giving too much away? Oh, screw it, the coat came off and hung on the back of the chair. If she was going to throw him out, he could grab it as he ran like a rabbit for the door.

"You didn't do anything," her shoulders lost some of their rigidness and she seemed to relax a smidge. "You just reminded me of someone I thought I'd forgotten all about. Something in the way you said or sounded or stood, I don't even know myself." Now she walked to around the counter, pulled out a chair and sat next to him.

"We all have baggage," he began, and she shut him down with a look. He was to listen and no more.

"Yes, we do," she granted him, backing off a half step, "but I thought I'd left all of mine at the state line. I thought it'd been thrown off the train a thousand miles and twenty years ago. Then you come waltzing into town, all dead and everything, and resurrect the ghosts." She got up, leaned over the counter, he couldn't help but stare at her figure as she did, and grabbed herself a cup motioning for the twenty something to please grab the coffee pot as she walked by.

"I didn't mean to…" What? Die? Be found and brought back to life? To what? He couldn't finish a thought he'd never seriously considered.

"This is not about you!" exasperation overflowed and spilled onto the floor, "What is it with men? They always think everything is about them!" She turned face to him, the better to glare. "You were just something that happened, like a scent out of the past, or a torn picture in the bottom of the drawer, you sparked a nasty memory and nasty reaction. I'm the one who is sorry." She finished and drank deep of her coffee to buy time and breath.

"Jeannie, come here a minute."

Why did that name sound familiar?

"You two should meet, officially," Maggie smiled as the young woman came to stand between them, "Jeannie this is, shit, I don't even know who you are!" she realized with a combination of embarrassment and a laugh.

"Padon, Padon McKenzie," he bowed the introduction.

"Well, Padon McKenzie, this is Jeannie Walton, she pulled your ass out of the cold abyss of death, into her pickup and back to life."

He stared at this tiny woman. She couldn't be much more than five foot and a wish, though built like a gymnast under her flannels and jeans. He tried to imagine her dragging his cold, dead carcass into a pickup truck. It was a hard picture to paint, she was obviously much stronger than her appearance and tougher than her braids would indicate. Something to keep in mind.

"You're the dead guy!?" She grinned ear to ear, looking as pretty as a spring sunrise over the ocean.

"Apparently, that is who I shall be known as, as long as I stay in this town," he guffawed and grabbed her in as much of a bear hug as he could manage. She took a second, unsure of how to react, and then hugged him back. As they separated, he wiped the tears that had sprung into his eyes and were now running as fast as they could down his cheek. "I don't know how you thank someone for your life," he blubbered hugging her again. "I guess I didn't know how much it meant to me..." he let the words float away aimless and shrugged his verbal incompetence.

"It's OK," embarrassed at his overzealous display—though what else could one expect from the person whose life you'd saved — and looked at the floor. She'd just done what anybody would've done if they'd come across a dead guy on the side of the road. "Nice blanket," she recovered.

"I guess I'm going to keep it," he laughed.

They spent the better part of an hour deep in conversation and gratitude. He expressed undying thanks, her embarrassed, Maggie poured coffee and laughing. Then it was time to get out of the way and let these fine folk work.

His thoughts followed his footsteps towards the Doctor's house and warmth. He was filled with a sense of contentment. Well, he was pretty sure that was the sensation of content; he couldn't be certain as he'd never had the feeling before. His life had been a contortion of overload: Pleasure, pain, joy, sorrow, depression. Lots and lots of depression, ecstasy and ego, but never contentment. He liked it.

It appeared his kerfuffle with Maggie had been smoothed over. They were on friendly speaking terms. Misunderstandings left to fester only bred anger, mistrust and loathing. It was better to air them out, let the sunshine cleanse and purify and if not rectify, at the very least, allow things to end on a pleasant chord. He thought they could become friends.

It was a strange thought; one he didn't think he'd ever entertained before. And it was mortifying. In his entire life he didn't think he'd ever thought of any woman as a friend. They were territory to be taken, conquered and abandoned for richer, greener pastures. Win them over for a night, a week, a month, but don't give them anything of yourself they could claim or hold you with. It was the game. It had always been the game.

Had it been that way with his wife? His daughter? Now he had to wonder, to re-evaluate. What had his life been worth? Had it all been just empty, ego driven, conquests of fluff? Shiny objects to capture his attention for a brief moment before another came along? God, he was shallow if all that was true. And did that make his art, his songs, what he had thought was his soul, just as shallow and empty?

Was his music shallow and without merit because he had only written from want? Was it just a lure to catch the prettiest fish? No! It had to be more. Look at the joy it had brought to his fans. Though they were never legion. There were hundreds, sometimes thousands, and they loved his songs. His old songs, he corrected himself. The ones he, himself, thought just love jingles meant to sell the idea of love masquerading as lust, and joy as want fulfilled. But were they? The feeling of contentment had fled him as surely as his wife and child years ago. He was bare bones and little else. He was tired—weak. The cold and emotional purging had taken their toll. He wanted only a bed with a thick down comforter and dark. A place to burrow into and hide in his shame. He was a sham.

Nobody could talk him out of a good mood quicker or more completely than he could. Stick with your strengths, boy.

He was in a sour mood when he closed the door and wrapped himself in the warmth of Doctor Caldwell's home. It was quiet, though it was always quiet in this home. No blaring TV shouting incoherent banalities, radio playing songs nobody listened to anymore, just filling airspace. Half a phone conversation with the sound of one voice giving half the conversation and allowing you to fill in what was being said on the other end: just quiet. He liked it, he needed it. She must be out seeing patients or shopping or hanging with Janet.

He stopped himself short of entering the kitchen and pouring himself a heavy shot of forget, choosing the better route straight into the bedroom. He required sleep and escape, not escape and hangover. He knew the dreams would come. He could never escape himself completely but maybe he could hide for a while.

Padon considered staying awake. It was early. There was no necessity to slip between the sheets. Hell, it was only dusk. But he was sapped and what would putting off the inevitable do? Exactly! So, why not face it. Maybe he could have his dose of nightmare, wake up, exhaust himself, then find some restful sleep. It was a plan, not a good one, but a plan.

CHAPTER NINE

Sleep was an elusive cat, to say the least. His body was tired from the walking, shoveling and healing. His emotions drained from the café, dancing a tightrope with Maggie and meeting Jeannie. He should have been asleep before his head hit the pillow, but his mind had been neglected and now wanted his attention. It has been the curse of the creative mind for centuries that when the body and soul wished only rest, it wished to play. It was the petulant child, the Muse, dancing and singing, prodding and begging, whining and crying when everyone wanted to sleep. And it would not be denied.

The nymph danced on his nose and rolled through his head, bobbing and weaving, so he couldn't catch what she whispered and put pen to paper. Just out of reach, tantalizing, seductively pulling his attention here and there. The scrap of an idea. A chorus of wonder. "Try to sleep," she whispered in his ear, taunting. "Try and you will miss all I am giving to you. A song of love, a poem to describe indescribable beauty. Here are the words you've been looking for, for the past ten years. Here is that chord you could never discover. Just come play with me."

So, he scribbled on a scrap here and an envelope or anything close to hand. Put pen to pad while the laptop took its time warming up and rebooting. How could anything that was supposed to be so fast start so slow. Why did the goddesses and godlings tempt and torture him so; he was quite certain they were stealing his sanity for barter. And yet, he was just as certain they were handing him a new life, if only he could be patient enough to wait for a bite before jerking the line.

This was what he used to live for and had forgotten. This is what used to keep him awake for days with wonder. Trying to capture beauty and story, elusive and grand, to make the ink tell the tale. For years he wrote to get away from what they wanted. He wrote with anger and spite. If they wanted pretty love songs or happy tunes of drinking and carousing, he would write dark, morose thought-provoking dissertations on the condition of man. He wrote not from the soul, not from the heart, but from self-loathing and pain.

He'd neglected the chase of a lyric, a line, a chord that fit like a hand carved puzzle piece into that verse. The butterfly net has holes in it. If only he could weave something better. The vision of Maggie beckoned him, imploring him to bring her into the song, just as dream Jeannie sashayed by, reminding him, he owed her life. Sleep would not be captured until the illusive rhyme could be found and only then could he rest.

The guitar was behind the table in the parlor. Did he dare run out to get it in only his skivvies? "Of course," said the Muse, "you need to be dressed for writing not write for dressing. Grab it. Grab it." Seductive as a five-hundred-dollar call girl, "I'll wait right here for you. Right here, in this nice, warm bed. And then we will sleep. I promise you."

Near naked he put ear to the crack in the door. Silence. He could make if before anyone came back home. Maybe they slept already. Maybe if he could run as quiet as night, he could be there and back before discovery.

Silent as a whisper he dashed on toes, heels never making contact with wood, to where he knew the Gibson patiently waited. It knew he would come; he always did. Padon knew it as well. He didn't know if the ancient guitar could hear the Muse or if it could feel his want, his need, but it knew. How long had it been since the call of the Muse was so strong, so full of promise he couldn't resist any request she made? Ten years? Twenty? When had it been so full of promise?

He grabbed the guitar by the headstock from behind the table and instantly shifted it to his left hand where he could get a better grip on the neck. Shadows passed outside the windows; someone was approaching the front door. If he didn't want to be standing in the hallway in his underwear holding his guitar in one hand and hope in the other, he had to hurry.

The front door clicked open just as he silently hushed his bedroom door. Leaning against it, breathing slow, deep, calming lungsful of air until his heart stopped pounding on the anvil of his ribs. He was afraid it might break several if he didn't calm it. On cat's paws he crept to the bed and began to softly strum a few exploratory chords. Yes, yes, these would support the lyric just perfect.

CHAPTER TEN

The bags under his eyes lay testament to the elusiveness of sleep, yet the crooked smile that played about his lips and merriment within those eyes belied a deeper truth. He may not have slept, but he was not the least bit unhappy about it. The embodiment of comfort in the over-sized sweats she had found at the dry goods store. Columbia emblazoned across the chest and down the right leg, all the way to his stockinged feet.

She knew she should chastise Padon for working all night, yet she also knew it probably did him more good, psychologically, than any-thing she could have prescribed. She watched him from where she sat at the dining room table as he poured his coffee and plopped a couple slices of bread in the toaster. She couldn't be completely certain, but she thought she heard him humming, quietly, to himself. He'd hum for a moment, turn his head sideways, look out the window, hum almost the exact same thing again, though with subtle differences, and smile. She didn't know if he was aware she sat in the next room.

The toast popped just as he finished humming and with a flour-ish his hand grabbed both with one effortless move, setting them on a plate, butter applied and now a good shaking of the cinnamon/sugar top-ping. Plate in one hand, coffee in the other he glided to the dining room and settled into the chair across the table from where Doctor Caldwell sat in amusement.

"Good night?" she inquired, coffee cup in both hands and almost to lips.

"Very, thank you," he paused for a moment as if collecting something important from where he'd hidden it many years ago, "and I do mean, thank you." He sipped and bit, chewed thoughtfully, finally, "you have no idea what you — well, you and this town, I guess, as it seems to be a community effort — have given me." He smiled to himself, yet it shone on all the world before him, true joy. "You gave me life. I don't think you saved my life," he shushed her before she could get the words to her lips, "though that is a fact as well. No, you gave me life. As surely as if you'd birthed me here in your office." His eyes moisten slightly, he caught the action before it could discomfit.

"I wrote a song last night." He stated it as if it is the most profound thing anyone has ever uttered. "I've written a lot of songs in my life," he continued munching — and she could swear she heard him humming under the words, chewing and sipping, as if he can't stop himself — then nods, "I guess a couple hundred. When I first started to write songs," he went on unbidden, "they were to pick up girls, to impress them enough they'd want to kiss me right on the mouth that had sung the words to them. It was wonderful." a tinkle of laughter escaped his very masculine mouth, "It was fun. It was innocent, believe it or not. I was young, they were young. The sun shone. There were no problems or pressures, just innocent pleasure and joy. Youth is such a simple, pure, naive time. I'm glad it doesn't last forever but we don't take near enough time to enjoy it while it is passing through our fingers." He stopped for a heartbeat and stared at the past in the reflection of the polished surface of the table.

He looked up, from under a bowed head, sheepishly meeting her eyes and they both nodded in agreement. No one knows youth like those who are well past it. The perspective of years brings all the angst of youth into focus, not with yearning but with understanding and serenity. No, they didn't want to drive down that bumpy road again, but it was fun to look at the pictures of the trip.

"Then I had a regional kind of hit, nothing I did, it wasn't because I was so overly talented or that the song was brilliant, just lucky somebody on a radio station decided they liked the song. Then others picked it up and life changed," he murmured, "and I wanted it to stay that way." Embarrassment and admission fill the words, "I wanted the admiration, the money, the small-time stardom. I forgot about the music.

"I spent some years chasing another hit. Writing what I thought people and radio stations would like. Rewriting a song I'd already written, grabbing for the brass ring, trying to hold on to something I never really had. I was a fluke." She leaned forward to reassure, to grasp his forearm, but he pulled away. He nodded thankfully but apologetically, he no longer needed to be reassured of who he is; and who he was. Truth will out.

"It's funny, then I spent years showing them. Showing them, I didn't need them. I didn't need the praise, the adoration, the life. I'd write to spite them. They'd come to dine on love songs and drinking and I'd serve sour tales of debauchery and the harsh reality of the human condition. But it wasn't the human condition, it was mine." He barked a bitter laugh and shook his head. "It is amazing how lost we can get in ourselves and never know we're off the path." He grabbed his plate and both their coffee cups as he got up from the table and walked into the kitchen. "Got time for another cup?" came from the counter.

She looked at her watch and at the wall clock ticking in the hallway. Not really, she thought. "Yes, a quick one," she lied, though just a crumb.

He sat back down, sipped and confessed, "Do you know what it's like chasing greed? And not just financial greed but artistic greed, to whore oneself not for art, but for what it brings. It sucks the soul right out of you. Not all at once, no, you might notice that, but little by little. You never feel it, you drain like a gas tank in a car but there is no gauge. Nothing to tell you that you are almost empty, and no place to pull over and fill back up. You wake up one morning, or afternoon," he smirked, "and there's nothing there. No want to get out of bed. No wish to write, to perform, to practice, to create. You don't care. Yet you walk on stage that night and find you can fake it. They don't even notice. The crowd, they don't care. They came to hear the radio. Radios have no soul, no humanity. They just play the same thing over and over. And so can you. You just have to play what they want to hear.

"Then one day you can't. You are in the wings and they are announcing your name and you freeze. And you remember, you remember when she left, and you didn't care. You remember when you finally did, and it was well past too late. You remember when you filled the hole with booze and sloshed your way through a month of people booing. You remember when you woke up in some flop with just your pants, shoes, shirts and guitar. Always your guitar. No socks, but the Gibson remains.

"I'm sorry, you have far more important things to do than listen to the sad tale of an old washed-up performer," he apologized and reached for her cup so there is nothing to anchor her to the table.

"I do have to go, I have people who need me," she half-heartedly apologized, and she rose from the seat, "but I'll be back this afternoon. Try to sleep. I want to hear more, I truly do. Please…" She allowed the plea to move her to her coat hanging on the peg by the door. She looked back to see him, head down, standing by the sink.

It had been an amazing transformation, from the tired yet almost gleeful person who had come to the table and the one now standing alone, looking out the kitchen window. She wondered, was this normal for the artistic. This roller coaster ride from joy to hell and back again. Was it every day? Or just when creating? She would need to keep a close eye on him. She didn't think he was suicidal, but did one ever know for sure. Creative people were known for manic depression and who knew where one could wander when at the lowest ebb?

He heard the door close and his shoulders slumped as he leaned against the sink. What the hell had brought that on? She wasn't a priest and he wasn't Catholic Why did he feel the need for confession. He was tired. He'd been up all night fine tuning the song and that always played hell with his moods. And this was a song he had been searching for. Not a hit. Not a song people would flock to hear him play. Just truth. And truth was beautiful and astounding; and unbelievably revealing. Shit! Could he even play this tune for anybody? Certainly not yet.

He thought about going back to bed. He lay the dish towel over the drying dishes and slumped against the counter, for just a second or two, before he stood, straightened his shoulders, turned and walked to the back bedroom. A shower and a walk, that's what he needed. And as he passed the wall mirror entering the room — a haircut.

He'd never had long hair, not even in his halcyon days. Shoulder length but no more. He always thought he looked like a goof with hair too long. He thought more so now. He remembered seeing a barbershop off one of the side roads just off Main. Shower, walk, haircut, write. It sounded like it should be a good day. "But they all started off that way, didn't they?" shouted his voice of doubt and pessimism. It was a dour man who stepped into the shower hoping the hot water would wash away his mood.

Winter would last forever. That was his assessment. He'd been here for almost two months according to his calculations. The first month or so in a coma, and probably the warmest he'd been since arriving, and a few weeks of rehab. He was definitely getting stronger, but not warmer.

The wind bit his face and exposed neck, all the skin it could find. He turtled into the leather, but the wind found him and battered his tender skin. He had always been a warm weather person, setting up tours north of the Mason-Dixon May until October, and then fleeing the north wind towards Alabama, Louisiana and Florida. You could live comfortable without a roof over your head along the coast. And it suited his temperament and thin blood. And now look where he found himself, almost froze to death in the damn mountains in the middle of winter. Yeah, that god he never believed in had a wicked sense of humor. His pace quickened as he turned down Main towards the warmth, he hoped, of the barber's chair.

He stopped to wonder, what if the barber was a hack, no idea what he was doing? He hadn't seen a lot of men in town, not yet, and the few he had he hadn't noticed their doo. He guessed that was a good thing. Maybe if he hadn't noticed, it was because their haircuts were fine, they didn't stick out like an abomination nesting on their heads. Then again, what did it matter? He was in the mountains in the midst of winter surrounded by people he didn't know and, once the weather turned, would probably never see again. So, what if he looked like a half-shaved calf for a couple weeks, it would be comfortable and much easier to care for. Just stop thinking and keep walking. It's freaking cold out here.

The fifty something, well-coiffed—he was happy to see, though who cut his hair? —gentleman sat reading the morning paper as Padon walked in. He nodded, folding the paper and got up from the single barber's chair.

"Morning," he welcomed, "need a cut?" Stating the obvious was always a decent way to begin a conversation. He could just as easily have said, 'cold out, ain't it?' and accomplished the same purpose.

"Yeah, getting a bit shaggy. Don't want to scare the women and children," Padon grinned as he removed his coat and hung it on a hook by the door.

As Padon sat in the chair and the barber, with a flourish, flew the cape around him and tied it close around his neck, "Just a trim, or a little more?"

"A heavy trim should do." And he closed his eyes.

"You're the dead guy, ain't ya?" And the clipping began. He was an old school barber with scissors he clicked as he talked and a comb that smelled of hair product. It took Padon back a hundred years to when his dad used to take him to get his hair cut amidst the scent of oils and gels and cigar smoke and old men discussing the matters of the day. And women. Every woman in town was the subject of discussion. Was she? Did she? Would she? Dirty old men talking about things they didn't know about as if they were experts. More perverts, but they chatted on and gossiped worse than the women they rambled about. At the time Padon thought they were the center of the universe. They knew everything. Now, they were just a joke from the past. He chuckled.

"Not so much anymore," chided Padon, "I'm recovering." They both snickered.

"What the hell brought you up this way? Especially in winter?"

The barber makes conversation as easily as a line cook makes eggs over easy.

"Stupidity, if I'm to be honest," shrugged the cuttee, "I have always had this morbid love of backroads. You know, the road less traveled. Get away from the highways, see America," he imitated the TV commercial for real America and laughed.

"Yeah, always a good idea until life finds you and then..." the throat cutting mimed, though with scissors in hand it was far more realistic than intended.

"Car broke down, tranny again, or so Bobby says..."

"He's pretty good," the local defended the local.

"Oh, I trust him, just saying, that was his verdict and there I was, dead in the water and not a soul in sight. Didn't appear to be any towns. Couldn't see any ambient light." the barber nodded the wisdom of the observation, "So, I could freeze to death in the car or start walking and freeze to death while seeking help," again he shrugged the obvious. "I chose to hoof it and hope."

"I guess you made the right decision," The barber nodded approval.

"With a shit ton of help from a lot of very kind, and strong, people," acknowledged Padon.

"That Jeannie, she's a heck of a lot tougher and stronger than she appears," chuckled the barber. "Little slip of a thing that can kick your ass up one side of Main, stop for a beer, and kick it back down the other. Comes from having four older brothers," he filled in, "who are now very respectful to their little sister." He laughed as he removed the cape and turns Padon, so he can see the handiwork.

Padon nodded his approval and handed the guy a twenty. "Too

much," says the man.

"Buy yourself a beer over at Merle's," Padon said as he grabbed the door handle. "Thanks." As the door closed behind him. The bitter cold bit him right on the back of the neck. Well, there was something he hadn't accounted for—apparently long hair served another purpose besides being pretty or making a statement. He pulled up his collar as he took the side street away from Main, so he could explore the frozen tundra.

The sound of the saw, or was it a lathe of some sort, drew his attention and eye to the small garage behind a small single-story craftsman home. As he slowly crept up the drive and peered around the late model Chevy, he saw father time in flannel working a table saw in the garage. The garage door wide open, the whine of the saw and the clouds of exhale mixing with sawdust. The ancient gaze guiding the piece of wood as surely as his hands, carving it into Padon could only guess what, but if intensity could build, this was going to be phenomenal.

"Whatcha building?" Padon walked, hands out in a half wave, curiosity blankets his countenance.

"Not sure just yet," the beginning of time grinned, "either an end table or a small house."

"Ain't you cold?" asked the city boy.

"Nah, not too bad today." And he took the piece of wood separated from its former self and tossed it into the open door of the wood burner in the corner. "That beauty does a nice job of keeping the winter out there. Be too hot in here if I closed the door." His attention returned to the large piece of plank in his hands.

"Mind if I watch for a while?" Padon was still sticking toes and fingers in the water. It's chilly but he thought he'll get all of him in soon enough.

"Not much to see, but suit yourself," his voice is clear and robust as youth belying the years carved into the rest of him. "Know much about wood, do ya?" he asked not taking his eye off the whirling blade.

"Not a thing," replies Padon, eye on the same object.

"Well, then, that makes two of us," laughed the maker of all things. "Never could do a damn thing with this stuff but burn it, but you gotta keep trying. Be honest, can't even put a nail in straight." All the wrinkles pulled up and hid his eyes in the creases, Padon believed it was a smile. "I always thought if I keep cutting and measuring, angling and hammering, soon or later I am going to have something I can be proud to show folks. Want a beer?" he asked turning off the loud saw.

"Hope you don't mind a bottle, but with this," he gestured at his massive display of facial hair, "anything else just doesn't work. Well, maybe with a straw but who wants to drink beer through a straw?" He chuckled as he handed Padon a beer. "You're that dead guy, right?" Asked the man who had outlived the reaper.

"Yeah, though not sure how true the name is as I seem to be partially alive." He sipped the beer and held his hand to his mouth to feel the breath.

"I guess, though when Jeannie brought you into town, she was certainly screaming about a dead guy and Doc Caldwell was needed right now." His ageless eyes assessed the visibly still living in his garage, "Looks like doc done good work." He laughed and sat on a work horse away from the red hot, pot-bellied stove. He gestured for Padon to take the one nearer the stove where the warmth was stronger.

"How you feeling?" It's as good a place to start with a stranger as any.

"From where I began this visit, remarkably well," Padon looked at the bottle then out through the open garage door to the small town nestled there. "I don't know if it is Doctor Caldwell's extraordinary healing powers or the restorative immersion in this town." He shook his head and grinned. "People are people wherever you go. We all have the same wants, needs, greeds and deviancies, we are tied to our primal drives, yet, this town seems to thrive on decency. More than any other place I've ever been. You guys go out of your way to do what's right. If I'd have broke down any other place, in these conditions, and someone came across me like that, they wouldn't have got out of their car, let alone drag a corpse to their truck, load it and drive it hell bent for leather into town." He gazed into the depths of the ages and saw the spark in the primordial pools of those eyes.

"Well, Jeannie is a bit headstrong, comes from…"

"I know, her four older brothers." Padon finished.

"Guess you've heard a bunch of the gossip and history of this town and her folks," Padon shrugged a nod. "Most of us came here to get away from what you describe. Lotta the town had been poorly treated out in the real world and they found their way here. We just want to be neighborly, lend a hand, have beer and a cookout, share what we have. Because what's the use of having something, money, skill, knowledge, a talent, if you just keep it for yourself?" Asked the man who was as old as his obsolete ideas.

"You know, someone's going to come up here sometime, discover you folks and call a paddy wagon to haul all of you off to a nice sanitarium." Padon finished his beer and put the bottle in the half-filled case of empties. He shook the hand of Chronos and nodded his thanks. "But I sure have enjoyed meeting every one of you crazy bastards. Good luck with the cutting. Watch your fingers." He embraced the ancient carpenter—probably knew Jesus—and took his leave. He knew he'd find his way back again and, maybe, he'd cut a few pieces of lumber when he did.

Chapter Eleven

As Padon made his way through the back streets of Rock Ridge his mind perused all the folks he had interacted with in this bizarre reality. They were happy, content, existing in this little town in the mountains. No one was rich, at least not to outward appearances, but no one wanted. People helped each other, they worked together, barter the coin of the realm. If you were in need of anything there was someone who could provide.

It wasn't bliss. They weren't a Stepford community — automatons just walking blissfully unaware through life. No, they were people who had lived, and apparently been shit on hard, and wound up here. There was joy, but now that he stopped to think about it and really consider all he'd met, there was also grief hidden deep in their eyes.

They were not depressed and hiding behind plastic smiles and platitudes. There was no threat, like some horror flick — everybody friendly until the sun came down, and then they would feast on human flesh!

They were as genuine human beings as he had ever met. They all carried their sins and abuses but fought to keep them from sight. Not out of shame or guilt, but they saw no reason to advertise. They had made a conscious decision not to live in the past, to leave their baggage at the station when they'd come to town. The hurt was still there. For some closer to the surface than others. Others were better at burying the pain, but it was there. And though they'd pushed it down, they did not deny its existence.

He guessed if he pushed, everyone here would open like a flower in the morning sun, displaying all the beauty and the black marks as well. They didn't wallow. They moved forward. They lived not in anguish but in spite of it. He could learn a great deal from these people, though he didn't think he would be here long enough. He would collect what lessons he could and take them with him when he left.

He had wallowed. Lord, he knew how to wear that like a skin-tight diving suit. Not in the pain others had inflicted on him, but in what he, himself, had created. He could forgive anyone any sin — anyone but himself. He expected far more from himself than any other human being. And he had failed miserably and massively. Some people forgot their trespasses as soon as they walked past them. Not Padon, he chained himself to each sin like an environmentalist to a bulldozer, and neither was going to get loose or move. Shit, Padon, just stop and enjoy the moment if only for the moment.

It was a lovely small, mountain town, with wonderful people, well, at least the ones he had met thus far, but they seemed a good cross section. He should go to the bar some night, that's where the real people with real attitudes would be. Liquor was like varnish remover. You couldn't hide your imperfections with a belly full of booze. He'd proven that several times in his own life.

He didn't know why he had to pull back the curtain on this nice, quiet, little burgh — yes, he did, he was a cynic when it came to the human race — and he had to expose their imperfections. He had to do it for himself, to show no one could be this decent. It was in his DNA. He was a shit and wanted to know everybody else was just as big a pile. You could see in their eyes, they were hiding something, buried their sins where no one could excavate them. Well, he had a pick and a shovel, and all the time in the world. He'd play their little game. He had nowhere to go and all the time in the world to get there, but he would find out where authenticity was buried.

Doctor Caldwell and Janet were sitting in the parlor when he entered and whatever they had been discussing came to an end with his entrance.

"And what do we think I am doing wrong," he hazarded.

"Nothing," replied Janet, far too quickly.

"We were just discussing," Doctor Caldwell smoothly corrected, patting Janet's knee, "that we think with you improving all the time, maybe you should see about finding some kind of employ. It would help with your rehab, give you some purpose and lend a feeling of worth. Jobs are good. We're pretty sure we could find you something part-time that wouldn't be too taxing."

"You want me to work?" he wasn't sure why, but he found the thought repugnant. Maybe that was why his voice had cracked like a walnut on the word.

"Nothing permanent, just something for you to do while you heal," Doc said reassuring, "Just something to occupy mind and body. I think," and she glanced at Janet for reassurance, "you need something to do. What do you think?" Well at least she was asking his opinion not giving it to him.

"I think I haven't had an actual job, job, since I was twenty — some kind of menial labor sort of thing. I'm not even sure what it was. I

play music. I write songs. I perform!" he emphasized the last with a ve-
hemence that came from desperation. Were these two serious? They
wanted him to get … a job? It was ludicrous, it was insane. He wasn't
sure he could work for someone else. He hadn't in so long. He was afraid
the first time someone told him he was doing something wrong or to pick
up the pace, or whatever they said to menial laborers, he would snap and
tell them exactly what he thought of them, their job, their lives. And that
would probably not be a good thing.

"Oh, I'm sure you're trainable," poked the Doctor, "Hell, they've
trained chimps to simple tasks. You might find you enjoy getting out of
your head and just allowing muscle to take over for a little while. It's
good for the soul. You know, come down here with us mortals and see
how we live," and now she couldn't help but laugh. "It might help in your
writing," she nudged, "I've heard that artists sometimes need a shake up
to remember why they loved their art in the first place. Maybe this would
get you back to your roots." He wasn't sure if she was mocking him,
goading him or was sincere.

So wrapped up in this crazy idea and discussion no one had
heard the front door open or the footsteps that entered the room.

"I could use a hand at the café," came a familiar voice. "Wouldn't
be much, some bussing, dishwashing and clean-up kind of stuff, but if
you're just looking to keep your hands busy, I could probably occupy you
for a few hours every day."

Padon was shocked! Was this some kind of conspiracy? Had
they plotted this out for days? "Every day?" was all that passed his lips.

"Well, maybe not every day every day, but most, I mean, if you
want. It's up to you," she smiled imagining him as her employee and
sweeping the floors. For some reason she found it endearing and attrac-

tive.

There was something he was missing in this plot, but he couldn't put his finger on it. She was offering him work, to help him, but it felt like more. Something in the words that weren't being said, something sensual. No, he was reading more into this than was being offered. It was the way of this town. They helped each other when they were down. And if you wanted to delve into the psyche of the town what better way than to work menial jobs where he would blend into the woodwork. He could observe without being observed.

'I'll take it," he surprised himself as much as the others. "I'd be good for me, and I need something to do or I might get into trouble." He smiled a wicked grin and the deal was done.

The smile Maggie threw him was — what? — predatory? Where had he seen that before? She took the days repasts into the kitchen and returned, hat in left hand, right hand scruffing up her short-cropped hair. She was well aware it gave her a boyish cuteness, a charm about her that was sensual, and it obviously was her choice to wear it that way, yet she seemed determined to pull on it until she could find the femininity.

"Anybody heard about a shindig coming up for Mr. Carpenter?" Maggie asked the other two women.

"No, what's going on?" asked Janet.

"We think it's his birthday soon," she said through a puzzled expression. "Nobody is quite sure as no one was around when he was born. And I don't mean just here," she directed at Padon, "I mean on this earth. We are all quite certain that he was the first human being on the planet. There are some who believe he helped God name the animals and probably most of the stars in the sky," she guffawed her little joke. "Oldest man you ever met."

"Does he live a couple blocks west of Main in a small white, craftsman with a single car garage?" Padon thought it could be the only person they might speak of in these terms, "Likes to play with wood," he finished.

"That'd be our Mr. Carpenter," nodded Doc Caldwell.

"Tough old bird," remarked Padon, "Seems to enjoy the cold, that's for sure." He shivered remembering his visit with the ancient human and the freezing breeze blowing through the open garage door. "Is his name really Carpenter or do you call him that because of his penchant for ruining good wood?"

"No, that's actually his name," Janet laughed, "and he only ruins it when he introduces machinery into the process. He actually is an excellent woodworker, when he uses hand tools. But he has this great desire to conquer the machine. We believe, most of us believe, it is because he lived so long without machines, they not being invented at that point, that he will never conquer them as it goes against his natural inclination to feel the wood." A smug half grin and glower at Doctor Caldwell as she evidently disagreed with this assessment.

" I thought he just was using the woodworking to keep himself warm," joked Padon.

"No, he's an excellent woodsman," defended Doc, "If you go in the café — which apparently you will be doing with some regularity — most of wood carvings and decorative accents are his," she jibed back at Janet and nodded to Maggie acknowledging more than had been said.

There was something going on between these women. Padon was quite certain they had colluded to get him to this point and kindled his interest in the café, Mr. Carpenter and who else might be in this town. Almost as if they were plotting to make him want to stay. Well, good luck with that! He'd had folks try to tie him to this town or that, this girl or those friends his entire life. He wasn't someone who set down roots. He floated free on the next breeze. He was the road and he was motion. Not someone who settled down. And it ain't happening here.

He'd stick around for a little while, but the itch would come. The road would call, and he would answer. He knew himself too well in this aspect. He might actually want to settle into a small town like this, where people seemed so welcoming and kind, but he couldn't. It wasn't in his DNA.

"I shall make note when I am there," he promised.

"There are other examples around town," Maggie chimed in, "I'd be happy to show them to you some time." She shrugged her indifference as to whether he would accept the offer or not. She was playing it cool. Or maybe she really didn't care. Maybe all this suspicion at their motives was something born of his own ego and wandering mind. No one had complimented him on his genius in how long? No one had told him how wonderful he was. How they loved his harsh, raspy voice, his songs, his rugged good looks, his massive talent. He might be thirsting for ego stroking and he was willing it on her. Maybe he was imagining her attraction to him. He could just be kidding himself and setting himself up for a big comeuppance and embarrassment. Hmm, that was something to consider.

"I'll talk to my boss and see if I can get time off, though I'm just starting a new job and don't think it would be right to be asking favors first day on the job," he challenged her.

"Oh, I've heard your boss is a sweetheart and quite kindly," she responded, "as long as you work your ass off while you're at work." She allowed the word to put her hat on and zip up her coat, making ready to leave. "See you tomorrow."

Chapter Twelve

He changed the rhythm of his step as it the crunched in the snow — his slow plod reminded him too much of the night he 'died' — and picked it up to a midtempo. The new kid walking his way towards his first day of actual employment in more than forty years. He would be lying to himself if he didn't admit some trepidation. Shit, he was scared to death. Yeah, he'd come to know Maggie a bit, but they weren't buddies or lovers. She was now his boss, and he hadn't had one of those since his wife left. And he was the lowest of low men on the totem pole. First days sucked.

The funny thing was — he ran the mind fart around the old brainpan a few times — in music every night was the first day. You walked into the venue and didn't know anybody, and they didn't give shit about you. You were just another slinger on the stage trying to get laid and selling liquor to the boys. That was the job. And everybody would love you for the moment, for the eve, maybe for the night, but next Wednesday they wouldn't remember your name. And weren't all that sure they liked your music. 'Where was that CD that guy gave me? I should listen to it sometime.' Hell, if they didn't like you, they forgot your name on the way home.

But that was different, wasn't it? First off, he knew what he was doing when he walked into a joint and onto a stage. He knew what was expected and if it sucked, well, he was gone the next day. It fit like most of his relationships. Here he was expected to fix what he'd done wrong and show up again the next day, where he would find he could discover new things to screw up. It was nice. It was marriage. Every day he would discover a plethora of new ways he could improve himself and his attitude.

Why in all hell had he agreed to this? He didn't have to do this, this work! (and his immediate thought was of Maynard G Krebbs). He was on the mend, rehabilitating from dying. No one would think less of him if he preferred to lay on the couch or in the bed recovering from his recent death! No one could fault him for rising like a very tired, old and beat up Phoenix from the ashes. Slow and easy, walking a little further each day. Meeting and greeting the town that had saved him. And weren't they now responsible for him? Wasn't there some culture that believed if you saved someone that you were now responsible for them? He didn't have to work — they owed him for not letting him die, damnit!

Yeah, tell that to Maggie. And why did he give two shits about what she thought? He wasn't staying. He wasn't going to marry her and settle down, raise a family grow old and die in her arms. Shit, they were both old already. Well, he was. She was cute. Yeah, that was it. She was cute. Not something one would say about a woman in her late forties, if he was any judge. And she was strong. She'd survived whatever had happened before she'd landed here. They all had.

This town was like a rehab center for what life had chewed up and spit out. And that included Doc Caldwell, JoAnn. Padon hadn't considered her, but she was here and that meant she had it bad somewhere before winding up here. Or did it? He'd only met a few folks. And no one had actually told him they'd been beaten and dragged, left by the side of the road, until they'd rolled in here. There was just something about them. Some sadness behind the eye, behind the smile, something purposely not said. He didn't know if everybody knew everybody else's secrets, or even if they cared. He only knew he didn't. He had to wonder; did he need to?

He stood at the door. The new kid in class. Was he supposed to enter in the front or was there a back door, in an alley or at the side? Hmm, he probably should look before … Maggie opened the front door and stepped aside so he could come in.

"Early. I like that," she said, closing the door and locking it again. "I forgot to mention there is a side door for employees to come in and leave by when the front is locked up." He started to say something, but she stopped him, "My fault, not yours. Just so you know tomorrow."

"Come on into the back and I'll introduce you to everybody and get you an apron."

An apron? He had to wear an apron? What the hell had he got himself into?

Every muscle in his body ached. Someone had beaten him from his head to each and every toe with a baseball bat and then run him over with a truck. How could clearing tables and washing dishes wear a man out so thoroughly? As he swept the last of the fallen table scraps into the dustpan and dumped them into the large waste can, he couldn't guarantee he would ever stand again. Damn! He used to haul sound systems up and down three flights of stairs, play for four hours and make love 'til morning light. What happened to that guy?

He got old and died. That's what. And now this town of mad scientists had reanimated his corpse and was intent on working him to death again. How long had he worked today? Eight, ten — had to be at least twelve hours.

He gazed up to the clock setting on the counter. Three hours? Three lousy hours? That was it? Are you shitting me? This was not going to work out, that was now an irrefutable fact.

And it hadn't been busy. It was the morning rush, that was all. They still had to set up for lunch. He'd be buried by one o'clock. And there was Maggie, a self-satisfied smirk playing around her lips as she sized him up. Well, fuck her. She wasn't going to beat him. Others had tried and had underestimated his will and ability to overcome pain and exhaustion. He rubbed his bad leg out of habit as much as need while he forced his back straight and stretched the few remaining working muscles.

"How you feeling?" She actually sounded concerned.

"I'll live," he responded, "though I may not want to." He finished honestly. "But I'll make it through the day."

She looked him up and down deciding whether to turn him out to pasture, work him more, or put him down. Her better angels settled on both shoulders. "Nah, you had a good workout and a really good start, let's call it a first day and you go rest. Jeannie's brother Herb is coming in and it doesn't look like it's going to be very busy. I'd rather have you rested for tomorrow; it's going to be a busy day. It's Saturday, and everybody comes around on Saturdays."

He wanted to argue, he really did, but he just couldn't find the energy. He concentrated as hard as he could to stop his fingers from shaking as he untied the apron, sluggishly lifting it over his head and placing it in her outstretched hand. God, even that hurt. "Thanks, I'll get stronger, I'll get better," as he slipped on his, now, extremely heavy, leather coat.

"You're coming back in, aren't you?" It was a statement of fact.

He wanted to answer with all the male braggadocio he could summon but there was none there. He was just a tired old man right now with nothing left but a few ounces of pride; and they were leaking out his shoes.

"Yeah, too stupid and proud to quit." He walked out the door and turned left down Main.

Maggie smiled as she watched him walk back in front of the Café after turning around to head in the right direction. He was very tired. No, he wasn't Doug and she shouldn't treat him as if he was. Doug had been the super asshole, control freak, who'd almost killed her before she escaped his domination. He had cost her dearly, but not all. Maybe there was hope after twenty years. She immediately chastised herself for the foolish old woman she was. What the hell was she thinking? She had to get ready for lunch.

She considered backing off Padon tomorrow. She'd been like a watchdog all morning. Not standing over him, watching and criticizing every move, but he knew she was watching. It was simple work, nothing that required a month of training, but it was strenuous and necessary work. If the tables weren't cleaned promptly and properly, they couldn't be sat again, which meant that a waitress might lose a turn and that meant money out of her pocket. This was a small place in a small, insulated town, nobody thought they were going to get rich, but you like to have a little jingle in your pants.

He had shed his musician pride at the door, she'd noted appreciably, and slipped on worker pride easier than he'd slipped on, and figured out, the apron. He was slow at first, and that was fine, so was the café.

He was overly cautious, not wishing to break a cup or a plate. Started at the crash of tableware as it co-mingled in the bus tub, and immediately turned to survey the dining area to see if he had disturbed any of the diners or waitstaff. He was conscientious, she liked that. And she knew he wanted to fly as he walked to the door but had forced his feet forward and his will through the portal. She couldn't tell if he was more frightened of working, something he obviously hadn't done in quite some time, or of disappointing himself. Or her, hmm. You never knew a man's motivation but any way you saw it he had acquitted himself well. No, he was no Doug. He had more character, and though he didn't know it himself, he was a better person than he gave himself credit for.

She'd seen it in the way he had jovially interacted with the customers once he had settled into the job. They all knew him as "the dead guy' and he went along without complaint. They'd get to know his name soon enough, let them enjoy their town humor for a few days. No harm, no foul. If he couldn't laugh at himself, he wouldn't be here long. This was a town full of folks who had survived and thrived. They loved to bust chops and laugh at the idiot in the mirror. It was good for the soul. And everyone in town had their well-kept, well-known, poorly hidden just below the blink of an eye, secrets. They all knew they all loved each other because of their imperfections, not in spite of them. It was a good town.

Time, it always came down to time. All will be known with patience. Ah Grasshopper, you will know all when you have truly waited between one breath and another. Shit! As he made his way back to Doc's house, Padon considered stopping by Father Time's garage for a beer and maybe a little conversation, but his body immediately rejected that idea as insane. It was past eleven AM and he needed to lay down and die again. He thought death humorous at that moment and appealing. Bone tired and ready to drop, he slogged his path to the warmth and welcome of Doctor JoAnn Caldwell's doorstep and the bed beckoning like a light of hope from the back bedroom.

Chapter Thirteen

Sluggish and tired he awoke as the hall clock struck four. He should get out of bed. He should restart the day. But he was so comfortable, and he knew if he moved it would hurt — everywhere. So, he lay for a few moments longer and enjoyed the perfect quiet of the house. He was alone, and that was just fine.

He ran the tub as hot as he could stand and slipped under the steam into relief. The hot water leeched the aches from his back, his legs, arms and soul. How could cleaning and carrying dishes for a couple hours hurt so much? Oh, that's right, because he hadn't done any manual labor for forty years and he was just coming back from a month of being in a coma. Yeah.

He carried amps up and down stairs, his guitar, but that was five minutes of any physical exercise, not hours of work. He was weak as a newborn and just as cranky. He'd wanted to walk away before he'd walked through the damn door. But there she was, opening the door to the den of the dragon, and he'd stepped through. Apron on, musical and artist pride swallowed, worker pride engaged. His father may not have given him much, but he had instilled a work ethic in his son. 'If you are going to do something, and you tell someone you're going to do it, don't half ass it. If you're not going to give any chore your best, leave it for someone who will. If you didn't do it right, then someone else would have to do it over.' All of it ran through his head as he eyed the front door of the Café with longing in his every fiber, but he'd made a promise.

And now, he had made it to here, and the hot felt so soothing he had to force his nose above the waterline, or he would drown in ecstasy. But what a way to go. The world turned, the blood flowed, the pain lessened, and the shame returned. Then the irritation. Why should he feel shame? Hadn't he been dead less than two months ago? Hadn't he been resurrected and walked upon the earth? Why should he be shamed by how quickly his muscles had atrophied? It was natural. He was a work in progress, and very early in that progress. It was time to be forgiving of his weakness, of his limitations. He was getting better and stronger every single day; he would progress much quicker if he would quit beating himself up.

He stretched a few more kinks out of arms, legs and back before he grabbed the towel and dried himself. As he toweled off and caught his reflection through the steamed mirror, he was still a bit taken aback. A scarecrow had more definition than his body did. He was a stick figure and he could see every single stick poking against the skin. He might be back, but he had to fill out and build up if he was going to stay. He required sustenance. He dressed and headed towards the kitchen.

He fixed a sandwich from yesterday's leftovers and a tall glass of ice-cold milk. Delicious. It's amazing how you can forget, and then recall, how much you loved simple pleasures like ice-cold milk. Sitting at the dining room table he caught the reflection of the Gibson leaning against the bedroom wall where he'd left it. He should practice. His callouses were mush and his fingers got confused going from chord to chord. It wasn't that far of a trip. They shouldn't get lost, and they'd traveled that road so many times it should be familiar. Well, familiar and knowing were two different animals. He also found he was having trouble chasing down lyrics in his brain. He caught the tail end of this verse but couldn't seem to pull out the head or body. Thank the goddess for choruses. Yeah, his muscles weren't the only thing on him to atrophy.

He swallowed the last of the sandwich and gulped the final swig of milk. It was time to start pushing life back up on the tracks.

His scales were clumsy, if he was being gracious, and the songs were hiding behind mountains of dereliction. It was frustrating, infuriating and satisfying when he stopped. It wasn't good. It was nowhere near where he should be, but he was crawling. And that was better than laying still.

His life was now being defined by small successes and triumphs. He got stronger as the days passed, thanks to the work at the café. He made half days through the weekend. Monday, he made it until dinner hour before collapsing in the back and Maggie had to send him home. By Thursday he'd made dinner and Saturday he'd opened and closed. It was his greatest triumph to date.

Everyone was going to Merle's for a beer after work and they invited him along. Even Maggie seemed to be encouraging him to come, but he was done in. He admitted to himself a cold beer would be most welcome but so would the comfort and quiet of home. And that was how he thought of JoAnn's house.

He thanked them all for the asking but declined as he slipped into the leather, zipped it tight and wrapped a scarf, donated by some forgetful traveler, around his neck and pulled his stocking cap over ears and just above eyes.

JoAnn sat at the table with a small glass of brown liquid in front of her. She turned as he entered and motioned to the other glass across from her. Padon maneuvered himself into the chair and poured a healthy dollop of Kilbeggan. They clinked glasses in silent toast and sipped.

"I believe my first paycheck is going to go to replenish this," he nodded at the half empty bottle.

"You might want to see the size of the check first," she giggled and took another sip. "You're kind of late tonight," she ventured. She didn't want to push him about his life, but she needed to know how he was feeling and to try to stem his desire to heal too rapidly and thereby do more damage.

"It felt good," he allowed as the whiskey made its way to tired muscles and warmed the innards. He was tired, and his muscles were limp, but they didn't ache today, well, not too much, and he did, in fact, feel good.

"I know you think it is none of my business, but I am still in charge of your health care and need to know how you're doing," she pushed a little harder.

"If you would've asked me a week ago, I would've told you I was pissed you didn't let me die."

"As a matter of fact," she began to say something, and his look stopped her.

"But that was a week ago. I was weak and tired. I didn't realize how weak and tired until you three," he pointed an accusing finger right at her nose, "finagled me into working at the Café. Don't think I didn't realize what you were up to." Again, the finger of accusation, "Maggie just happening to show up when she did, and everybody coming up with this wonderful idea. I thought I was going to die, either from the work, the stress or choking on my own words. You proved your point; I could do it." He sat back and stared at the whiskey as he swirled his glass. "I'm glad to have proven something to myself, as well," the words contained a peace she had not heard in his tone previously. "Maybe I'm not such a waste of time as I'd been led to believe. And believed. I don't mind admitting I didn't think I would last the first day," he smiled.

"Neither did any of us," she chided, "I sat in Maggie's office the whole time just in case … well, just in case."

He looks at her with mist filling his vision, "I didn't know that," the words barely fell from his lips.

"You weren't supposed to," she lifted her glass a quarter inch and tips it towards him, "but we weren't positive you were up to it, physically."

He laughed hard and slapped the table with a crack. "Neither was I!" he choked through the laughter, "I thought I was going to die from exhaustion and shame. It's hard," he continued in a more sober tone, "to admit some things to oneself. To come to terms with the possibility of giving up something you once loved. It was hard admitting to the guy staring back from the mirror that I'd lost my love of music. And, I guess, with it, my love of life." He choked off a sob with a swig of whiskey.

Silence smothered the dining room, even the hall clock quieted her tick-tock, as the two sat, facing each other. His respect for this woman had grown and intensified so much over the last few weeks, not because she saved his life, but she had worked so hard to give it back to him. He was not in full possession yet, but he'd made a substantial down payment. He owed her, and Janet, he amended, and Maggie, and everybody, apparently in this town, for his second lease on life. Not living. Life. He chugged the last half inch of warmth.

"Want another?" he asked lifting the bottle and measured the content with one eye closed. "I feel like celebrating a little. Everybody was going to Merle's for a beer," he began…

"And why didn't you?" she was truly curious.

"I was tired and just wanted to be here," he gestured with both arms and honesty. "How about we put on a little music and talk, maybe I'll ask you to dance. Though it will have to be a slow tune, I don't jitterbug like I used to."

"So, what are we celebrating?" She asked as he poured a wee dram more into her glass.

"Life, and the return thereof," glasses clinked, sips smooth and warm. "l'chaim, and to health," he grinned, "mine especially," he toasted himself.

"I know you are feeling better, but you are not healthy nor anywhere near," she cautioned. "Understand it is going to take some time before you are one hundred percent, or anywhere near, for that matter. It takes time for the human body to recover, to mend. You are not recovering from surgery, you don't have to wait for muscle and tissue to heal, though there is a some of that as well, but you are coming back, literally, from the brink of death. We still don't know if any damage was done to internal organs or what might be permanent." The seriousness of her tone halted any smartass response he may have been tempted to give.

Padon hadn't thought of permanent damage. He thought once he began to feel better, once the pain began to subside, he would be good to go. This required some readjustment, again!

"How long?" he asked.

"Was a Chinaman," came the Pavlovian response.

"What?"

"Nothing, just a, never mind," she shook herself. "It could take up to a year for you to fully recover and for us to know how much, if any, damage has occurred."

"I have to stay here for a year?" he wanted to shout but it comes riding a whisper.

"You don't have to stay here," she said with slight indignation and a little hurt in her tone, "but we have to keep an eye on you. I would suggest you plan on not doing any traveling for at least six months though". She completed the thought in her head: 'If you think you can stand us that long.'

Padon sipped and allowed the liquid a few moments on his tongue before he slowly swallowed. He nodded to himself as if coming to a decision and satisfied with it. "I can do that," he smiled a bright, joyous grin, "if you'll allow it."

Is that what he was concerned with? She wondered taking her own nip to allow her brain to catch-up with reality. He probably hadn't set down roots for more than a week since he was child. Even though he was married, he had traveled constantly. He might have had a home base somewhere, but his home was his vehicle and the road, not the house. She was forcing him to accept he had to set down roots, if only for a nominally short period of time. It was being gleefully accepted. Life was forcing him. Circumstances compelled his course. He had to accept. It gave him an out. The decision had not been his, it had been taken out of his hands and he couldn't be happier.

"Think Maggie will keep me on?" his concern coated each word.

"I don't see why not?" she shrugged. "As long as you don't screw up too bad," she chuckled.

"How about that dance," he asked as an old favorite from his childhood came on the radio. It is 1971 and he is in fifth grade and his

140

first dance.

They stumbled around the dining room and hall for a minute before realizing neither of them had the knack for dance. He bowed, she laughed, and just for a minute, for the flash of a second of life, she was twenty something and he was a nervous young man, unsure of himself or where his feet should go. It was sweet, and it was fantasy. She'd never known such a boy and she'd never been such a girl. But it was nice.

They returned to the table and sat for a few heartbeats in silence, each lost in their own past. Maybe both thought about what had never been and what would never be. She was too old, he was too … him. And it was all too late. But she liked him, just him. Oh, she loved the song about her and Janet, and she knew she would love his music. But it was him. It was his refusal to lay down and die, his acceptance of the job at Maggie's, his self-mocking style. She knew — it was possible he might begin to know — but she knew, he was a good man. He just needed the opportunity to show it. Especially to himself.

Through patience and will power she forced his eye from the glass to her own where she held it as surely as if she held it in her hands. "I must admit, I thought I was going to have to tie you down or drag you kicking and screaming into this idea." A crooked half smile showed her relief.

"If this was two months ago you wouldn't've stood a chance," he grinned back, "I'd've been three miles out of town before you finished the first sentence." He tipped his glass but did not drink, lost in what had brought him to this point. "See, I been running my whole life. I always thought I was running towards something, the next gig, the next check, the next record or song, the next girl," he added reluctantly, "the next escape," finished the admission. "But I wasn't. I was running away from everything. From home. I started running away from home when I was thirteen. They kept bringing me back and I'd begin planning the next great escape.

"I hated my life. My parents fought constantly. Everything I did was wrong or stupid or a waste of time, theirs, not mine. I was expected to find a dead end, no future paycheck just like the old man, but it was not for me. So, I started running. And every time someone or something tried to tie me down in one spot, I shed the chains and ran."

Now he drank deep and emptied the glass. He stared hard at the bottle as if it is the truth, all he had to do was open it and let it flow. He looked at her. She shrugged. He poured. "I ran from my wife and daughter. I tell people she left but I'd left far sooner. She just had enough balls to call a spade a spade and her husband a drifter. I ran from my own damn child — can you even imagine? Guess I never admitted that to anyone before." Repulsion shook its head and remorse came too late. "Not even me." He set the glass on the table without imbibing.

"I have been on the run for forty years and all it ever got me was tired. Well, I'm tired, and sick of me. Maybe dying is the best thing that has ever happened to me. Maybe I left me by the roadside, froze to death. Maybe this ain't no town at all but some kind of afterlife. I don't have a clue but I'm going to stay to find out. For once in my whole life, I'm not running."

His eyes locked with hers as he made this solemn promise to himself and she nodded her witness.

The hall clock struck two and broke the tired trance of two people who had overstayed at the party. His morning to end of night shift rampaged through his tired bones and he realized breakfast is only a few hours away. It has been never that he worked seven days in a week, but

142

he made another promise before he left to come home, he'd be in tomorrow. Today, he corrected himself. He needed some shut eye and he needed it now.

He opened the Kilbeggan and carefully poured the dark liquid from his glass back into the bottle, maybe tomorrow or the next day. Right now, bed called, and he would do his best to answer.

"I'll be extra quiet when I leave in the morning," he said walking toward the back of the house.

"I can give you a doctor's note excusing you from work, if you'd like," she spoke to the empty chair, but it is the man down the hall who answered.

"I told Maggie I'd be there, and she promised it would only be a half day, if you're concerned about my health."

"Would it matter if I was?" she asked the brown liquid in her own glass. "Don't kill yourself again," She said loudly to the closing door, "I'm all out of miracles and don't think I can put humpty dumpty back together again.

"Promise." Closed the door.

Chapter Fourteen

The half day had gone smoothly. It was Sunday and that meant brunch. He ran food from the kitchen to the banquet tables set up along the wall. Eggs, bacon, sausage, French toast, potatoes, sliced beef and ham, fruit and cereal, a pasta dish, homemade of course, and a hundred very satisfied stomachs. He had started at ten this morning and he looked to be done by four thirty. It would be a welcome short day.

Padon cleared tables and kibitzed with the customers, most of whom referred to him by his nickname. They laughed and kidded each other and him. He had never known the feeling of inclusion, not even in his band days. He'd been the leader and songwriter. There had been a revolving door of people who thought he could get them to the next level of their own careers. He'd never belonged in his own band. It made him chuckle and shake his head. He had never bothered to stop and consider this, but it was truth.

Everyone who came through the door knew Maggie and Jeannie. They waved to the cooks in the kitchen, Wally and Ralph, a couple of African-American fellas with fast hands, machine-like precision on the griddle and wits as sharp as the knives they carved the beef with. He had gotten into a few verbal battles and throw downs, but they'd cut him to the bone, smiling the whole time, not working up a sweat. He was way out of his league with these two—too fast, too smart, too cunning.

Ralph had been a stockbroker back east in some huge concern and found they were doing some shady shit under the table with investor's money. He did the right thing, reporting them to the SEC and was immediately rewarded by being tossed out on his ass without much more than what he'd squirreled away in his own investments. He was banned from any investment house of any repute and barred from his career. They got off scot free. Guess it paid to have friends in high government offices, and Congress.

He'd had enough and left it all behind. His home, his career, his wife and his former friends, all of whom had disowned him and couldn't remember ever having met him. Now he flipped burgers, eggs and steaks and had never been happier. He didn't know what had happened to the company or his former life once he left, he didn't care. He'd heard through a grapevine or in the paper that his wife had married one of the partners and both had gone to jail for drugs and embezzlement. He didn't care about that either. He was happy here in his new life. He liked the people, they liked him, and nothing else mattered.

Wally had been a musician back in Chicago. He had played in some of the big blues outfits until his habits caught up with his talent and then overtook it. He lived on the streets for a while and then got tired of dying slow, so thought he would speed up the process and had jumped from a bridge into the Chicago River in mid-winter! Damn near froze to death — something he and Padon shared. A cop jumped in after him and pulled him out. When he stopped shivering, he decided he needed a new view, so he hitched out west with nothing but a few changes of clothes and a wish to live. Somehow, he wound up here. Rock Ridge, a little town of white folks who didn't care about his past as long as he didn't care about theirs. They all were looking for a place to live.

Padon was quite sure everyone in this town had some kind of story, some reason for winding up here. He was not alone. He had landed on the island of Misfit toys. It made him smile.

They were middle-aged, young and old, ancient, like Mr. Carpenter, and everywhere in between. They had lived hard and full. And somehow, they all fit together like a well woven carpet. Each adding color and texture to this tapestry. It was truly an interesting pot.

He liked them. They weren't trying to impress. They weren't racing for the last dollar or last piece of ass. They had put their ladders away and choose to live like human beings. It was like some old hippie commune had grown up and found out how to make the whole, damn thing work. He shook his head as the thought carried him, and he carried plates, silverware and glasses, into the kitchen.

Harvey the dishwasher grinned a sunbeam his way as Padon set the dirty dishes within his reach and unloaded them so Harvey didn't have to, then rinsed out the tub. Harvey whistled an almost familiar tune and his feet danced as he rinsed dishes, loaded them into the racks and pushed them into the dishwasher. He was as happy as any human had a right to be. The man loved his work.

It made Padon stop to consider every time he interacted with Harvey. How could a man take so much pleasure in washing dishes? Simple, thought Padon, he found joy in the simple things in life and routine kept him in rhythm. Now Padon laughed hard and did his own little clumsy two-step with Harvey as they went about their work.

The last of the diners waved their goodbyes as they exited into the frigid mountain air. Padon collected plates and glasses, walked them back to Harvey and then returned to the dining room to wipe down tables and set them for the next day's business. He was tired, but he had learned there is tired and there is good tired. He was good tired. They broke down the tables and stored them in the back and Padon grabbed a cup of coffee and sat at the counter to relax for just a moment.

Maggie eased herself into the chair next to him. She was a fine-looking woman and a very hard worker. If she expected a lot out of her employees, she expected more out of herself. First in, last out. He respected her and, he had to admit, was attracted to her. He needed to check that at the door — she was the boss. He nodded to himself to check off that box.

"Tired?" she yawned.

"Wore out," he admitted swallowing a gulp of black coffee.

"Well, ya done good," she nodded, "and I don't mean just today, you've been busting your ass all week. I'm impressed and out ten bucks." She grinned.

"Who?" he ventured.

"Harvey, of all people, he was the one who swore you'd make it. He believed in you when no one else did," she shook her head, "Even the cooks thought you'd quit by Tuesday, Wednesday at the latest. You've impressed a lot of folks here. Thought you might want to know," she got up and walked to where the half full coffee pot waited on the burner.

"Guess I should thank him for the vote of confidence," he nodded thanks for the fresh cup of coffee. "Nice to know someone thought I was worth the bet."

"Oh, I didn't doubt you, not really," she added before he could object. "I just didn't think someone who'd made his living as you have would care for the day-to-day working-class lifestyle." She gave him a half-cocked grin of approval. "Most musicians I've run into couldn't

147

seem to lower themselves to be part of the proletariat they claim to support and sing about. They like to make a lot of noise about how noble it is to own weary, working hands and how humbled they are by those who own them, but they just can't seem to find a way to be part of these fine, fine folk. Nice to sing about hard work, to paint the portrait of the strong arm wielding the nine-pound hammer, just not interested in the swinging."

Padon wanted nothing more than to argue the point, to show her how she was so far from the truth it was laughable. To expose the flimsiness of her case, but he couldn't. She was absolutely right. Oh, there were exceptions, but they only stood to prove her point. Hell, he'd known some musicians who wouldn't carry their own damn guitars. Not many, but enough. And he knew enough who had never worked a real job, never put in a twelve-hour day in a field or a factory or construction job. And never would.

He, himself, hadn't worked more than a few years in his teens before making his living in bars. But wasn't that work? Setting up in the afternoon and tearing down at three in the morning? It was a long day, depending on how much equipment one needed for the gig. And the travel, the shitty accommodations, all for very little money, most times. But chasing a dream is far different than working to support a family and put a roof over the heads of those you loved.

Most of the musicians who worked the road had no other home, no wife and kids, no responsibilities other than music. When you took the worry, the burden of carrying a family on your shoulders, of supporting those you loved, out of the equation, it was a different pony.

Yeah, they worked hard when they worked but they only worked for themselves, for the goal of getting signed, recording and finding some fame. It was all me. He knew some who had family back home, but not many. The lifestyle didn't agree with responsibility. Wives soon tired of being home alone with the kids while he was running all over the country playing in bars full of single women who thought he was a star. Not just some guy playing music and avoiding cutting the grass, taking out the garbage and painting the back bedroom.

We are nomads, he thought, always have been, always will be. The Muse and the Music were jealous lovers and will not share with anyone for any length of time. For the first time in his life, it made him sad to think of it.

"Sounds like you had a bad experience," push the conversation her way and away from his discomfort.

"I've seen life," she disclosed, and blew on the hot coffee.

"Is that what keeps you here?" he stuck his toe in the water.

"Life," she said purchasing some time, "and hope."

They hadn't noticed but the two of them seemed to be the only ones left in the café. All the other employees had skedaddled without so much as a "see you in the morning" not wishing to disturb the conversation. It was a good crew. They cared about each other and each other's privacy. It didn't surprise Padon in the least to find they'd left without a goodbye. They'd quench their curiosity in the morning or whenever Maggie decided to spill her plate of beans.

"I knew you when I lived in Maine," she stopped and reconsidered, "Not you, you, but another version." She restated and began again, "Though I think I might have seen you perform years ago up in the northeast," she smiled shy, "you played at a bar in Portland and I was underage." She chuckled a memory. "But it was a few years later I met a guy who played beautiful music and sang songs to fill the heart and soul with longing and want. And I did. I wanted him to sing about me the way he sang about love. I was very young and very innocent and very, very stupid, and impressionable. I guess many of you can do that, but I didn't know many of you, I knew him.

"He would sing me songs, I would melt. What I didn't know was how many others melted along with me. He was always going to settle down with me. We would get married, have a family and he would slow down his touring, maybe just play regionally so he could be home." She sighed and stared at the vacant and abandoned building of her past re-membering when it was full of life. "I would've done anything for him and almost did." She stopped, sipped.

"You don't have to tell me this, it's really none of my business," he gave her the out, she refused to take it.

"Nah, it doesn't hurt like it used to. The callouses are pretty tough now, the scabs healed over, the past has flowed out to sea," she giggled like a small child who has said something very funny, but only to her, "We make mistakes. We either stop and correct our course or we don't and," she completes the incomplete. "I kept making the same mis-take over and over, and he kept manipulating. I take responsibility for all of it. I was smarter than that, just less mature than I needed to be. I want-ed to believe. You can't be manipulated unless you are a willing pawn—at least at the beginning. Sooner rather than later, you lose that control but at the start you can walk. I lay down like a puppy. Made it easier for the next guy, Doug, to manipulate and hurt."

"I think you might be being a little hard on yourself," he gently reprimanded. "You were just a kid, and in love. We all do dumb things when we're in love!" he insisted.

"Did you?"

"I don't think I was ever in love with anything but music and anyone but me." Well, if honesty is on the menu, he might as well have a large serving.

She stared at him, shocked by his admission. She got up to lock the doors and closed the blinds and grabbed a bottle of bourbon from behind the counter. She threw him a questioning look. He shrugged acceptance. The train is out of the barn, might as well ride for a while. "When did you admit that to yourself?" she was truly curious, almost as curious as she was about the man himself.

"Honestly?" he considered, "About five minutes ago." He watched her pour the bourbon into two coffee cups and set the bottle on the counter.

She sat and scrubbed her short brown hair with both hands, a habit he found endearing and just damn adorable.

"Why don't you let it grow out?" he asked gesturing with his coffee cup to her hair, "You play with it all the time, pulling and scrubbing, like you're trying to make it longer. Why not let it?" He grinned though could not imagine her with long hair. The cut fit her physically and her personality. He wouldn't change it.

"Too much trouble," she cast the words into the ether, "I haven't been much of a girly girl since I came to my senses. I was then, when I was in love, and when I allowed myself to be flushed. I didn't like her, she wasn't very strong," she reconsidered the statement, "No, I just don't think she knew how strong she was. Girls weren't supposed to be strong; they were supposed to be pliant. Do what your husband/boyfriend/lover wants. Don't make a fuss. Guess I was brought up on the tail end of that bullshit. Guess I should've listened to someone other than the woman who had ridden that rail her whole life, my mom. It was what she knew.

She wasn't a bad person; she just didn't know any better. It is hard to break old habits.

"I am much more forgiving of her knowing how hard it can be. It took me some time, and pain and suffering, to learn that. But I know it now." She shot the bourbon and chased it with a gulp of coffee. She did not shudder or gasp like a child. She drank like an adult, as if she enjoyed it.

"Was it that bad?" he took a sip, not that he couldn't shoot it, he just preferred to enjoy allowing it to coat the rails.

"Worse," she snorted, "but it is water so far under the bridge a whale just shit in it." She snorts again as she pours just a tad in the cup. "But I prefer not to wallow. I got free of the vortex, licked my wounds and ran as fast as I could away from the agony. I don't live for the past, it accomplishes nothing, it stops you from living. It's like being caught in a time loop you can't escape from. I escaped and have no desire to return." She sipped this time and stared out the closed blinds.

"I spent a few years hiding from my past, working in restaurants and bars. The places that don't care if you have experience. They'll train a turtle if they think it can serve. That's the beauty of this business and why it draws so many who have a past. You can wash dishes, learn to cook a decent burger and not burn the fries, and if you've got a personality, learn to wait tables or bartend. It's a great business for starting over. Nobody checks your app. Nobody is concerned whether you graduated from college or high school or, shit, eighth grade. They just want to know if you're willing to bust ass. Don't get drunk on the job, don't take a smoke break during the rush, don't bring your bullshit into work. It's pretty simple. And you can make enough cash to live — most of it under the table. Even in a joint like this.

"If you're still around come summer you'll see. We get tourists. Not a ton, but enough. We don't want too many. They screw up the traffic and the town. We're not a well-known mountain town. People stumble across us more than plan on a visit. Del's can usually handle what shows up, even on the holiday weekends." She laughed, and it was pleasant to his ear, like church bells.

"I can't guarantee anything at this point," he stated flatly. "Doc says I am looking at a long rehab no matter how I feel. My body isn't up to what it used to be." He sounded frustrated, but his tone also contained resignation and, she might be wrong, longing.

"Is it so bad? Staying in one place? Is it so frightening?" Now she's pushed, and she knew it, but the bourbon gave her courage.

"Yes," he admitted, "it is. The question is not whether it is frightening, it is whether I can deal with the fear — whether I can overcome my predisposition to run." He felt as though he pulled his guts through his teeth. Why does honesty hurt so much? He only assumed this is why he has avoided truth for so many years. This woman made him want to be honest with her and that made him want to run farther, faster and now. He stayed put.

"Interesting," she poured another slash in each glass and returned the bottle behind the counter. Maggie sat down again. She waited.

He knew what she wanted. She wanted what they all wanted. What his parents and friends wanted. What every girl, every love, every human being wanted. They wanted you to walk away from your dreams, from what you'd spent your life pursuing. They wanted you to be like them. To amble through life, picking up your weekly stipend, your bribe for not dreaming. To sell your soul to any bidder willing to take your happy ass in. They wanted you to be just like them. They hated people who were different. The odd ones. They always did. In high school, college, the local bar, they disparaged everything you wanted. Because they couldn't have it. They mocked your dream. They punched you when walked down the hall in school. They spit on you when you walked down the street because you had the balls to chase something they couldn't imagine. That's what they wanted.

It's what he referred to as the "why dontcha's." Why dontcha get a real job? Why dontcha grow up? Why dontcha settle down? Why dontcha get married again? Why dontcha find your daughter? Why dontcha, why dontcha, why dontcha? Why dontcha get off my ass and leave me the fuck alone? That's what he wanted to shout, but when he looked into her face, into her eyes, he couldn't. Because that's not what she said, not what she implied. She asked out of curiosity. And he didn't know the answer, that's why he wanted to strike out at her, at life, at anything.

Maggie watched as the spark became fire and the blaze of anger roared behind his eyes. She had inadvertently blown on banked embers and brought some memory or old flame back to life. His past, or something or someone from it, stampeded across his face. His features tightening in suppressed rage and an attempt at control. She could tell his immediate reaction was to lash out at her, at anyone who would push him, ask him why, but he was fighting that instinct. As the world orbited the sun, he gained control. She was impressed. She had seen that play out in another's eyes long ago, it promised hurt, pain and punishment. She almost winced with memory but held. And so, did he.

Padon sipped his bourbon and set the cup down slowly, carefully on the counter, then with the same deliberation picked up and sipped from the coffee. Deep breaths and focus lay testament to the restraint he exhibited. Now, a calm wrapped him, and his posture and demeanor relaxed. He was back. It was an amazing exercise in self-control, and she was impressed.

"I don't know why I am the way I am," he began softly, with a calm she would never have believed just moments ago. "It is something deep within me and always has been. I think my problem, if one can refer to it as such, is I found many reasons to fight, to rebel, against authority, people defining me by their lives and standards, normal. It is not natural to me. What is etched in my soul is to run, to be free of society's constraints, to not fit in. I fought what others wanted of me." He sat back and took a healthy swig of the bourbon.

"I have never wanted to be anything but what I am. Never found any reason to change.

"Since I was a kid, I have sought out confrontation, the argument, the fight, always against the authority. I didn't mind taking on the world, I looked forward to standing against the wind.

"However, I wanted to be left out of my parents bickering and battles. I had no desire to be in the middle, to be the reason. So, I hid in my room when the fights started. I put on my records, closed the door and blocked them out with music. Music became my oasis. My forest pond. Where I could hide. My safe place. And when my old man got pissed one day for me doing just that, he smashed the small record player that had been my salvation. My depression was overwhelming. I crawled inside myself and created my own room with my own music." He sipped the last of his bourbon but hung on to the cup and stared into its depths. Deep, cleansing, fortifying breaths.

"And people have been trying to take that away ever since, to destroy what I had built. Every person I ever knew, from my folks to friends to girlfriends to my wife and daughter, wanted to invade that space, my space, and take it over, take it away." He stopped his diatribe wondering if he sounded whiney, childish. He didn't want it to come off that way, but he could not think of any better way to tell her.

"I know what this sounds like," he attempted to save some dignity, "like a child crying over someone taking away his toys." She sat patient as a stopped clock. "But this, music, writing, performing, has always been my refuge away from all the world's cruelty, from people." He held out his left hand with the callouses displayed on fingertips. "My music was my life." The world was spinning somewhere out of control but in here it had ceased. "And I pissed it away," he finished with the finality of death. "I took it for granted, I wasted what was given. Now, I don't know if I can find it again. If I stay here, if I stay to heal my body, do I lose my purpose?" He was lost, confused. Maggie wanted to reach out, to hold him, but she remained as if part of her seat, rooted in place.

"Maybe I'm not supposed to know this," she prepared to throw the lifeline, "but Doctor Caldwell and Janet were in for breakfast a few days back and she told me you wrote a beautiful song about them. Is that true?" She searched his face for life and saw the glint of flint striking steel and a spark of hope.

"I guess they liked it?" Yes, hope and a little pride.

"They loved it. It was all they could talk about," she blew gently on the fragile flame.

Baby steps, pray to the Muse, and take baby steps, He got up and downed the last of his coffee.

"Thank you for the conversation. I appreciate your concern," he took her right hand in his left and gave it a gentle squeeze, "I truly do, and the job, but I need to work this out. I'm still trying to come to grips

156

with the whole dead guy thing. The left turn life has taken and whether I'm actually alive or this is some kind of weird purgatory. You all might just be forcing me to face my life before I wind up some place I never considered believable." He slipped into the comfort of the leather and scarf, pulled his hat down over his head, "Either way, it's been a blast so far and I sincerely hope it doesn't come to an end any time soon." He hugged her and walked to the side door.

"Neither do I," she said to whatever spirits might be listening.

Chapter Fifteen

He took the back way, as he hoped to avoid any folks he knew if he took Main. The sound of the saw drew his attention and his body followed. Mr. Carpenter was, as usual, in his shirt sleeves and cutting firewood. His breath steamed out of ancient but strong lungs and he hardly took notice of Padon's approach. But take notice he did.

He looked up as Padon closed the distance, "You look like shit," he grinned, and nodded to the cold beer chilling in the snow.

Padon grabbed two and unlocked the liquid with a quick twist of each cap, and handed one to Mr. Carpenter—who set it to the side— before sitting closer to the warmth of the wood stove.

"You know, I can't say I was happy, living a good life, rolling in comfort or even doing a good job of getting by two months ago," Padon took a deep draught off the bottle, "but I hadn't died and was fairly content. Or so I thought." A deep breath, another tug, "Now I don't know who or what I am.

"Do you ever stop and wonder what the hell does any of this mean?" He snorted at his own insipid question. "Sorry, just feeling lost and sorry for myself. Whatcha building today?" He slipped off despondent and into a nice deflection.

"God only knows," said the ancient carver, "and he has not seen the necessity of informing me," he grabbed the beer and took a slow pull, "so I keep cutting hoping something will occur," he grinned.

"You know I've seen your work down t' the café, you do beautiful woodworking, why you screwing around with these machines? They obviously don't agree with you," he asked sincerely interested.

"Those who refuse to change, to adjust, to grow are doomed to mediocrity," the wisdom of the ages pontificated, "I know how to carve, to whittle, to create with a knife, chisel, mallet and wood, but I don't know how to do this. But I'll figure it out or kill a lot of trees trying," he grabbed another piece of planking and inserted it into the saw, attempting to maneuver it into some kind of pattern as he ran it through the thin blade.

"I may be wrong but that almost looks like something," Padon stared hard at what Mr. Carpenter held in his hands.

"You might be right, dead guy, it does sort of look like a tabletop or something, don't it?" He grinned ear to ear at his handiwork before he threw it on to the scrap pile. "But not enough."

"You are either the right guy or the completely wrong guy," said Padon looking at the small mountain of ruined wood, "but do you ever stop to wonder if you've been wasting your time on something that just didn't mean anything in the first place?"

"Oh, like this?" chuckled the ancient wood devastator.

"Or chasing a dream you should've given up on a long time ago," confessed the sinner.

"I would guess that depended on the dream and what I thought I would, realistically, get out of it. What it would mean to my life," said a thought full of time. "I mean, if all I ever really wanted out of life was fame, fortune and ease, and I didn't get that, I would think myself a failure. But if I thought my dream would bring contentment, joy, creativity, satisfaction, a reason to get out of bed and be excited every morning, I would consider myself a glowing success. It is up to you to define what failure, success and worth is.

"I would think in your business if people were entertained, if the songs touched them and made them think or laugh or cry, if you were pleased with the songs or stories, that is success. I would hope, though you may have begun wanting money, that at some point you would want to perform for the love more so than the financial gain," he sent a questioning glance towards Padon and hit him direct in the forehead, "That to give your songs to fifty people, who loved and appreciated them, would be far more satisfying than to ten thousand who didn't. Of course, I could be wrong, I can't carry a tune with both hands, a pail and help from the Mormon choir."

"I know I used to, before, yeah, before," Padon admitted.

"Sometimes you got to go back to where you started, go back to where the dream was, and find out if it's still there," time finished the thought and then watered his parched vocal cords with amber liquid.

Damn old people always seem to have wisdom, why can't they ever just say they don't know. Because they do. They have had years to learn and make these mistakes before we got to them, admitted the young buck again.

"I haven't cared about the money for years; I don't know that I ever really did. The problem came when I stopped caring about the music." He tried to remember, "I don't know when that happened. It sort of drifted away a little at a time. I can't say I was aware it was leaving. Somehow, somewhere along the line it disappeared, slowly, dissolving into apathy. I don't know," he finished helplessly.

"It's like any kind of relationship, if you don't pay attention to it, water it, feed it, work at it, it dies," confirmed the old man. "Life isn't easy, you have to work at all aspects of it for it to be enjoyable, fulfilling. You have to love and give your all if you want the relationship to last. I bang my head out here day after day, but not all day. I have to give time and effort to my hand tools, to my skill with wood or I would lose it. I don't consider that time to be a chore or work. It is something I love and when you are spending time doing something you love, it is joy." He turned off the saw and the quiet of nature filled the garage, it was deafening.

They sat for a few minutes lost in their own contemplations before the embodiment of time rose to go work with his hands. "Son, I don't know what you're feeling or going through, but you seem a decent enough fellow to me and I think you'll work it out." He gave Padon's shoulder a squeeze before going in the house.

It was snowing as he made his way back to Doctor Caldwell's house. Big, fluffy flakes gently riding a barely felt breeze. It was cold. When wasn't it here? But the beauty of the falling snow warmed him inside if not the exterior. He shivered slightly and hunkered down inside his leather wondering if he would ever be truly warm again.

He hadn't bothered to try to remember the night this all began, though the memory itched just out of reach, begging to be revisited. The human mind was a complicated entity, blocking out painful events so as to lighten the load of life. But he wanted to remember. It was necessary for him to relive what had been such a momentous moment in his life. The mind didn't forget, it just chooses to block the occurrence it found too distressing. It was a defense mechanism he was well acquainted with; it defined his life.

But if he was to heal, complete and thorough, he had to heal body, mind and spirit, and that meant an unpleasant trip down memory lane. It wasn't the memory of how it happened. He knew that. He had to remember why. He could remember in minute detail the car giving up the ghost, the wave of despondency as he immediately recognized his situation. There was every chance his impulsive need for back roads was going to cost him his life.

It didn't have to be that way. Years before, during one of the few happy periods of his marriage, his wife had cajoled and nagged him to keep an empty coffee can, candle and a pack of matches in his trunk for just such an occasion. He had diligently carried that kit with him through five different cars and decades of travel. He had never used it. So, when he bought his newest old beater outside of Lubbock, he left the can and all the memories associated in the trunk. It was the last thread to her, and he'd cut it.

As he sat in the chilling vehicle, he could hear her laughter. "Stupid," she laughed. "Stupid, prideful, moron. Such a simple solution to avoid certain death, but you just had to have it your way and spit on common sense. Enjoy the slow freeze as you die." She would enjoy hearing how he died. It would give her a measure of satisfaction knowing she'd been right. Well, it was the least he could do — give her this parting gift.

The cold invaded the car, invaded his bones, invaded his soul. He couldn't feel his face, and his fingers hurt when he attempted to bend them. He could feel the scalpel of frigid cutting into the old wound deep in his calf. He was going to die without a fight — just lay down on the bench seat, not bother to lock the doors and let death just come and steal his life without even calling for help. It was the most pitiful thing he could have imagined.

What the hell was he doing here, lost in the mountains, as far from civilization as he could get and still be on the planet? He'd come to die. The realization came as clear and cold as the icy air. He'd gotten off the highway to come here, to this spot, to die. He'd had enough.

He began to cry as he stood at the corner of despair and truth. It was time for more than a little honesty in Rock Ridge. He'd come to the mountains to die, in a tragic, hopeless, futile gesture. A stupid last statement of how vain his life had been.

His music was gone. He could still play, but why? There was no joy in his songs, or in his performance. He'd divorced himself from the love he'd taken for granted years ago. He stuck around, played shitholes for coins and shame, just out of pure pigheadedness. There were no worthwhile gigs behind him and none coming up in the foreseeable future. He was done. He was tired. He was through fooling himself. He acted like he was something when he knew in his bones, his frozen, aching bones, he was nothing.

He fought the depression and lost. His father was right. He was just a dreamer who didn't have the heart nor the willingness to make that dream come true. He would never give all of himself to make it happen. He just didn't have it in him. He would never give himself completely to anything. Always fearing the rejection. If he held back some of himself, they could only hurt him so much. Yeah, nice plan.

He couldn't even be honest enough to commit suicide in an honorable way. No, he had to come here. He knew this piece of shit machine was on its last legs. He knew it would not survive a trip through the mountains, so it would appear as if this had all been some horrible mishap. He died trying to get to the next gig. No one would ever know there was no next gig. There hadn't been a next gig for a long time.

It was time, just close your eyes, his brain told him, and let it happen. It'll be easy. Drift off to sleep and never wake up. Dream becomes reality and reality can go fuck itself. He closed his eyes.

What the fuck was he doing? His eyes popped open, his will kicked in and his brain, sluggishly behind, caught up and threw the survival switch.

A life spent fighting the great monster — depression — was not to be thrown away because he was tired, tired of failure, tired of fighting the same fight, banging the same head into the same walls. Was he just giving up? Just like the old man? He had given into life and worked a job he hated, to live a life he hated, to go hang out with people he didn't care for or respect, but they were close. As close as the bar up the street. It would've taken too much effort to change his life. To find some joy. It was easier to go with what crumbs life gave him. To die slow. They didn't suffer depression in the old man's day. They ignored it.

Isn't that what Padon was doing? Dying slow, letting life freeze itself out of him? Squeezing him like a toothpaste tube until they could throw away the husk? How pathetic had he become? If he was going to die anyway, why not truly make one grand, stupid, useless gesture and try to save himself before he did. At least people would know he tried. He hadn't given in to the inevitable. He hadn't quit on himself.

Knowing it was too late but unwilling to fade into obscurity without standing on the heaping pile of shit that was his life, he declared, "I Lived! I Mattered! I Am Here!" He zipped up the leather, pulled down his black knit cap and opened the car door to the bitter death that awaited. Depression wasn't going to win this one.

The elderly couple that puttered down Main would've thought the figure seated on the park bench overlooking the small pond was a statue, had they not lived for the past thirty years in Rock Ridge. They loved their little burgh. It was quiet, peaceful, everyone left each other alone. They also were there if you needed them.

They were bundled, head to toe, against the cold early evening air, and though the figure sitting there had a leather coat, knit hat and scarf, still they thought he must be cold just sitting there. They should check. He was so still they thought him either sculpture or dead, but that thought was betrayed by the puffs of breath coming from his nostrils. He was alive but looked to have fallen asleep. That couldn't be. They conferred with each other. It was far too cold to sleep out in the park. They would check on him.

Padon opened his eyes to the sight of an elderly man and woman inches from his face and just about to shake his shoulder. It startled him the rest of the way out of his reverie. He jumped where he sat which had the effect of startling the couple, who jumped back as far and quickly as two old people might.

"Are you OK, young fella?" ventured the elderly man.

"Yes, yes, thank you," he sputtered, "guess I just got lost in a daydream for a moment." He attempted the explanation, "it's just so restful and pretty here." He stammered on when he should've quit.

"Not a good day for getting lost in dreams, too cold," the old woman chastised. "Go warm up before you freeze." They laughed as they continued their own stroll towards a warm fire and a cup of cocoa.

How long had he sat there? His legs felt stiff and the cold had found its way through to each bone. What the hell? Had he almost froze to death trying to remember how he'd almost froze to death? Wouldn't

165

that be a bit of a kick in the cosmic nads!

He stiffly stood, he knees popped, his leg rigid, shoulders and elbows ached from the cold. He stretched them out as best as he could. How long had he been sitting here? He could not recall coming here. He'd headed home after he talked with Maggie. A talk that had brought up some uncomfortable truths. He'd stopped to talk to the ancient wood worker, Mr. Carpenter, and headed the couple blocks home. Instead, he wound up in the center of town, staring across a frozen pond at what? His future? His past? Death? Truth.

Though he may never share with another human being what he came to discover, he would still have to discover all that was hidden in his own soul. He had to know, for himself, why he walked so close to death. And not just now but apparently most of his life. How can one live if you are concentrated only on dying?

He knew about depression. More importantly, he knew about his own. He had lived with it like a snarky, ever-present, over-bearing roommate as long as he could remember. And, unlike his old man, he couldn't ignore it. Couldn't pretend it didn't exist. He fought it, every step of the way. It was exhausting. But he'd kept it at bay, or had he? Maybe he'd lied to himself his whole life. Maybe he'd been kidding himself. Maybe it was winning, and he hadn't noticed.

Facts came to the surface quicker than he could scoop them up but scoop he must. Scoop and separate in levels of importance if he was to continue to breathe. The world had become one huge, persistent mirror. One that saw into his soul, into his motives and it was not about to let up on him.

Yeah, he wasn't certain what this town was or where it might be in the spiritual realm, but it forced him to face some very uncomfortable facts. And, whether true and or not, he began to believe he would never leave here until he faced them honestly. Shit! The Universe decided to have a little fun and torture some self-realization out of him. Well, if that was what it took, then he would man up and face witnesses, judge, jury and plead his case.

He had to find some warmth, a hot bath, a little whiskey, unknot some muscles and grab a pen and pad. It was time to write. He knew. The necessity was on him. He had to open the wounds and let them bleed out on the page. It was time for some self-doctoring, bring on the leeches and let them do their level best. If the universe was going to force self-examination, then let the autopsy begin. Scalpel!

He slipped into the almost scalding water, submerged as much of himself as possible without drowning. The moist heat soaked deep into his bone and muscle and loosened knots of frozen pain and relaxed mind and body.

His mind wandered, thawed and unchained. Free to inspect ideas and words, concepts and truth, lies and preconceived notions. This is where the songs lay, deep and buried under the refuse of life. Like hidden treasure or jewels strewn in an overgrown valley. He would need to chop through the wild. There were phrases and chords, lyrics galore if he could only unearth them. He would. He knew this territory and was expert at excavating the word.

He liked Doc Caldwell. He liked her as well as he had ever enjoyed any human on the planet, yet he still had been glad when he returned and found her gone. She — hell, everyone he met in this town — had a way of looking at him, examining him, forcing him to look into himself. It was not something they said, it was that they made him want to examine his life, as if that was some kind of kindness. Sometimes he just wanted to be alone and not think about how his life had been an abject failure. How every relationship was based on the most superficial basis. Even what he'd had with his own child.

Time to get out of his head and into some lyrics. He had an idea:

You were always your mother's favorite

Though you never knew

You were always your mother's favorite

If only it was true

It wasn't much but it kept floating around in his head. He'd chased it for a couple days. He wasn't sure he liked it. He didn't know if it was going to come to anything. He never did when he first stumbled across lyrics laying in the deep grass. If he trimmed what didn't fit, he could fashion himself a nice song. It was a sculpture of word and chord. He loved the process. He stared through the walls, past the bare branches of the trees, into the darkening sky, up past the moon and into the deep black nothingness of space. If he stared hard enough, concentrated deep enough, left himself open and vulnerable, maybe the Muse would take pity and give him the one word he sought. Or maybe she would laugh at his impotence and tease.

He whispered a rueful chuckle. This was all so preposterous. He had never been one to live in remorse or regret. He'd made mistakes — a plethora. He had his sins. He wore them like scarlet letters in his heart, pressed between the pages of a tattered and torn scrapbook like dead roses, the scent and beauty beaten out of them. But he'd made them, he could not change the past. It was what made him, him.

He didn't care. He was damn near sixty and they no longer had the weight and bearing they'd had twenty years ago. If anything weighed down his spirit it was the fact he made those stupid, callous, selfish decisions because of the music, his music, his love, his sacred chalice. He sold all he had for his dream, and he lived it. Both dream and nightmare, but he owned them, lived them and, yeah, and then what?

He'd walked away from it. He played like a whore. He gave up on himself. He wrote in ink, not blood. The chords died out too quickly, they didn't ring true. The empty vessel sailed rudderless, without direction, banging into rocks and deserted islands full of flavorless fruit and tasteless water. He hadn't noticed his taste buds had died. The sweet and tangy left the dull flavor of sand in his soul. That was the regret. That was the sin. That was what he paid for now. He could live with the rest, hell, he had forever, but this was too much. This was the sin he died for. What he had, literally, killed himself for.

He collapsed on to the floor, curled into the most primal position known to man and wept. Wept until there was no more. Wept until he was spent and hollow. The husk that had been a man, spilled himself on the hard wood and prayed to the only god he believed in: Music.

Chapter Sixteen

Doctor JoAnn Caldwell dragged her tired old ass through the front door and closed it with her back. She leaned against it and allowed the warmth and familiarity of her home to fill her. What a day! She didn't know if there was something in the air or if the town was just passing through a low mystic, spiritual, transcendent point. Whatever the hell that meant. Or it could just be people were worn out from the icy blasts from the north, but they were definitely cranky and in need of counseling. And she was the town counselor.

People sometimes didn't get sick, they got sick of something — loneliness, cold, life, impending death—an old people's ailment—isolation and need of human contact. So, they became part-time hypochondriacs. It was something to do when winter dragged on and spring refused her entrance. She handed out placebos by the handful, wrote some scribble on a prescription pad and headed to the next house. That patient wanted to talk her ear off, complain a bit about everything in the universe and the cycle repeated. It was busy work and exhausting; it was also necessary.

What this town needed was something to break the monotony. A party or a concert or a blowout booze fest. Or a combination of all the above. Hadn't Maggie mentioned it was old man Carpenter's birthday coming up? And even if it wasn't, they could make it so. Yes, a party, something to take the collective town mind off cold and snow and nowhere to go.

As soon as Janet showed up, they would get to work on planning. Janet loved a good party as much or more so than any human being on the planet. She was a good person to have around when plans were in the works. Hell, she was good person to have around no matter what. She just loved Janet; she should mention it more!

In the kitchen she lit the flame under the tea kettle and picked a nice Earl Grey to get her blood flowing. She wondered if Padon was back from work. She could check but if he was, he was either writing—which would be good—or sleeping—which would be better—or thinking about life—which would complete the scene. No, she would leave him be. If he wanted or needed anything he would emerge from his den and say so. She was pretty sure he would've heard the door open and close. So, she assumed he was busy.

Janet returned from her errands a half hour later. She had delivered prescriptions to the shut ins and, of course, that involved much soothing, talking, reassuring and comforting. She excelled at all. Tea was made, poured and sandwiches built. They sat at the dining room table and munched in silence only broken by sips and slurps.

"Where's your boarder?" Janet finally asked around a bite of ham and cheese.

"Don't know, he wasn't here when I came home. Maybe out on a date," she grinned.

"Thought he'd be too tired for such after working all week," shrugged Janet. "He's been working his tail off over at the Café."

"Yeah, I know. I've been a little concerned with all the hours, but

Maggie assures me she is not driving too hard. She said she had to try and slow him down. He's driven man," she sipped and glanced towards the front door as if expecting it to open any minute. "He's definitely trying to prove something, either to himself or to her or to God and the world. I'll have a talk with him. I can't have him pushing so hard he undoes everything we've done."

"They'd make a nice couple," observed Janet off hand with her usual keen eye.

"Who?"

"Now who do you think I'm talking about?" Snorted Janet as she picked up her cup, "Padon and Maggie, of course."

"Yeah, when pigs fly," snorted Joann.

"Why?"

"Do you honestly think Maggie will allow anyone to get that close to her?" Glared the doctor, "I love her, she's as good a person as anyone could hope to meet, but there's something hidden deep in her — some horror that haunts from the past — that won't allow her to let any man close." She nodded a quick approval of her own assessment.

"Why didn't you ever get married?" came from out of left field.

"What?"

"Why didn't you ever get married?" asked Janet again, "you're a good-looking woman, probably were cute, adorable when you was young, how is it you never found a guy willing to put up with you?"

"I did." She said quiet, final. "Long time ago."

"What? I mean, how come I never knew? I swear, you are like someone I never met! All this coming out all of a sudden. Damn! What happened?" the questions came flying like geese from winter.

"He died." Time stopped. Janet wanted to but refused to ask.

Time will begin again, or it won't.

"In the war, he was a doctor. The bombs hit the wrong camp. He was under them. Friendly fire, they called it," she sighed a breath held for fifty years, "What the fuck is friendly fire? He didn't come home — not much left of him. Left his remains over there." She shrugged and admired a star in the far distance out the side window.

"Never wanted to try again?" pushed her friend of many years.

"Nah, I knew what true love was. I knew how it felt, the touch of his hand, the feel of his skin. I knew the scent and taste of it. It always seemed like I would be disrespecting, sullying that, if I ever tried again. I never wanted the shine to blemish. It was perfect. You don't ask for that twice in one life. It would be greedy and wrong. I get everything I need from those who need me. It's a symbiotic relationship, I love my patients, they respect and need me. We live off each other from a safe distance. It's satisfying without soiling my sweetest gift."

Silence wrapped the room, the house, the world. A silence so profound they heard a scratch, a movement from the back of the house. They stared in horror at each other, jumped up from their chairs and raced to Padon's room.

The found him on the floor in a fetal position unresponsive and comatose. His breathing shallow, his pulse steady but slow. He didn't seem to be in any pain but there was really no way to know. She couldn't ask the insensate man.

"Help me lift him into the bed and let's hook him up and see what we see," she instructed her assistant. She could only do the most rudimentary tests, as she did not have a medical facility, only an office, but it would give her information she didn't have now. The EEG and PET scans would give her some indication of brain activity and the EKG would tell her a little about his heart. Other than that, she would have to rely on a lifetime of observation and experience to tell her anymore. It was time to play doctor at a much higher level than she had in years.

Padon felt himself rise. At first, he thought death had at long last come for him, but soon realized what he felt was physical not spiritual. They were lifting him into bed. He wanted to help, to tell them there was no pain, that he had collapsed from mental, emotional and psychological exhaustion. He had overloaded on healing. He couldn't open his eyes, his mouth or move any muscle to indicate his condition. He could hear them talking but could not respond. This might be the final straw to his insanity, trapped in his own body. His claustrophobia began to kick into overdrive.

In the background of the screaming inside his head he heard the calm tones of Doctor Caldwell and Janet. Cool as two cucumbers in ice water they went about their business. If they were frightened or becoming frantic, he would never have known by the tone of their voices. They discussed his condition as if he were a fish they'd caught and were discussing how to filet it. It was the most reassuring thing happening in his mind.

"He doesn't seem to be having any difficulty breathing and his pulse is still strong, though slow and measured," came the facts from Janet.

"Well, that's good. That's a good start. Let's see if we can learn anything from the mighty machines," her tone light, unworried and unhurried. The doctor, if she was concerned, hid it well.

"Honestly, if I was a betting woman, and you know I am," chuckled the doctor, "I would think he worried and worked himself into this. He is one of those who has to prove himself to himself every day of his life. I guarantee he knows every single thing he has ever done wrong—in his mind—and to whom, and lives with it every day.

"I always thought that was probably the true definition of hell, living with your past. If you have a conscience, if you are a decent human being, if you care at all, you carry all your sins with you. All the time!" Her voice rose almost to a yell before Janet shushed her and pointed at the prone figure on the bed. "Sorry," mouthed the doctor.

"I just know people like this. They carry it with them, twenty-four -seven. Some people carry baggage. Some carry anvils. He looks to be an anvil guy." She shook her head and read the squiggly lines being spit out by the humming machines. "This all looks fine. Let's hook up some IVs of saline and 5% dextrose solution. We'll keep an eye on him from there," she checked off other considerations and decided enough would have to be enough, for now.

"Oh, and we'd best call Maggie and let her know he won't be in to work tomorrow. She'll need to know that." Now she nodded her head affirming her mental litany. "I need a drink."

It was just after eleven when Maggie stormed through the front door. Her usual disheveled self, more so with hurry. "What the hell happened?" she snapped as she threw her coat over the back of a chair and looked from one woman to the other.

"Would you like a drink?" Asked Janet holding up the quarter filled Kilbeggan. A quick nod and a glass was filled and set before her as she sat.

"Maybe you could tell us about his last week or so working at your place, which would probably be the best place to begin," said the doctor.

"I didn't do anything. You said to work him but not too crazy. I did what you said," her defenses were up and in place, ready to repel all attacks.

"Now don't get your dander up," calmed Doctor Caldwell, using both hands in a shushing manner and to keep Maggie in her seat. "No one is blaming you for anything. I just need to know about his schedule at your place. I know what he was like when he got back here. When he went to sleep, when he got up and his eating habits. I don't know how he was at your place." She sipped and sat back.

From his place of coma on the bed Padon heard women's voices like a murmur in his head. A word here, the scrape of a chair on wood, a raised voice and more, but not quite picking up on the conversation.

"Well, he doesn't know how to slow down. I mean, at first, he was just keeping up, doing a good job but didn't have the energy. Like you told me," she nodded to the doctor, "but as he got a little stronger each day, he pushed harder. Like he knew he was getting better — healing — he could feel his strength returning. I tried to keep the brakes on him, giving him busy work and none too taxing but he wouldn't have it. So, I tried to placate him without killing him. He is a worker," she shook her head in admiration.

"It was like he had to prove something to himself, like, that he was still alive. That he still mattered, if only to him. He's pleasant enough. I don't mind saying, I was worried he would be a sour puss coming in there," she smiled, "you know, sacrificing himself to prove a point. Mr. Big Time Musician bussing tables and scraping dishes." She dared them to criticize, but they remained quiet. "Anyway, he doesn't mope or drag. He bullshits with the customers. They love him — by the way — does his work, proves everybody wrong. There was a bet as to how long he would last. I lost," she frowned at her financial loss, "but he works his ass off. And a cute little ass it is," she added under her breath.

Janet and Doc shared a glance. OK, not quite so under her breath as she thought.

"He was so proud of himself yesterday when he worked the double and refused to take today off. Kept claiming it was only a half day, seven hours, and he could do it. I'm not sure who he is trying to show his stuff, but they ought to be impressed. I was," she admitted. "There's a lot of young kids who couldn't keep up with him. Bet it ain't doing his hands any good, but he doesn't seem concerned."

"No signs of weakness or lightheadedness?" Probed the doc. "Never saw him unsteady on his feet?"

"Nope, not that I ever saw."

"I think we are just going to have to put this down to mental and physical exhaustion for now," supposed the doc. "I can't see anything that would've caused it but him. I think we should keep him in bed for a couple days and see how things go. Right now, he is comatose. I've got him on fluids and am hoping he will come around by morning. That's the trouble with these kinds of things. There's no way to know for sure except time."

"By the way Margaret, the town is feeling winter SAD and I think we need some reason to get everybody out of their houses and have a party. A mental vacation from themselves. I thought between the three of us we could find a reason everyone would buy into and show up for. Didn't you tell me Mr. Carpenter was closing in on his two hundredth birthday or something? What say we have a blow out this coming weekend and see if we can't wipe off some of the cobwebs and dust off these old folks—and the young ones as well—and get drunk?" JoAnn raised her glass to be met by the other two, eyes glistened with mischief and merriment and toasted a wonderful idea.

The murmur of female voices rose and fell with intensity, and re-lief, and landed near laughter. It was reassuring even to his fevered and claustrophobic mind. He tried to relax but found it impossible. This was his worst nightmare come true. He had been claustrophobic ever since some kids had locked him in a laundry chute when he was eleven. It was cramped, and he couldn't breathe. They laughed and taunted him and then left. Went to their houses. They left him locked in an airless laundry chute with no idea when the folks who lived here would be home. He was catatonic when they found him four hours later.

And now here he was, trapped inside his body. It was tight, and he couldn't breathe. His mind raced; his pulse was a rocket blasting into space. He couldn't break free. He tried to concentrate on something other than what was happening. He hummed. Inside his head, he hummed.

Tuneless at first, just a sound, a distraction, a vibration to bore through to the surface. Soon it morphed into one of his Irish tunes, a reel — fast, crazed, whirling — then rock and roll. He needed something with more power — a raucous, wild, loud, piercing, tear-down-the-walls anthem to break through all resistance. He heard footsteps. Had one of the women heard his humming? Had they heard the music? Had it saved him again?

Someone stood next to him, he could feel the presence, the breath on his face as they leaned in close. And then he could feel the cool as the medication flowed into his veins, the medicines providing a sopo-rific effect. And the world went dark.

They screamed for more, but he had none to give them. They didn't care. It wasn't a call for an encore anymore, it was a demand for blood. His. They would have all he was willing to give — in fact, they had that in spades — and all he was trying to keep. There would be no holding back.

He had played every song he knew; some he half knew and others he was making up on the spot. He played the half dozen songs they had come to hear and loved, over and over, but it didn't satisfy. They wanted him, physically, creatively, spiritually, on a platter. They would devour all he had, all he was and spit out the bones.

The stage manager pushed and pulled him back through the wings and back onto the stage, duct taped his guitar around his waist and yelled for him to play. The demonic faces, filled with hate and hunger, filled his vision. They pawed at the stage, threatened to overcome the security, who, apparently, didn't care and were not going to protect him. They would have him. All he could do was play and hope.

His bloodied fingers attempted chords and riffs, his tattered vocal cords rasped nonsensical lyrics and guttural utterances. The pick glued to his fingers tripped over strings and banged on the flat top in a percussion of the dance of Hades.

He'd died, and this was his eternity, playing songs he hated to people he loathed without cease. All the beauty and soft ripped from the melodies. Sensual lyrics of love now grotesque and perverse. Filth streamed from his mouth in pornographic diatribes. There was no esoteric, profound symbolism just grinding, gyrating superficial banging. He wept. They laughed. He prayed. They blasphemed. The Muse lay prostrate, gutted and dead on the floor of the stage, sacrificed to their wants. He was disgusted.

When he pleaded why, why was this happening, they screamed it was not them who had forsaken the Muse, it was him. He killed her. They *had not bastardized the music. He had sold it for beers and a flop. He was torn from the stage, ripped piece by piece into semi-conscious shreds and devoured. They would have much more than their pound of flesh, they would have their fill of creative energy-unused, promise-unfulfilled, artistic expression-unrealized. If they could not have his soul, they would feast on his flesh.*

The nightmare could not end because he could not break free of the drugs Doctor Caldwell had given him to force his sleep. This was the ultimate definition of hell. Consumed by his own passion.

He opened his eyes and immediately shut them. Brilliant light streamed in the window, piercing his brain and intensified his headache. Well, the pain proved he was still alive. He would discover if that was a good thing or not. This dying thing was getting old, either do it or don't, but whatever controlled the universe had to make up its mind. It was wearing him out.

He tried to turn over but found his arm restricted by the IVs and the cocoon of covers wrapped tightly about his body. It was constricting, and his claustrophobia began to kick in until he realized he was free of the prison in his mind. He could bear the physical, and would, until freedom came with the footsteps down the hall.

He could tell by the scent it was Janet. She always smelled fresh as ocean and mountain air. He assumed it was her body wash. She was a lovely fifty-something woman, with the figure of someone who had lived and the intelligence that living brings. She was smart, funny and very quiet and reserved, but there was always mischief boiling behind those calm brown eyes. She would accept no shit from no one, especially an old, broke down musician.

"Don't pretend," she admonished, "The machines tell me you are awake, and they don't lie." She busied herself with tugging at sheets, reading printouts and checking IV bags. She sternly whacked his hip, "Want a cup of my famous coffee?"

"Dear God, yes," he grinned, opening his eyes with a nod of thanks.

She padded out of the room and returned within seconds with a steaming cup of coffee, a slice of toast — lightly buttered — and a small bowl of fruit. Nothing to upset a tender tummy.

"How long was I dead this time?" he joked, though only marginally.

"From what we can determine, maybe twenty hours. Give or take," she glared at him. "We didn't know you were here, so, we don't know how long you laid on the floor before we found you." She held the cup, so he could sip, and he almost spit it out.

"I'm late for work!" Well, she had to give him responsibility points, if none for intelligence.

"We took care of calling you in," she chastised and pushed him back onto the bed.

"Shit, she's going to be pissed. I told her I would not let her down," he mulled as he gulped the fruit.

"She can be a very understanding woman, sometimes," she added and scowled his way. "But she expects you to take care of yourself and return to work as soon as you're up to it. But not before!" she added in case he had any crazy man thoughts happening in that empty pumpkin atop his neck.

"How long?" Came the plaintive plea, begging the judge for leniency.

"A week," she slammed the door of hope, "and don't get any ideas about trying to slip out before then or I'll strap you into the bed, got it?" Right eyebrow raised in challenge and promise. She took the empty bowl from his quivering hand back to the kitchen.

"How's the patient?" Doc asked as she donned her heavy coat in preparation to see to her appointed rounds.

"Not too bad for someone who keeps dying on us, but he'll live," exasperation fills the room.

"Please be kind and keep a compassionate eye on him while I soothe the town," she grabbed her black bag. "Maybe I should stick my head in, just to check." She walked to the back bedroom while pulling on her gloves.

"I have to go check on some folks," she said sticking her head through the half open door, "I would appreciate it if you would listen to our lovely Janet and try to stay alive until I return," she turned and walked heavily down the hall. Point, Doctor Caldwell.

Chapter Seventeen

Janet returned to grab the small plate, now empty of toast, and see if he would like more coffee. Of course, he wanted more coffee, and her company if she wouldn't mind. She returned with two cups of the steaming black liquid, she set one on the nightstand for him and one on the small wall table for her.

"What the hell is happening?" he opened the salvo with the big guns. "I mean, I've never been the healthiest person in the world but never died quite so often." His eyes begged her for answers.

"Well, I ain't no doctor, the doctor is, well, the doctor, but I am guessing once you died the first time you needed to take better care of yourself to keep it from happening again," her smirk stung but he asked for it.

"I thought I was taking care of myself," he answered sheepishly.

"Well, you were until you started killing yourself at the café," she chastised, something she apparently exceled at.

"I was just trying to pull my own weight," he defended.

"Yeah, Well, you don't weigh as much as you used to," she finished.

"Am I allowed to practice my guitar?" Petulance is always childish, but she allowed it to pass.

"As long as you don't start rockin' and rollin' and dancin' all over the room, I guess you can have it," she walked to the other side of the bed and carefully picked up the instrument and handed it to where he was now sitting up in the bed.

"Thank you."

Where did he put that pad from the other night? As long as he's going to be stuck here, he might as well see if he can dig up some of the love he used to have for writing. The nightmare from his drug induced sleep was still very near the surface of his mind. He decided what he had to discover was, was something lost or abandoned a long time ago, and could he rediscover it or was it lost forever.

He wanted to write—just to write—not for fame, fortune or getting laid, but to create something from nothing. To fill the blank page with meaning. He used to be good at that.

He could hear Janet puttering around the kitchen and dining room, more than likely preparing things for when JoAnn returned home. They made an excellent team, he thought, and probably would have made an excellent couple, but life goes its own way. Love comes in many colors, shapes and conditions. You just had to grab what was offered.

And what was being offered? He had no idea. This town seemed to be offering him a second chance, a family—that was love, wasn't it? —friends, a home, all the things he never had. They offered everything except what he had chased his entire life. They could not give him fame or fortune. They could not help him tour or chase a dream long gone. So, he guessed it was up to him to decide what he wanted.

The problem was he knew what he wanted, what he craved on a visceral level, what he'd sold his life for. And even though he knew it could never happen, certainly not at this later stage of life, it didn't stop the want. It was an addiction, a sickness, that glimmer of hope. That thought that if he could just write that one song, come up with that combination of words, and feeling, he could ride the wave one more time.

That was the rub, wasn't it? To decide to settle here, to live the rest of his life in one place, surrounded by the same people, day after day, was anathema to everything he had sacrificed his life for. He would chafe at the bit every day. He would never stop wondering if he could have had one more turn at the plate. One more chance to hit that home-run. His feet would itch. He was quite certain within a year of trying to settle down he would hear the road seductively whisper to him. And, sooner or later, he would answer. That was the curse.

But was that true? What had he sacrificed? What had he given up? A job he would have hated? Living in a town he just wanted to escape? Retirement? Security? He never had any want for any of that in the first place. He had given up nothing. Sacrificed nothing. He had settled for his own greed and lust. His ego and want drove him, not some altruistic, benevolent quest. He had played for himself, driven himself to achieve what he wanted, and the rest of humanity be damned. He hadn't given up anything he wasn't already trying to divest himself of. He had fed the monster and the monster was him.

But if he could just find that one song, that message, that touched people, he could make it all up. To himself, to his family, to the naysayers and doubters, he could show them. They'd finally see he was everything he told them he was, not some loser. If only…

He set the guitar to the side of the bed. He no longer wanted to play. The pad of paper slid to the floor. He should sleep. Rest. Stop pushing so hard. He should…weep and seek clarity. Damn it!

Normal depression is bad enough to deal with on a day-to-day basis. Why don't you smile more? Are you OK? Sad? Everything will be alright. You're just having a bad day. Why do you have to be such a negative Ned all the time? Why can't you be happy? Yeah, why can't you. But you throw in a physical ailment, like dying, and the fight is on.

He had never really gone into detail with people he knew about his depression, because he'd learned early on people didn't want to know. Asking, 'how are you?' Is their way saying something rather than ignoring you. It was not meant as a question. They don't want details. They don't want to know you are drowning and not sure you'll make it 'til the end of the day. They want fine and move on.

Add in a physical injury and the depression finds a way to bore into your bones and try to eat its way out. The single chance he had at digging his own way out was a tried and true one, as true as any method could be when it came to this. He had to write. To force himself not to quit, to put pen to paper and chords to words. It had, years ago, been his only salvation. Liquor, drugs, meditation, exercise, nothing helped sooth the savage beast like music. It was true. He picked the pad up from where it had come to rest on the floor.

Blank stared hard at him from the page—challenged, teased, dared him to put down the pen. There were no words, no clever twist of a phrase. No tune wandering lost in the backwoods of his brain. Nothing. The Muse was dead. He'd seen her butchered on the floor of the stage and then torn to pieces. He had been torn asunder alongside her.

But that wasn't true, was it? He was here in the bed, weak, beat to hell, constantly dying, but here. Alive. And if he still lived then how could a godling, like the Muse, be dead? She had to be here somewhere. In his head. In his heart. In his soul. As long as he lived, so would she.

He had to resurrect her, bring her from the ashes like a Phoenix, and she would reward him with music.

The only way to shake this damn depression was to write but he couldn't write while he felt this way. Catch 22, again. He would work his way out. He would not quit. That was the problem, wasn't it? He would never quit. It was why he was laying in this bed right now. He was supposed to ease his way into the whole 'work for a living' life change, but he had to push. Had to prove himself to everybody that he could do what they he couldn't. He had to show them he could do the double and then seven hours without sleep. Yeah, he was superman, and he would show them.

He had shown them alright, shown them how to literally work yourself to death. Push, push, push just like he had done on the road for so many years. Drive for twenty-four hours. Set up. Play the gig. Sleep for two or three and drive another fifteen or seventeen, and start it all again? He was an asshole about showing he could outdo anybody. 'Is it insane? No one has ever even tried to do this before. Let's go. Shit yeah, hold my beer.' It should have been his motto.

And then exhaustion and depression kicked in, so he would drink it away and the depressive hangover would attempt to kill him. How many mornings had he woken up feeling the press of a steel barrel against his head, and he didn't even own a gun, but he could feel it. Taste it in his mouth. Feel the death. How many times did he go to sleep assuming there would be no morning? And his answer always was to push, push harder. Maybe he could work the depression to death.

Well, now he had no choice but to slow down, to allow his body to heal. And maybe, just maybe, allow his mind to heal for the first time in his life.

If the words weren't coming, he could at least practice what had been written before. Lift the Gibson off the floor and let her settle into his loving embrace. A tiny bit of tuning and his hands roamed free. He didn't think, he played scales and instrumental meanderings, songs he written and songs he learned, songs with lyrics that he hummed. He wanted to let the mechanics of playing, the muscle memory, take over. After two hours he put the Gibson to the side of the bed, again, and eased his legs over the other side. He could stay here no longer. He wasn't going to push. He slowly, carefully made his way to the kitchen for a glass of milk and a sandwich. Certainly, they couldn't begrudge him that?

"Where do you think you're going?" came from the front parlor.

How did she do that? She couldn't possibly see him from where she sat. She would have to be able to see around corners or through walls. He was beginning to believe in magic. The woman had some kind of Voodoo powers that allowed her to feel when he moved!

"I heard the floor squeak." Jesus, now she was reading his thoughts.

She came around the corner of the doorframe, scowl well in place and loaded for bear. If he'd had the energy, he would have stood his ground, but he knew he was defeated before he could utter a word. So, why not whine and lie a bit.

"I didn't think anybody was home," he began his slow trip to hell, "and thought I could probably make it to the kitchen for a glass of milk and something to eat." That part was true.

"You could've called for me," she chastised as she shooed him into the dining room and pointed to the nearest chair.

"Damn it, I can't just lay in the bed all day doing nothing!" Frustration reared its pretty little head.

"You weren't doing nothing, and I was enjoying the nothing you were doing," she smiled. "Sit," came the command. "you're very good with that thing," she complimented. "You must love to play."

"I sure used to," he muttered.

She set the milk on the table and bustled back into the kitchen to see what she could pull together for him to eat. She returned with a plate of cut up chicken, some mashers, corn and a slice of bread. "When did you stop loving to play?" He stared at her, how had she heard what he'd said? "I have excellent hearing," she answered his unasked question, and read his thoughts again, "it's how I heard the floor creak when you were sneaking out of your room." She sat across the table from him.

"Am I expected to eat all of this?" His eyes might be bigger than his stomach right now, but this plate was bigger than his body.

"I'll help," Janet said as she reached across and grabbed a piece of chicken. "Why don't you love playing?" She pushed.

"I don't really know," he said honestly, "it sort of slipped away while I was busy trying to be a star. I started playing for the money, not the love, then when things picked up speed downhill, I played for surviv-al. Then because I felt trapped and it was the only thing I could do. I kept thinking I could play my way out my bad choices, but it turned out play-ing was my bad choice. Or so I became convinced." He shrugged, "Now I am not so certain about it, or anything. I have to concentrate on getting back to one hundred so I can see clearly. Right now, I feel like I'm stand-ing in dense fog with no way to know where north is." He shoved a fork full of chicken, mashers and corn into his mouth and chewed thoughtful-ly.

"What I heard sounded like someone who loves what he does." She scooped her own fork in for a landing, "I'm not an expert and wouldn't know an E chord from a piece of fish, but I heard some passion coming from that room and you can't deny that!" She clamped her teeth around the food.

"I haven't played, really played, in so long, it just felt good, satisfying." His eyes focused on something she can't see.

"Maybe because you were just playing for yourself, just for the sake of it, not for me, or Doctor Caldwell, or your millions of adoring fans," she snickered.

"Maybe, and maybe I just forgot why I picked up the damn thing in the first place."

"Because you loved music?" said the kindly doctor's assistant.

"To get laid," said the honest musician, then laughed loud and hard.

"What's so funny?" Came the shout from the whoosh as the front door closed.

"We're talking about getting laid," laughed Janet.

"Well, I might want in on this conversation," chortled Maggie in a sensual and wicked voice.

Padon attempted to stand as she entered the dining room, but she pushed him back into his chair and sat next to him. She unbuttoned her coat but didn't remove it, just shoved a concerned look his way as if she could see inside him and how he is repairing.

"How's the patient," she asked Janet without taking her eyes from Padon.

"A pain in the ass who doesn't listen to orders very well," she feigned exasperation.

"So, about the same as he is as an employee," Maggie shot back.

"I'm sitting right here," said the object of their scorn.

"Ah, you're a big boy, you can take a little ribbing," Maggie spoke to him as she would a five-year old, "but seriously, how do you feel? You've been causing quite a stir of concern for someone who's only been in this town for a couple months," she presented him a crooked half smile to take any sting from the words. "You have got to stop dying, people are talking."

"I shall endeavor to make this the last time, the very last time," he bowed from a sitting position.

"Good. Now on to important matters, where's Doc Caldwell?" She threw the question out to both parties not caring from where information came.

"She should be home," Janet listened as the clock struck eight, "very soon. Just checking on a few more of those with seasonal depression and neediness. It is becoming imperative to do something to take the mind of this town off the cold, snow, and housebound."

"I stopped by Merle's and talked to Dave on my way here. He thinks a birthday bash for the ancient one is an excellent idea," Maggie said as she got up to go into the kitchen to retrieve a cup of coffee or tea or whatever else might be available. "We have much to discuss and plan, and not much time to do so if we are really going to try and do it this weekend. I figure I will do the food," she clicked off the obvious, as she has the best comfort food in town.

"We can start, and she can catch up when she gets here," and with that Janet dug a pad of note paper out of the buffet and two pens.

Padon yawned and excused himself, knowing he was not needed here, though they invited him to stay, it was half-hearted. He returned to his room and pulled out his own pad of paper determined, more than ever, to write something tonight. Where was that song, Your Mother's Favorite?

The words formed painstakingly slowly but they began to come. Sometimes writing a song or, he guessed, any creative endeavor was like archeology. Pick a promising spot and start to dig, excavate, work around the dirt and rock until you find something and then carefully unearth and see if it is truly worthwhile. A word here, a whole phrase there, scratch out this section, move the other.

The murmur of female voices intensified in the dining room, now joined by Doc Caldwell, and he was curious as to what they were planning so studiously yet refused the distraction. If they wanted him to know they would pass on the info. Though the idea of a party certainly appealed to him. It was the last thing he thought of as he fell into a deep, and thankfully dreamless, sleep.

The predawn silence whispered to him and he woke. It was still pitch-black outside. The small mountain town of Rock Ridge did not waste resources on lighting a town asleep. He lay in the soothing dark for several minutes. Padon had never been an early riser, it was not his time of day. He lived for the night, waking at the crack of noon and easing into the flow of society. But his mind was clear, and his body didn't hurt.

Flipping on the small bedside lamp he wondered what he should do. Not much. He couldn't practice or cruise around the Victorian, or he would awaken JoAnn. She needed her sleep as much as he did. Sometimes he was amazed by the energy and spirit of the woman. She had to be mid to late seventies and chugged along like a small tugboat, pushing and prodding her town towards health. It was a hard push.

Writing would not be too noisy, maybe he could find some of the lyrics that he'd been chasing the night before, here in the quiet of morning. He had scratched at the pad for a while the previous night but the

192

sound of laughter and conversation from the dining room had distracted him. It was perfectly still now, nothing to scare the words from where they lay hidden in the brush.

The pen took on a life of its own, it flowed and skated across the pages. He caressed the words, called to them, coaxed them with coos of love and reassurance. They would not be slaughtered on the page. They would not be wasted and sacrificed for wants. They would be loved and nurtured, caressed and coddled as a child. They would be given as a precious gift to others, who would love them as much as he did. And they came.

Like a flood through a deep valley. Building and flowing, raging like a river gone wild and free, cleared of all the clutter that had gathered over the years. Deadwood and underbrush swept away in a torrent as cleansing as the flood of Noah. He rode the rushing tide, danced to and hummed the music that flowed over the top of the lyric, and still more came.

He hardly noticed as the pink of dawn peeked over the mountain and grew into brilliant sunshine and full morning. He didn't hear Doc Caldwell get up and start the coffee or Janet come through the front door. He didn't hear their soft conversation and the clanking of pans or rattle of dishes. He only heard the sound of songs in his head.

A soft tap on his door and the scent of coffee roused him from his cerebral concert. His stomach growled. What time was it? Did it matter? He kipped out of bed and slipped on his sweats, cracking the door. Janet smiled and handed him a hot cup of joe. He nodded his thanks and said he would be out in a minute. She smiled. It was beautiful.

The pure white beamed from the pure chocolate face; her eyes danced when she smiled. Had he bothered to notice before now? It was going to be a good day. He actually felt human, and content. Is this what content, bliss, felt like? He thought he might enjoy this sensation for more than a morning.

Small talk filled out breakfast. The doctor kept a watchful eye on Padon but did not question his health or how he slept. She would let him be an adult and tell her if something was wrong. Padon could tell it was killing her and he dangled her on the hook for just a few more minutes before breaking the news that he was fine. As fine as he'd ever been.

He ate like he'd never seen nor tasted food before; he was ravenous. He couldn't remember the last time he had been this hungry. It was as if life had only now landed on his shoulders and he could partake in all its glory. He wanted nothing more than to gorge himself on life and joy. He wanted to stuff himself and go back to his room and play. He had songs to finish and tunes to write. And daylight was a wasting. He smiled, an actual joyous smile.

"Just so you know, no, you three didn't keep me awake at all last night with your cackling and secrets," he kidded.

"We attempted to keep it to a low roar," Doc shot back. "How did you sleep?" Well, he'd opened the can, she was going to taste the contents.

"As well as I ever have. Better," he added thoughtfully. "I woke rested and without any pain," and then reconsidered, "with pain but not so much to cause discomfort, if that makes sense," he shrugged.

"When you have been through great pain and rehab, it takes much more to get your attention," the doctor appeared satisfied. "You're not immune to pain, but you're also not as sensitive. I'm very glad to hear you had a good night." Janet nodded her approval as she began to collect plates.

"If it is alright with you both," he put his hand on her wrist staying her motion, "I would like to clean up from breakfast. I promise not to overexert myself, and I don't think these few dishes will do that, but I have to contribute for my own self-worth."

The two women shared a look, silently discussed their thoughts, before they nodded in agreement. "As long as you don't push," said Janet as she put the plate back on the table. "If you feel tired at all you stop, and you call me. I ain't going nowhere, my job, right now, is getting you up to speed," she reprimanded, finger waggling and scowl firmly in place.

Dishes done—he walked with a bit more spring in his step at the accomplishment—Padon returned to his room, letting Janet know first, of course, so she would know where he was. He grinned at the absurdity but loved the fact they cared so much. He wrapped himself in their concern and love, he picked up pen and paper and that old Gibson.

The hours passed but time has no meaning to the creative spirit, it blocks all clocks, the chimes do not ring, the tick has no tock. The fingers dance, the pick strikes the proper chord found on the hard wood of the fretboard. The phrases move as needed, flowing from the front of the song to the end, a word here, a concept there becomes a verse or chorus and they weave into a beautiful quilt. A rocking, body shaking, rouser or a story so human you could reach out and touch the participants. He gloried in the writing, knowing no one would ever hear but not caring. Today was not about pleasing an audience it was about the doing, the making, the shaping.

He thought of ancient Mr. Carpenter, tossing wood into the stove and he realized even the failures served their purpose. If only to keep one warm until success could force its way in. He had concentrated on his failure for too long, thinking it defined his life. It hadn't defined, it had helped shape. Failure is only failure if you continue to make the same mistakes. He'd heard that somewhere and he made the decision to hold it close to his breast. Maybe have it embroidered on a damn pillow, so he could sleep on it. Change is in the air, and he would be that change.

Chapter Eighteen

He laughed at the pompous ass staring back at him from the mirror. So, you think you can change overnight? Moron. Just because you died, does not mean you get to come back a completely different person. You were not reborn, you were revived.

He would need to commit to the long haul and understand he would need to crawl before he ran. He had never thought beyond the next show, the night's drive, the next woman and the next escape. Now, he had to focus on a future he couldn't have seen with a telescope two months before. And one he couldn't imagine still, as he had no idea what form it would take.

Yes, he wrote songs, but for what reason? To write, he answered himself, and wasn't that the first step to change his life? Wasn't he supposed to realign his priorities? And what better way than to return to the beginning, to the theoretical reason he had walked this path in the first place.

Yes, he'd gotten off the path, lost his way in his own ego and self-indulgence, but that didn't mean he couldn't find his way back. He had to absolve his sins to his art, find the purity of what was supposed to be his first love. He would shed what he'd become, to become what he should have been.

He would not consider fame or money as success—he never had; well, he would not start now. Success would not be something measured by some nebulous standards created by nameless, faceless entities he did not know nor had ever met. Success would be measured by his own definition. And that would be by quality. Simple. Honest. How did it make him feel and how did the song affect others? Did the song lift those who heard it? Could he truly change or was he bullshitting himself and everyone else? Time would tell. And time told him it was naptime. Now was not the point in life for overload. It was the time for slow and deliberate.

He slept through the lunch hour and Janet saw no reason to roust him from what she knew he required most. Rest — rest the body, mind and soul. Let it heal. She admonished him not to overdo, and she had to abide her own counsel. If he didn't stir by dinner, she would wake him, but that was hours away. She would check on his vitals in a while.

He slept, not deep as he hoped, but skimmed along the surface of REM. Dreams tantalized, promised gifts of songs that would take him far from here. And just as quick he would lose them. He was frustrated, and he woke tired and grumpy. He required a change of scenery.

Disheveled and rumpled, bags fully packed under his eyes and ready for pickup, he found his way to the parlor where Janet sat, curled up with book in hands and cup of tea at her side.

"You look like shit," she greeted him.

"If I look as bad as I feel, I wouldn't blame you for running," he fell onto the sofa. "I need a change of pace. Think I could find someone to take me into the mountains, driving not walking, to see a sunset and something other than town?" He knew he asked a lot, but he asked, not whining, not demanding, and not quite begging.

"I'll clear it with Doctor. When are you thinking?" She never looked up from her book.

"I don't know, tomorrow or the next day," he shrugged nonchalantly, "It wouldn't be strenuous. I'm not talking about hiking or camping out — just a drive through the mountains and someplace to sit quiet and watch the sunset behind them. And that would be the thing, I would want to try and find someone who doesn't require conversation. Just quiet."

"There's Joe," she said thoughtfully running through her internal rolodex, "Claims to be some kind of Native blood, Ojibwa, or Cherokee, or Iroquois, or something, though he's pretty B and B for anyone to take him serious," she smirked.

"B and B?" he asked for clarification.

"Blond and blue-eyed," she filled in the gap. "Wanted people to call him Indian Joe but no one would, too much respect for the indigenous folks we know around here. And I wouldn't let them if they tried. I got this thing about names, words and their effect on peoples thinking," she nodded the finality on that. "Don't know why folks can't be happy just being people. Why they got to try and appropriate somebody else's culture, but folks do it all the time. Wannabe's we call them. Not happy with their life, or feeling too privileged, or guilty or something so they claim to be black or Native or some race they ain't. Someday, somebody is going to explain to everybody on this damn planet there ain't but one race and that is the human one. Take the color out and we're all the same, bland, boring and no flavor, but the same.

"Me, I like who I am. Who my folks were — where we all came from and what it took to get me here. If you claim to be somebody you ain't, then you are just spitting on all the folks and hard work that brought you to this point. You are denying your forefathers and foremothers, and everybody in between. The idea is not to deny who you are but accept everybody for who they are," she had made her point to the world, "but that's not what you asked." She smiled.

"Joe does know these mountains as well as any. He's been here for a while — fifteen years, I'm guessing—and spent most of it wandering around up in the mountains. He isn't real talkative, just enough. Let me check with him and see if he'll take you," she put down her book and picked up her cell phone.

It's funny, Padon realized, he hadn't thought about his own phone since coming back to life. It no longer held the importance it once did. He should ask if anybody found it on him, by him or in the car, or wherever. Surely in two months someone had tried to contact him. It might even be important. He made his way to his room and tried to remember if he had seen the damn thing since he returned to the land of the living.

He looked through his backpack, guitar case, sundry clothing and odds and ends. Hmm, no phone. Maybe the computer bag? Nope. Maybe he left it in the car? Lost it while walking? Laying down? Being picked up by Jeannie and thrown in the back of her truck? He would have to make some enquiries. Back to the parlor — maybe Janet could shed some light on the mystery.

"Joe says he'll take you to a few of his favorite spots day after tomorrow, Thursday. He says it is supposed to be clear and not exceedingly cold, so, it should be good for viewing all the way around." How had she heard him walk back in his stocking feet? She said she could hear the squeak of the floorboards, but he heard nothing and, thank the godlings and Muse, his hearing remained perfect, unlike many of his contemporaries who were near deaf. There was something spooky about this woman. He was seriously beginning to think she had some hoodoo.

He may not believe in religion, but he did believe in hoodoo!

"Fantastic!" he enthused, "I promise I won't do anything stupid. I just need a change of scenery for my brain and spirit." He sat back on the couch and studied her. "I don't suppose anyone found my cell, did they?" he asked, mental fingers crossed, though not too hard.

"I wasn't here the day they brought you in," she thought, hand on chin and stared at the ceiling, "but there was a box of stuff you had on you. I know there was the guitar, your computer bag and pack, but I don't recall there being a phone. You should check with Jeannie and Bobby. They picked up most of your stuff when she found you, and he towed the car," she clicked them off on her right hand.

"Tomorrow," he replied wearily, "not sure I even want to find it. Probably no missed calls, no texts, no messages," he frowned as he got up, looked at Janet's empty cup, grabbed it and headed for the kitchen. "I don't think I want to know that no one has missed me enough to call looking for me. I'll make you some more tea and get myself a cup as well."

"I want the orange pekoe," she called after him. "That other stuff makes me pee too much and keeps me up all night."

"I can smell what it is," he chimed back, "Think I'm going with the Earl as I need to stay awake for more than ten minutes if I am going to finish anything."

A few minutes of steeping, a dollop of cream and just enough sugar, not much, just to sweeten, he returned to the parlor with two cups of steaming liquid.

"You need rest to heal," she reprimanded.

"I need to write, to create, to be on stage, to heal," he retorted. "It is where I have always taken refuge or solace. It is my 'safe' place," he air quoted, "It has been the only place in my life that really never lets me down. Even in a bad show, a drunken bar filled with animosity and disregard, I can block all that out when I play. It's like you climb inside the music, the lyric, the magic of the melody and it is a fortress, it holds back all the evil, the grief, the hurt, life gnawing on your bones, it all goes away.

"You can walk on the stage with a hundred and three fever, aching so bad you can hardly walk or lift your arm, and two minutes in, you feel like you're sixteen. It heals you." His silly grin reminded her of a boy on Christmas looking at a shiny new bike. "The day my wife took our daughter and left me with a half bottle of milk, some old meat and cheese, one chair and a note, I walked on a stage and gave one of the best performances of my life," he sighed a single snort. "Sad, isn't it? It is the only place I have ever truly enjoyed being. And now, here I am, in the middle of some kind of dream or purgatory, in this little village in the mountains, freezing my ass off and content to leave it that way." He shook his head hard as if trying to loosen the insanity from the walls.

"It ain't such a bad place—this town," her hands swept in the whole of the outdoors, "We look after each other, and protect each other, and bury and remember each other. We are just here," she shrugged at her verbal impotence.

"I'm not trying to run it down," he responded, hands up to ward off or surrender, "It's just that I have spent my life doing something, something I once loved as dearly as life, and now I am not sure who, or what, I am." He sipped his tea, stared hard at the bottom of the cup trying to read the leaves settling there.

"Maybe you need to take some time, not be in such a hurry to return to what you were running from. Rest a while—collect yourself, your thoughts—try to find true north." She watched the dark out the front window. She didn't want him to think she was pushing him to do something he never wanted to do. If you don't like mushrooms, you don't like mushrooms. And no amount of somebody shoving them down your throat is going to make you love them. She tried to nudge him into not deciding before he knew all the facts of his wants and now, his needs.

"Maybe you're right, maybe it's time for me to stop making snap decisions based on how I think for one moment. I just buck every time I think someone is trying to run my life," now he chuckled, "'cause I've done such a magnificent job of that myself." He got up, teacup in hand, walked to her and kissed her softly on the cheek. "Thank you for caring. I'm going to go rest and write."

The lyrics flowed; the melodies lingered. He couldn't write fast enough nor play well enough to capture all that was being given. But he did his best and prayed he would find what he'd missed as he smoothed over the scratches on the pages. He would buy another legal pad or two tomorrow when he moseyed into town to talk with Bobby and Jeannie. He shouldn't, but he now wanted his phone. He wanted to share what he was crafting and that meant phone calls—apologies, begging, cowering, and pleading, but it would be worth it. He just knew it would.

He slept well and woke early. He woke hungry and recalled he'd only had a cup of tea for dinner. The hunger would be assuaged. For now, he could see the thin pink of dawn crawl over the mountain rims and felt the excitement of anticipation. He would find his phone, he knew it in his gut, then place a few calls. There had to be one or two agents who would still deal with him — a bridge only singed or not completely burnt to the ground. Surely, there had to be one person who would listen to the new tunes and want to record. Then it would be a tour, a limited one to start, to prime the pump, wet the whistle. Maybe he could do Europe yet this year. They wouldn't be booked up in the fall yet. Yeah, he would find the phone and put all this together. He hadn't been this excited about a project in thirty years and he was going to take it for all it was worth.

He dressed as warm as his clothes would allow and, quiet as he could manage, slinked out the door into the frigid morning. The icy air embraced him. It acted like a morning bracer, and his step was lively and full of promise. First stop the garage. It was seven thirty, Bobby should be there by now. He could catch him before he got busy.

Bobby was just opening the door to the office as Padon walked up. Of course, he hadn't unlocked the door. It wouldn't have been locked. Padon smirked. Bobby beamed at the sight, just happy to see Padon once again. They chit-chatted for several minutes and caught up on how Padon was faring before he could slip in his question about the whereabouts of his phone.

"Don't remember seeing any phone," Bobby thought hard, "but if it's still here we can check under the seats and all. Worth a try," and with that he grabbed the Buick's keys off the wall and bounded out the door.

Fifteen minutes later they warmed their frozen hands by the small wall heater in his office dejected by their futile search. They had gone through every inch of the car. No phone. Padon thanked the mechanic and promised him another beer as he pushed out the door toward the café and Jeannie.

It was breakfast rush when he arrived, and they sat him at the counter with a cup of coffee and a stern warning not to pick up a bus tub or even a fork if he valued his life. Five minutes later a plate filled with eggs, bacon, potatoes, a cinnamon roll and toast was slapped down in front of him. Wally waved from the kitchen window and Padon mouthed his thanks. He was starved, and the phone could wait.

As the rush slowed to a trickle all the employees had to come by and say hello, and asked the same questions over and over: when would he be coming back? How was the health? Was he done dying? Would they have to retrain him when he came back? A little ball busting and a lot of love. He bathed in it and it refreshed like a cold mountain stream. He had never felt so much a part of something. And it saddened him that he would soon leave this behind, but such was the life of the traveling troubadour. After ten minutes of good-natured ribbing and arm punching, all returned to work and Padon sat with Maggie at the counter. There was just something about the woman. She was not what most would consider beautiful, not in a magazine sort of way. She was hard and slim from work. Solid. The crinkles around her eyes and around her mouth added depth to her good looks. The sprinkling of grey and white accented the dark brown of her hair. The woman had character and a steadfastness about her that spoke more volumes than had ever been written on beauty. She was attractive in a life-long way. He shook his head. Now was not the time to get involved in something that had no chance.

"Thought you were supposed to be recouping," she challenged.

"How can I ever get back to work if I just sit on my ass or lay in bed?" He leaned back on his stool and cracked a toothy grin. "Is Jeannie around?" He changed the subject, "I'm trying to find out if anyone might've found my cell phone and Bobby thought maybe she might have it."

"Maybe you don't need it, if you haven't thought about it 'til now," she suggested.

"I probably should let sleeping dogs stay lost, but it ain't in my nature," he waved away his own inadequacy. "I haven't made any contact with anyone for a couple months; they probably think I'm dead."

"Wouldn't be far from the truth," she sighed. "Jeannie," she called to the woman as she passed the open kitchen door, "Mr. McKenzie would have a word with you. Something about a phone." She got up and leaned over to give him a peck on the cheek before she left

Jeannie didn't bother to sit; she was cleaning in the back and they were one person short and he was sitting at the counter. "What's up?"

"I can't find my cell and was wondering if maybe you found it when you were carrying me to your truck?" he asked full of hope. "Or if it might have fallen out inside your truck," he tossed in for good measure.

"No...I don't remember seeing one, but I was kind of busy and not really looking for a phone," she considered silently for a moment and then, "Let's go look through the cab of my truck. I haven't had time to clean it out, so if the phone fell out of your pocket, it's still in there." She headed towards the back of the house to grab her coat and keys.

After ten minutes of searching seats, floors, cracks and crevasses they knew there would be no phone, but Padon looked for another five. Nothing! The phone was gone and so were all his contacts, numbers and hopes. Dejected they walked back into the café.

Maggie brought both cups of hot cocoa to warm their disappointment. "No luck, huh?" She dug for some tiny marshmallows. They always helped when she was a kid.

"Nope, must've dropped it when I was walking or when I sat down to die," Padon was especially disconsolate.

"You can get another phone, can't you?" she asked. "Herb's got cells down at the market and hardware. I think he carries about all the brands. He can probably hook you up with something," she tried to be helpful, but not too helpful.

"All my contacts were in there — my agents and bookers, the recording people, my connections," he skidded to a stop. "Doesn't matter, I was probably just kidding myself anyway. No fool like an old fool, my old man used to say," he shook his head and sipped the chocolate.

"No backup on your computer?" she threw him a life preserver.

"No, I only use it to type out song lyrics and stuff, so I could keep them in one place once they're written. Not really very good with the technical stuff. It's more a glorified typewriter," he sighed. "Ah well."

"Funny I thought you wrote on the computer, that's why you had it," Maggie kept the conversation churning along the track. She thought if he kept talking it might lift his spirit just a bit.

"No, I can't write a song on a computer, don't think anyone really can. A song, the lyric especially, comes from the soul, from the heart. It is of humanity, not machine. It has to be, for me at least, ink or lead on paper. It's organic, natural," he tried desperately to explain. "To have a direct connection between skin to pencil or pen and paper. The flow of words coming from your hand. The scratched-out word or phrase or verse that you can actually still see, because you can't be absolutely certain you don't want it, or it doesn't fit, until the song is done." He fisted his hands in frustration of trying to show someone how the invisible becomes visible without understanding it fully himself.

"See, it starts out with a feeling in your heart that can be translated to the head—not completely—just enough that words form to describe that joy, that sorrow, that moment in time. The love you felt for that girl that sparked a fire you hoped would burn a lifetime. And it has to come from deep inside, that is where the soul is, not in a computer. A machine that corrects as you write and wants to tell you proper grammar and punctuation. That is the least important thing in any song. A song is all emotion, sentiment. It's not fact and data. It is funk and soul, and all things rock and roll: a lyric that causes women to faint and men to cry, to remember and hope and dream and reassure! It's a story shared by someone with the universe. To be thrown upon the waves or the wind and carried to far lands by magic and love. It is the pounding of the drums of war — syllables that stir men's and women's souls to rise up and strike against intolerance and inhumanity. To demand rights and dignity and equality and it doesn't come from a machine! That is why music, for a large part today, sounds the same — repetitive and without merit. It is created by a machine, cranking out the same lyrics in differing order with the same chords in the same key so you can't tell one song from another. It's just a blur of surface scratches to bump and grind to, it's all body, no intellect or soul." His passion has now kicked into high gear and the revival is on.

"Don't get me wrong, I ain't against some bumping and grinding, but it is so much better, it means so much more, when there is some depth of feeling to it. Some love. Something shared. It ain't making love TO somebody, it is making love WITH somebody. That's where the song is. A computer can't tell you the difference. A crumpled piece of scribbling thrown in the corner of the bedroom can tell you everything and more," he winds down, stared at his cocoa and realized it is perfectly silent in the café. All work stopped; all eyes were on him.

There was a tension in the room you could cut with a spoon, it was so thick — and sensual. He has brought them all in and he didn't mean to. He just wanted his phone.

Maggie slumped back against the counter, "I think I need a hot cocoa with extra marshmallows." She stared at him with — what — admiration, want, respect and longing? She is not certain herself, but she hoped he would never find his phone.

"I'm sorry," he apologized sincerely, "I didn't mean to go on like that. I get caught up because I so love the birth of a song. People just think you throw a piece of paper in a machine and it spits out something meaningful. I guess I am just tired. How are your plans for the party?"

She almost spun out as she hit the brake and did a one eighty. "It's coming along," she exhaled a breath she didn't know she been holding or for how long. "This Saturday at Merle's, if you're not busy." She stumbled through without falling.

"I will need to check with my keepers," he grinned with appreciation. "Maybe I can get them to allow me a couple hours with the big kids." He got up to leave, the disappointment at not finding his phone still evident but dissipating. "I'm really very glad to have met you." He wanted to say more but didn't trust himself. It was time to go back to Doc's.

His mind had overflowed with information, disappointment, want, lust, loss, and wondered just what in the hell he was to do with his life. He feet knew the way, but his mind wandered. Without the phone he had no numbers to call, no tour to set up, no dream to chase. It had all the inside numbers, not the office numbers, but the numbers that took you through the jungle, the maze, directly to the guy or woman in charge. He wasn't sure how many were still out there, how many still lived or worked or had any influence, but he had a ton of numbers. And now he had some really good songs. And no way to get them to anybody who could do anything with them.

Yeah, he could start working the bars and the joints, coffee-houses and open mics, but he wasn't some kid just starting out with a lifetime to pursue an elusive dream. He was old, worn out, cynical and tired and not about to start all over again. He didn't have the passion or the energy, and in this business, you needed both in wheelbarrow loads.

And ignorance. That was something he couldn't regain. You had to have naïveté by the truckloads. You had to believe and trust. There was no way he could. He didn't trust himself, not completely. Yes, he'd had his epiphany, but that and a dollar would get you a cup of joe at Mickey D's. He still couldn't trust himself in the great, big, wide world. It was easy here, in a town not ten blocks long and fifteen wide, enclosed by mountains and safety. But back out there? Probably not.

And he knew he couldn't trust the people he was trying to get in contact with. They'd done him good in the past, but they had also taken him for a few rides, and he had no desire or the time, to do that again. Besides, he wasn't some kid with the looks that grabbed the girls by the want and shook them. Hell, he'd never been that.

So, then, what? Somehow, he was going to catch fire with the Geritol set? The songs he had composed were deep but not depressing, full of hope and love, but from a much different point in life. He loved them. They were his adult children, but teenage was what sold. He was bummed because he couldn't find his phone with contact information to people who, if they were still in the business, would love his new tunes, but wouldn't have any more of clue what to do with them than he did.

It was apropos of his entire life. He wrote, or was writing, some of the best, most heartfelt songs of his career and there was no place to play them, no one to hear. The wind bit his face and ears, stinging the skin. He closed his eyes against the harshness of the cold and life.

He'd fallen for it again. He had to laugh. Like some dumb, wet-behind-the-ears kid, just out of school and into love, just got laid for the first time and he was gonna sing it to the world. What a maroon! He pulled his hat down a wee bit tighter, zipped up his leather until it bit into his chin. He put his head down and headed for Doc's house. He knew where the bottle was.

When Joann Caldwell returned home, she found Padon slouched at the dining room table, eyes closed, head tilted back, arms crossed on the table and a glass of whiskey at his right elbow. The house was deadly quiet. Where the hell was Janet? Behind her she heard the front door open. She turned to see Janet as she came through while taking off her stocking hat and scarf at the same time. She was frazzled as she rushed into the house.

"Is he here?" she demanded, "If he is, I'm going to kill him!"

"Yes, he is, number one," Doc Caldwell spoke calmly, quietly, as she stood in front of the charging woman, "Number two, where were you?"

"Looking for him!" Her tone accusatory and lethal.

"Well, we are all together again let's settle down and find out what is going on," cautioned the good doctor. They stood and watched him for several seconds. His breathed deep, even, the small glass full.

"What happened?" JoAnn never took her eyes off the seemingly passed out figure.

"He went into town, going to check in with Bobby about his phone. If it wasn't there, he was going down to the café and ask Jeannie," Janet's anger had subsided. "He was gone longer than I thought he should be, so I went looking for him. Guess I was behind him all the way. He drunk?" The question hung in the air for just a moment before…

"You know I can hear you," he murmured from behind closed eyes.

"No, I didn't," huffed Janet, indignance flowed like hot lava., "I thought you were passed out, boozed up."

"No." he says softly, "actually I haven't had a drop, though I sure thought about it for a long time." He opened his eyes to take in the two women who stood with arms crossed just under breasts and glaring at him. "No phone, no luck, just me chasing my tail." He pushed two chairs out with his legs and both women sat.

"So, you going to pour or not?" Asked Doctor Caldwell and pushed over empty glasses set there for just such an occasion.

"Might as well be good for something," he acquiesced.

"Feeling sorry for ourselves today?" JoAnn mocked, but only to prod.

"I thought If I could find my phone, get to my contacts, make a couple calls…" he let the thought peter out.

"You thought you could hop back on that train to nowhere and ride for a little bit longer," Janet finished.

He poured just a wee dram in each glass. "It's early," he said to their questioning glances. He picked up his own full glass and with a steadiness that belied what he felt, poured ninety percent back into the bottle. Both women watched with a small amount of admiration.

He stared at the amber liquid and swilled it in its prison. "You ever seen a junkie who really needed a high?" he asked to their rapt attention, "Or a drunk with the shakes who would kill his own mother for a drink?" You could hear the earth rotate on its axis. "That's what it is to chase a dream." He set the glass on the table. "You know who the luckiest people are who play music? People who just do it because it's fun.

They play on the weekends, for their friends, around the fire. You know why? Because they don't have the dream. They know, they know they aren't good enough. They don't have the talent, the drive. They just play. And when their friends tell them they are so good they should be famous, they smile. That's all they do. They smile and say thanks. Because in their hearts and souls they know, every fiber of their being knows. And they take the compliment and shove it their pocket for when they need it and go back to their lives." He sipped, just a taste.

"But a dreamer," he chuckled sadly, "he gets off one stage and can't wait to find the next. To get that shot of applause, adoration, love. He forgot what it was to just play. To just write something because it had to come out. Not because he could take that song and sell it or turn it into fame, so he could tour the world. Just play. He's got just enough talent and drive to get him to here," — Padon held his palm flat about six inches off the surface of the table —" just enough to find a modicum of success, enough to solidify and make the dream seem real. Seem possible." He downed the rest of the liquid and turned the glass over on the table. "Enough to keep chasing and hoping and dreaming and chasing and…"

"I'm going to go write something, something goofy and silly and fun. A dumb song about love, and wanting, and passion and nothing more. I am going to strike pen to paper without a windmill in sight. To just play some music without a tour in mind or a phone number to call to tell them how wonderful I am and that I am back. Because I'm not. Do you know why, ladies?" his humor would not climb past his nose to light his eyes. They shook their heads 'no'. "Because I was never there to come back to."

He stood, bowed and made his way back to the bedroom, though he did not close the door. The sound of pen on paper and music came.

Janet got up, she needed to check on him, to let him know they didn't care about any of that. They cared about him. Doc Caldwell stopped her with a hand on her arm, "Nah, let him be. Sometimes, you have to let the wound bleed. And the blood of truth and honesty is a great purifier." Janet sat back down and they shared a look, a silent toast, a prayer, and a sip.

Dinner was quiet, filled with soft chit chat about the upcoming party and the change in town attitude. People required some distraction from time to time in these locked in mountain towns, and a party was just the right prescription. Padon had asked respectfully if he might be well enough to attend, as he liked Mr. Carpenter and wanted to be there for him. Doctor Caldwell weighed the person who sat across the table, took her time so he would understand her decision and abide by it. "Yes," she reached her verdict and pronounced sentence, "You may, but you are not to overexert yourself or stay too late." He leaned in toward her, but she stayed him with a glare, "Let's get you healthy so you can finally decide, with clear mind and somewhat healed body, what you want to do and who you would like to grow up to be." He sat back and nodded his head once.

Neither woman mentioned the sounds that had emanated out of the back room all day, allowing him room and privacy. Doc Caldwell had been in and out all day checking on folks, and Janet sat quietly reading in the parlor. They would've loved to have told him how much they loved to hear him sing and play. His playing smooth and expressive, his singing voice pleasant, passionate and the songs—oh my—the songs would not leave their heads. They had wormed their way into their brains and would remain forever happily in residence. They wanted to thank him, but no, they allowed him to play for the love of it.

He went off to bed early as Joe would come by in the morning to collect him and show him his mountains. Padon slept fitfully at first but soon settled into a lovely rhythm and pushed worry and dream to another night.

Chapter Nineteen

The morning was cold — what's new? — but bright. A brilliant yellow sun had crested the eastern ridge and scattered the clouds. The temperature was frigid, the sky warm and it invited. It was, and would continue to be, a beautiful day.

Joe waited patiently in front of the doctor's house, as promised, in his 1966 Jeep Cherokee. Padon snickered as he opened the door and slid inside. He held out his hand, "Padon", Joe shook it mentioned his own name — unnecessary — and put it in gear. They left the curb in silence.

Fine, thought Padon, if silence was on the menu, he'd have a full helping and be satisfied.

"Can we stop for a coffee somewhere?" Well, he'd start on that silence once he had a large coffee, "I'll buy," he added hopefully.

"Fair enough." They pulled into the one stop to grab two large black coffees.

As they exited town and entered the surrounding forest Padon took stock of the man behind the wheel. He was large, not obese, but all around big. Yeah, he had a gut, very few middle-aged men he met didn't — and Padon was kind of proud of himself for his svelte figure — but Joe was big through the shoulders and had thighs like small tree trunks.

He was sturdy. As blue-eyed and blond as any human being from Norway. If he had a drop of Native blood in him it was because the guy cooking his hamburger had cut his finger and dripped it on the meat. It didn't matter, he appeared to know where he was going.

The sun played hide and seek with the towering pines as they plodded through the two-lane panorama. Joe was in no hurry to get nowhere and Padon was riding shotgun on the meandering express. He rolled down his window halfway, so the scent of frozen pine forest could bathe his senses. Eyes closed he allowed physical full control over cerebral, permitting his brain to shut down and feel the world. It was peaceful up here in the frozen woodlands. Peaceful and quiet. They saw no wildlife nor hardly a bird in the air — just beauty.

"Wanna stop and walk around a bit?" Asked Joe after an hour or so of silence, without taking his eye off the road.

"Yeah, that would be nice," Padon said to the windshield. To feel the snow and rock beneath his feet. To make a connection with nature he never really had. He was a city boy, born and bred. He had traveled through the Rocky Mountains seventy or eighty times in his life, crisscrossing the country. North and south, he'd seen. He had been through the Appalachians and the Smokies. He had seen them all; spring, winter and high summer. Seen the fall explosions in the Adirondacks and Green Mountains, but he had never taken the time to enjoy them.

Mountain ranges were for driving through to get to the next gig. Sometimes they were easy. The weather was clear and the roads clean. Sometimes they tried to kill you with snow, mudslides and washouts, but he'd never felt the need to stop and experience them. He would now.

Joe pulled off the paved two-lane and headed up a snow-covered gravel logging road. No one had traveled it for some time as evidenced by the lack of tire tracks. Padon thought about saying something, maybe ask if this was a good idea—his past experiences with getting off the road well-traveled not turning out so well — but he'd put himself into this faux Indian's hands with the blessing of both Janet and JoAnn. He held his tongue.

Coming around a curve, they popped out of the deep forest on the bank of a small lake overlooking a deep valley that stretched on forever. Mountains walled in the valley for as far as the eye cared to see. A massive field of boulders pocked with stands of hundred-foot pines added texture and contour. A few clouds skidded across the reflected perfect blue of the sky on the surface of the placid lake. If there was a more perfect scene of serenity, Padon had certainly never witnessed it.

Joe turned the Jeep off, and they sat for long minutes absorbing the scene. Padon rolled the window back up as he opened the passenger door and stepped out into the pristine snow field bordering the lake. His feet sank a half foot before finding solid ground. Deep but not deep enough for snow to fill his boots. He warily stepped towards the lake, each footstep sinking into the powder, sometimes to his knees, but he continued to the water's edge.

Hunching down he put his hands into the melted ice filled lake. It was cold as to be painful, but he didn't remove his hands. Within seconds they were numb and still he left them in the water. Finally, the cold seeped up his arms. He pulled them free and stared at the bright red and felt the sting. He wiggled his fingers and blood began to flow once again. The pain was intense, but he refused recognition. He wanted to experience and experience he would.

Now he walked around the edge of the lake, to the far side, where weather had felled a tree and he sat on the trunk and gazed out over the endless valley. It flowed into him, the splendor filling him like a dry lake. A plant, almost dead from the drought, coming back to life, the leaves and stems reaching, once again, for the sun and sky. Rebirth, back from the edge. He took a deep, cleansing breath as if for the first time. The doctor smacked his ass and he did not cry out but gloried in the magnificence before him. He hardly noticed when Joe sat down, just down the fallen tree from him.

"The Shoshone called this Window of the Great Spirit," Joe said. "They roamed here back before the white man came. Them and the Arapahoe. This was their territory, though others came as well." He spoke with reverence and confidence.

Padon didn't know if what he said was true or if he was just making up bullshit for the city slicker in attendance. He didn't care. He could see if the Shoshone hadn't called it that, somebody should. It was a window on the soul of the universe. If there was a God, this is where He would sit at the end of the day and nod his head in satisfaction. He let the silence fill the void left by Joe's words blowing away.

He walked to the end of the cliff, a drop-off of a couple thousand feet. His head swam and the wind tugged at his clothes, whispering in his ear, daring him. But he was no longer one to be dared into stupid. He had gone there without provocation too many times. He wanted to come into contact with the spirit of Mother Earth without anything standing between them. Dizzy filled his head, his knees weak, but he knew, deep, down, they would not fail him. He never felt so confident and safe in his life. In the Mother's arm.

He smiled. He didn't think he had ever felt this safe anywhere near his genetic family. They had birthed him, fed him, clothed him but never nurtured him. They had sucked his energy dry. It was their way.

He didn't think they realized they were doing it, it just came natural. Dissatisfaction becomes life and the norm. If you eat hamburgers every day, from low grade, high fat ground beef, to you that is delicious, and you feed every generation after that the same deficient meal. If they would prefer something of a finer quality, you nip that in the bud, beat into the unhappy party that they are lucky to get a full belly. Your taste buds adjust, and satisfaction supplants any notion for excellence. He wanted excellence.

Time passed, he never noticed, but the cold stayed and he did notice that. Stiffly he got up, regretting the necessity to move, to find warmth, he nodded to Joe who appeared content to leave or stay. Maybe the cold didn't bother him. Maybe he had assumed the native persona so completely, so viscerally, he had adopted their capability to suffer the elements.

The warmth of the Jeep wrapped him, and he closed his eyes, thankful.

"I'm going to get back out of here and get back to the main road, OK?" Joe informed as he slipped the shifter into reverse. He glanced over at Padon for confirmation, his foot remained on the brake, the Jeep remained static.

"What?" came the word on a ragged breath.

"You want a rag? Or cloth?" The words carried no censure, just empathy.

As his face warmed Padon sensed the moisture running from his eyes to his chin. How long had he been crying? He wiped his face and pulled out a napkin from his pocket to blow his nose. Interesting. He was not embarrassed, just slightly taken aback.

"Affected me that same way first few hundred times I saw it," grins Joe. He shakes his head and takes his foot off the brake, "now, I just get a lump in my throat and butterflies in my chest."

They eased up the snow-covered log road to the dry pavement awaiting.

"So, you never up in the mountains before?" queried the blond haired Native.

"Hell, I've driven through the Rocky's at least seventy times," Padon said and turned his attention from the side window to his guide, "just never stopped to appreciate what was passing by my window. Guess I was always in too much a of a hurry, or too worried about the drive, the road, the conditions. Whether there would be a crowd? Would I get paid? Would they like the new music? Bullshit stuff. I should've pulled over and spent more time breathing. I should've worried less about the next big thing and concentrated on the now. Musical styles and tastes change but if you're doing something true and honest, it lasts." He chuckled at his own joke and returned his stare to the passing wonder.

"You want some lunch?"

"Yeah, I could eat. What time is it?" Absently made small talk.

"Almost four," came the response.

Shit! How long had he sat on that tree? Where had the time flown? Did it make any difference?

They pulled off the road onto another logging track and headed west, as far as Padon could tell, towards the sinking sun. By the time they stopped at another valley — though much smaller and shallower than the last grand valley had been — the sun was not much more than a hand span above the mountains to the west. Clouds moved in. Not enough to block, more to accent, the sunset. They sat in the Jeep, Joe handed him a bag with a sandwich, a banana and a small bag of chips, while setting another in his lap. He had a thermos, beat, dented, ancient, filled with coffee and, hmm, something that tasted an awful like, Tullamore Dew. Really? The 'Native' brought Irish coffee to share with the Scotsman? Ain't that America.

Brilliant yellow, blue and white morphed into spears of gold, surrounded by shades of pink and violet transforming and deepening into reds, mauve, purple and black as the sun slid below the tops of the Rocky's. What had been white topped mountains with deep green forests were now black and grey silhouettes framed by a darkened sky filled with dying colors, fading into blacks. It was breathtaking. He sat in stunned, mesmerized silence as the tears once again flowed from eye to chin. He thought if he kept this up, he would soon be encased in frozen tears.

In the dark quiet they sat in the Jeep. Padon thought he should say something, 'thank you' or 'wasn't that swell', but he couldn't find the strength or the will to shatter the perfect silence in this mountain chapel.

After a few more minutes Joe started the Jeep. Padon hadn't noticed him turn it off. Joe shifted into gear. The ride back through the pitch black mountainscapes, broken here and there by patches of fresh, white snow and differing shades of black, were wrapped in the stillness of a sensation of right.

Padon had no idea what was happening to him and he didn't care. He was in no mood to stop the transformation. He knew one thing — what he had been doing, how he lived for the past twenty years or so — when faced honestly, wasn't working.

As he stepped out on the sidewalk, he shook Joe's hand, thanked him quietly. This was not a time for effusive gratitude and asked if he was going to be at the party Saturday for Mr. Carpenter.

"Yes," said Joe.

"I'll buy you a beer," Padon responded.

"I don't drink," laughed Joe.

"I'll buy you a burger."

He closed the passenger door quietly and raised his hand in salute, thanks and good night as Joe pulled away. He stood on the sidewalk for several long breaths—wasn't that Tullamore Dew in the coffee? Whatever—stared at the crescent moon and the CO_2 leaving his body. It is a good night, indeed.

Chapter Twenty

The sound of voices died as he opened, then closed, the door. Within a second the cacophony rose again. The quantity belied the fact there were more folks here than just Doc Caldwell and Janet. Hmm, must be the final planning stages of the great party.

When these folks decided it was time to break the monotony, they didn't mess around. The entire town would be involved, it seemed, and there was planning, and conniving going on here, unless he was much mistaken.

There were easily ten folks crowded around the dining room table and spilling into the hallway. Chairs were helter skelter. Glasses were at varying levels of consumption. And guests were at varying levels of inebriation. It would appear the celebration had gotten off on a false start and there were no judges to restart the race. Ah well, if you can't beat 'em...

He skooched by the folks crowding the hall and made his way to the kitchen between hellos, hi's and introductions. He met Dave, the owner of Merle's, where the festivities would occur, and Betty from the yarn and dry goods shop, and he, finally, got to make the acquaintance of the famous Del. He knew most of the others, Maggie, of course, Jeannie, Bobby and Ralph were there to plan the menu. There were few other faces he recognized from the Café.

He pulled a small glass off the open shelf above the sink and found his way to the open bottle of bourbon on the counter. He poured just enough to be sociable but not enough to interfere with what the day had given him. He still wanted to capture that on paper and steel strings. But no sense being aloof.

There were questions about his health and when he might return to the café. It seemed he had been missed. Maggie swore on all that was holy she had not put them up to asking but he could tell she was glad they had asked. He deferred to the good Doctor. "Soon."

And they were back hip deep in the planning, laughing, indignation and all-around levity that came with planning a huge party. He could not get it through his brain how they were going to get all these people into one place. He could not picture any business in town that would accommodate.

Dave assured him they would squeeze them into Merle's. It would be tight, but they had done it before. This was not their first break-the-boredom-and-tedium-party they had thrown. It would be a hoot. Some would come early and leave early, some would come midway and others would show up late, it would work out. It wasn't so much a birthday party as a reason to party. Of course, he would show up, he promised, as he excused himself to go rest after a long day in the mountains. He could tell Doc, Janet and, especially Maggie, wanted to grill him, but this was not the time. Though he could tell it was killing them not to follow him into his room and put him to the question.

They promised quiet, and he knew they sincerely meant it as the words left their mouths, but he also knew it was an unkeepable oath. He smiled as he closed the hardwood door and hoped it would block the volume if not the wall of sound.

The small night light plugged into the wall next to the bed provided the only illumination in the room. That was fine. He wanted some sensory deprivation after overloading for the entire day. He lay, fully clothed, on top of the bed and stared at the sunset still sharp and brilliant in his memory. Tears flowed once more as he was submersed in the beauty of nature. The memory was so strong he could feel the cold on his skin and the scent of snow and tree.

How had he spent so many years traveling through mountain and hill, down by the ocean and along riverbeds and not noticed? How had he been so blind? He should get out of bed and go to his knees and thank whatever held this universe together for allowing him today.

Instead, the music called. The Muse danced, not out of reach, but right on the tip of his nose. She hugged him around the neck and did a pirouette down his chest and then flipped back up to lay beside his head. She hummed a tune so sweet, so light, he smiled. She sang, wordless but painting an image of the open valley and the copse of trees, the wind whipping and dancing in and out of the pines with her riding the fluffy flakes of snow. The sun brought light, so all could witness and then sink in the sky. The tones of color being played in minor chords, sweeping across an open sky, chasing clouds and geese. He could feel the joy on his face as he switched to majors representing the deepened colors and promise of a new day. She whispered in his ear, words and phrases. She wanted him to have them, to put them on paper and match them to the song she had sung. She knew he could accomplish what she asked, for she had chosen him. She knew him. She was jubilant and gleeful and wept with joy that he had come back. She'd missed him, but he was here and that was all that mattered. And then she was gone. She had left him to his work. He would have to finish what she had started.

He lay with his eyes open, not seeing the room but the song and all it evoked. It was wonderful. He no longer heard the voices from the dining room, the clatter of dishes or the laughter, only the song.

His fingers tapped on the bedspread and his right foot kept time. He grabbed the legal pad from the nightstand and let the ink flow like a beautiful skater across the frozen landscape of the paper. It formed the vowels and consonants, sculpted words to phrases as a skilled ice princess forms the dance. It would be a long song, not three verses and a chorus, but not Alice's Restaurant. Not too many notes and words. Just enough. It was a song of life, his life. It would paint his joys and sorrows, his highs and lows, heartache and bliss, it was him in three-quarter time.

He knew the chords before his pen left the paper and he picked up the Gibson and strummed with the fleshy part of his thumb, just loud enough for him to hear. He didn't want to disturb those in the outer rooms. He wanted to put this together.

He sat up the rest of the night, fine tuning the chord structure while he searched for, and found, better words than he had hurriedly scratched onto the pad. He moved the bridge to the end of the song. Yes, he knew it never went there, but his bridge to life came late and so it would be there. The final chorus would be sunset and contentment. The tune, the chords would remain the same and the lyric would paint his joy. People would sing that. Yes, they would, he thought, and just as quickly thought, maybe they won't, but that was OK. It was his song and if one person could feel it — just that one person — just the person it was intended for. He smiled again.

Breakfast was light as Janet and Doctor Caldwell gave him the highlights of the previous evening and the plans for the party tomorrow night. They laughed and giggled like two teenagers with excitement and anticipation. This would be a shindig folks would talk about for years to come. He sipped his coffee and nibbled a piece of toast with jam and butter and delighted in their plans.

Yeah, he was going to be alright. He was going to be more alright than he might have ever been in his life. Whether his plans worked out this time or not. Whether anyone paid attention or not. Whether they loved, hated or were completely indifferent or not, it didn't matter.

He chased a dream his entire life. Suffered, gloried, starved, feasted and hoped, never realizing he lived it. He'd lived something pretty damn good. The flops. The nights in his car. The driving for twenty hours to a gig that had cancelled. He lived it. The adoring crowds, the encores, the accolades. He had lived it. The success, the failure, the breakdowns and depression, the loneliness, the heartache, the desperation. He'd lived it. He'd flown high for a while and crashed like a meteor, but here he was. He lived it. Hell, if you listened to anyone in this broke down, town, he died and came back to do it all again. He fucking lived it.

And he would do it all over again. He laughed at himself. Pitiful, sorry ass bastard. Ha!

They prepared for their day and he prepared to sleep his away. He was tired, dog tired and required a nap. Yeah, old dog, still dig the lifestyle, dontcha?

A timid tapping on his door was just loud enough to rouse him. It must be Janet waking him easy, so she could shove some food and vitamins down his throat. She was very devoted to her work. And his care. Groggy and filled with dream remnants he stumbled to the door to let her know he would be out soon.

Maggie smirked at the half-dressed drowsy human who stared at her from the half open door. "Nice skivvies," she chortled.

"Oh, Jesus," he spurted in Spanish, covered his half nakedness like a young virgin.

"C'mon," she chuckled, "not like I haven't seen the likes of it before." She said to the closed door.

"Yeah, well not mine," he replied through the wood.

"Have now!"

He reopened the door, t-shirt on backwards and inside out, half tucked in his sweats and rubbed his eyes. "Is something wrong?" he asked, buying time to wake up. "What's going on?" he stumbled.

"No. I have something for you," she lifted her right hand in her coat pocket to show she had something there. "Come on out and I'll fix you a cup and you can worship me properly," she turned and walked toward the dining room.

He followed like the drowsy dog he emulated and sat, like a good boy, at the table while she went into the kitchen to find him a cup and some tea. She, definitely, took her time, built the suspense and drove him to distraction. Christ on a cracker woman, just tell me, he yelled inside his head. His face remained calm and relaxed and waited patiently.

She set the cup down in front of him, he nodded his thanks and took a long, slow sip. Two can play at this game, he thought, but he was wrong.

"When I saw how despondent you were the other day, at the Café," she began, "I felt horrible for you. You had searched so hard for your phone," she spat the word, "your lifeline to your life, that I couldn't stand it if I didn't try something." She went back into the kitchen to retrieve her own cup of tea. Why she couldn't have brought both at the same time was beyond Padon, but he bit his tongue.

"So, the Café was dead yesterday and Jeannie and I went back up to where she found you. We thought maybe we could be lucky and find it by where you died. We searched and dug for an hour," Her eyes bore into his own, so he would understand someone had gone to great lengths for him and he should not take that act for granted. He nodded. "But there was nothing." His shoulders slumped with the rest of him close behind.

"We gave up the cause and headed back to the truck, which was parked right by where she had pulled off the road when she found you," again she expected, and received gratitude, "I kicked something I thought was a rock and almost tripped and fell on my ass. I dug down to pick it up to throw it and I found this!" She handed him a cell phone remarkably like the one he'd lost.

He took it reverently in both hands, stared at it like it was the Holy Grail, and then, gazed into her eyes. His thanks so evident she was almost knocked back by the power of it. She hadn't realized until now how much he wanted, needed, this object. It was his ticket out. With this phone he could call for help, book a gig, have someone come drag him away from this miserable town. She saw him run, escape, fly free; it was in his eyes. He wasn't thankful to her; he was thankful his prison term was over. She wanted to smack him across the face.

Instead, she turned to leave, "I hope that makes you happy and it gives you your life back again," she said over her shoulder as she left the house.

He wanted to chase after her, to thank her properly, to show her how much what she had done meant to him, but he was dumbfounded and couldn't. Would the damn thing even work after laying in the snow for two months? Wouldn't it have frozen or gotten wet or whatever? It couldn't possibly work after all this time.

He pressed the button to turn it on. Nothing. Well, no shit, it had been dormant for over two months. The battery would be dead if nothing else. He ran into his room and dug furiously through his backpack for the cord. Of course, it was buried on the bottom. He plugged it into the wall and with a prayer to the cell phone gods plugged it into this phone.

He waited, nothing. Finally, after a small eternity had passed the charging icon showed on the face of the phone. He yelped and did a little jig. He should give it a few minutes to warm up, charge up, light up, but he couldn't. He held the power button one more time and, it came to life. He wanted to cry.

All the work he had done here, all the new songs — the piece he had written last night! All of it! He could now call someone. Tell them about it. Play it for them. They'd see. They'd hear. They'd know!

Shit, it was late. He couldn't call anybody back in New York. They wouldn't be in their offices. He'd text so they would find it when they got to their work phones Saturday.

For the next half hour, he furiously texted everyone he could think of: agents, bookers, club managers, studios and producers — all of them — they had to hear. He made rudimentary recordings of the songs and texted them as well. And then the waiting game would begin. It would be along night and morning, but he knew — he just knew — there had to be a reason he'd written these songs — that song — it couldn't be wasted.

He heard the front door open and close. He waited just a few moments before he came out to meet Janet, phone in hand. "Look!" he squealed like a five-year-old with a brand, new favorite toy. "Look what Maggie found!"

She looked at the phone, sniffed as she took off her hat and scarf, "Got your freedom back, did ya?" She sniffed again.

"It means I can contact people about the new songs — about maybe touring again. Maybe get back on the road for real." He could hardly contain his excitement.

"If that's what you want, then that is what you should do," she said as she removed her coat and hung it on the peg by the door. "I gotta get dinner going. Doctor will be back soon." She walked to the kitchen.

Doctor Caldwell was a bit more enthusiastic about the find, though still reticent in her fervor. "I'm shocked it still works," Bemused she inspected the lost and found item.

"I did some research online and it seems that the deep snow it fell in acted as an insulator against the coldest temperatures and since it never thawed, the phone didn't get wet," he grinned. " It's weird but I guess it happens." He shrugged and joy spilled from his face. "I've already sent messages to everybody I know back east," he continued, "I'm hoping they still remember me and want to hear the new stuff." Again, he had trouble controlling his glee.

"Dinner's ready," followed the ping of the microwave.

Through dinner he talked about what he was going to do, what he hoped to do, and where he would go first. It's as if he had forgotten everything that had happened, thought JoAnn as she listened. But that would be the way, wouldn't it? Thinking he would stay was stupid, selfish and unrealistic. She shook her head at her own foolishness.

She should be happy for him; it would seem he would finally achieve his dreams. She should be, but she just couldn't bring herself to be. She looked across the table to where Janet fumed, silently. Doctor Caldwell had known the woman for twenty years — this volcano was about to blow.

Back in his room Padon was extremely impressed with Janet's self-control. He was quite certain she was going to whack him at least once with either a pan or her hand, but she held. He understood their anger and disappointment — his joy at having a line to the outside world, to his world, was a slap in their faces. They had done so much for him. Shit, they saved his life, brought him back from the dead. Twice! Fed him. Nurtured him. Sat by his bedside and comforted him. For him to be joyous at leaving had hurt to the soul, but he had to know.

He knew. No one in his life had ever been truly sorry to see him leave, not even his own parents. Not his wife, not his daughter. He'd never had actual friends, just musical acquaintances, collaborators, band mates who had other goals in mind. No one had ever cared about him. It was a strange, befuddling feeling. He stayed in his room for the rest of the evening and prepared for what was to be tomorrow.

Chapter Twenty-one

The party was in full swing as he walked down the street, The Gibson case swung freely in the wind. He hardly noticed the bitter wind as it kissed his face and neck. He grinned and hummed as he made his way to the rear entrance to Merle's. He slid in through the kitchen and dropped the guitar off in the small alcove between the ice machine and the door entering the bar. He stood at the door and searched the crowd.

People had shed the depression of several months of cold and snow and, even though it was a false promise, the promise of spring was in the air. Well, in the bar if not outside. No one noticed him standing against the wall between booth and door. He was, for all intents and purposes, invisible. He scanned the happy faces and bodies moving rhythmically to the ancient sounds of the jukebox. It was nice.

Folks conversed and laughed with people who lived just up the street, but they hadn't seen without heavy coats, scarves, hats, hoods and gloves for months. It was as if they were meeting for the first time. Or a High School reunion thirty years down the road. They hadn't changed, they looked just like the last time they'd seen each other, oh, those many moons ago. It was funny, in a nice community way.

He didn't notice as the party's center of attention — though only peripherally — slid up beside him. Mr. Carpenter, for all his years, stood straight and strong, drink in one hand, the other on Padon's shoulder. It was as companionable a contact as Padon could remember. They stood and took in the activity without mingling. The music was just loud enough to dance to but not so loud one couldn't talk without yelling into the ear.

"Nice soirée," said the ancient man to the dead one. "Looks like the whole town showed up for me," he grinned, "though they don't seem to know I'm here."

"Oh, I'm sure they do," reassured Padon, though he knew it wasn't needed. "They are blowing off some cold and snow, dusting off the boredom and loneliness." They shared a knowing wink.

"Want a drink?" asked the old man.

"I know where the bar is," retorted 'youth', "but thanks. It's your party you should be enjoying yourself, not serving," chuckled Padon with good nature.

"I'm glad you came," and Mr. Carpenter gave Padon's shoulder a thankful shake.

"You know," began Padon on a completely different line of thought, "I always thought I was destined for great things. That I would find fame, and write great songs, be remembered for being a truly brilliant artist." He looked down into the ageless depths of Mr. Carpenter's eyes. He was lost for a few breaths, a little dizzied by the heights. There is nothing to hang onto out here in the cosmos. And then he was back in the bar. "It's funny how after years of chasing something you realize how unimportant it truly is. Maybe great things are overblown." He shrugged.

"Maybe some people do great things in small places and those are just as important," spoke the wisdom of the ages before he headed off to find another beer.

"When in Rome... " Padon mumbled to his imaginary band.

Beer in hand he made his way around the bar, stopped to say hello and chit chat with folks he knew from the Café. He spotted Wally sipping a diet coke over in the corner, shooting the breeze with Harvey the dishwasher, and wound his way through the crowd to join them.

"Nice party," he threw the words up for grabs.

"You playin'?" Wally's eyes steel with challenge.

Shrug.

"Got my bass next door, thought it might come in handy tonight," he offered.

Padon eyed him thoughtfully, a crooked grin made its way across his face. When was the last time Wally played? He thought Wally had told him he hadn't played since he sobered up. He was afraid it would bring back the want. Great things. He grinned big.

"Yeah," he nodded, "why dontcha get it and let's see if we can liven this joint up."

Wally beamed like the morning sun as he grabbed his coat and then shook his head, left the coat on the back of the bar stool. It's just next door, his body language said, and he slipped out the back. Padon made his way back to the kitchen and opened the Gibson. He made a quick check of the tuning while he waited for Wally to return.

Guitar in hand, Wally trailed with his upright, they made their way to the small, empty stage in the far corner of the bar. Surprisingly, no one seemed to pay them any never-mind. Another quick check of tuning between them and Padon said the key and the tempo and the feel. Wally nodded.

They eased into a midtempo swing in A — a simple 1-4-5, just to warm the fingers and get a feel for each other. There was no PA, no mics, just the two of them playing to each other for now, and it was comfortable. They were mixing the chemicals, a little bit of this, a touch of that, a dram of love and the sharing of music. It fit like a well-worn coat and they both settled in. It was going to be a long, good night.

It was three tunes before folks begin to take note, so laid back was the vibe. It just slipped under the sound of the juke without a seam. But now the folks in front were tapping toes and dancing a step or two. His fingers danced with them on the fretboard and Wally closed his eyes. He felt the changes coming and, unless Padon did something really out of character for the song, he could follow. Both musicians were in a zone and the audience was responding with appreciation.

A shot showed up for Padon and another Diet Coke for Wally. People smiled, grinned ear to ear. They were digging the songs even though they've never heard them before. It was good.

Slow love, slow song, slow dance. Shit, JoAnn is dancing with Janet. They're smiling and holding each other as only two old friends can do. There is love and then, there is love. Love filled the room. Mr. Carpenter nodded approval from the corner of the bar where he parked his old carcass, happy as a teen.

It was halfway through before JoAnn and Janet realized the song they danced to. They hugged each other, grinned and laughed and mouthed 'thank you's' to him. A few others picked up on the lyrics and the joy of the two women and soon he had to run back to the beginning of the song so more could enjoy and dance in celebration of the two most loved women. The ladies got a well-deserved standing ovation. Tears and hugs, love overflowed and spilled into the night.

It was time to throw in a few tunes they would know, something to sing along with, to wrap their arms around each other and relive some youth. Time to give back some of what he'd been taking. He ran them through the sixties and seventies and even threw a Glenn Miller at them just for Mr. Carpenter. He nodded his approval and another shot showed up to the stage.

Now back to his tunes and then it would be break time and time to face his future. They flowed through a rocker, another swing tune and his sing-along-bring-everybody-together-kind of love-hugging-hanging-arm in arm, feel good song. Break time finally arrived.

Butterflies, when was the last time he'd had butterflies? Well, this was truly important. He had to put all his cards on the table, and he was going to do it in a full bar to an entire town. How big were his balls, anyway?

The song faded into the sound of humanity. Wally leaned his bass into the corner and Padon took off his Gibson to lean it against the back wall. He took a deep breath to steady nerves and held his hands up in a gesture that begged silence. He was pleasantly pleased they responded.

"Thank you for your attention," he began, nervously but gaining on confidence, "can we get a nice hand for Wally on bass? Brilliant, and he's never heard any of these tunes before, amazing," he shook his head in homage. "We both appreciate you digging the music and not turning up the jukebox!" They laughed and shook their own heads 'no'!

"As you all know I was kind of dead when they brought me to Rock Ridge," he stopped to chuckle, and many joined him." Still cracks me up. Kind of dead in more ways than I knew. I want to thank some people, some people without whom, well, I wouldn't be here. Jeannie found my carcass by the side of the road and, rather than leave me for coyote bait, decided to wrestle a dead man into her truck and bring me here. I can never repay, never give back, never..." he wiped his eyes as he walked over to embrace her for several minutes, then kissed her and embraced her again. He was not the only person who wiped his eyes and thunderous round of applause covered the sobs of joy and thanks.

"And then there are the miracle workers—to the two finest, most wonderful human beings on the planet, Doctor JoAnn Caldwell and Janet Jackson," he shrugged, and his eyes twinkled.

Janet scowled and mouthed, "How did you know?"

"I asked someone, then asked two more because I didn't believe the first person." He laughed loud and long. "It fits, this town, these people, just perfect!" He hugged her deep and kissed her on each eye, each check, and hugged her more. Then he held on to Doctor Caldwell for all both were worth, tears flowed freely mixed with smiles and hugs.

"I was born five years before her. I was the first one!" Laughed the real Janet Jackson.

"Five?" said a voice very similar to Doc Caldwell's.

"They who sat by my bedside and nursed me back to health, or a reasonable facsimile thereof. They held my hand. Calmed me. Took away my fear. Fed me and shared their fine Irish whiskey. There is no amount of money or anything that I could give to show my undying — literally — thanks. I owe you more than my life. I owe my friendship, love and honor. Respect for the best, kindest folks I have ever known. It would seem I am surrounded by very strong brilliant, good women who are much smarter that I." He, again, nodded to them both.

"Got that right," said a voice very similar to one Janet Jackson.

The three embraced together and wept and embraced and hugged. Words will never do, but love said an awful lot.

"To Bobby for caring for my dead Buick. He's a good man and a better mechanic." He shook Bobby's hand while he motioned to the bartender to get Bobby another beer and anything else he wanted. "To Mr. Carpenter, the honoree this evening for not only being the oldest man on the planet but the most wise and honest man I have ever met. A rare quality." He tipped the glass of bourbon that has found its way into his hand from the ancient one who nodded his thanks.

"And to my friends at the Café, who took me in and taught me about the glory of hard work and shared burdens, I love you all." Again, another tip of the glass. "But there is someone who I must thank most of all, for she gave me the most."

"She took in a, literally again, broke down, worn out musician and showed me how to work. She was patient and forgiving and watched over me like a mother hen with a sickly chick. Maggie was a shoulder to lean on and had an ear to listen. She is, like apparently everyone in this small town, of the finest cloth and the sturdiest soul. She is also quite easy on the eye." He barked a loud and erotic laugh. Did she actually blush? Hmm. "One more thing, to tell you what kind of a person Maggie is, she knew how much losing my phone came to mean to me and rather than blowing that concern off, she and Jeannie went out into the winter, Thursday, knowing, after two months the chance of finding it was nil. They found it." He held up the phone for all to see the miracle. Thunderous applause and handshakes of congratulations, thanks, hugs to Maggie and Jeannie for being what this town was truly about.

"It was my connection to my world, to my path back to the musical community I knew, my friends and fellow players and writers. She gave it back to me." He nodded his thanks.

"I had come to these mountains to die," he said to the now hushed crowd. "I had given up. My career was in ruins and a pile of smoldering ashes of broken dreams and a wasted life."

Doctor Caldwell took a step toward the stage to stop this, but he stayed her with a look. "No," he whispers, "we are here to celebrate the life of a very brilliant and honest man, let us do that with honesty.

"I'd given up and just wanted to end the suffering. But you folks would not allow that on your watch." They nodded and murmured their agreement. "You pulled me, literally, from death's door and made me whole. Apparently, I was not the first to be saved in this amazing conglomeration of humanity." Again, much agreement and a few hugs, arms wrapping each other in shared salvation.

"I couldn't wrap my head around people like you. I had never met people like you. Never! In all my travels, over all the years. People who cared, not because of what I could do, or sing, or play, or what I'd been. You didn't know. You didn't care about that. You cared about me. Maggie cared about me. Just me." He stopped to wipe a stray tear that had gotten lost along his cheek.

"This afternoon I got this text from a well-placed A and R guy in New York City," he held out his phone so he could read from the screen and they would know he spoke truth, "Hey Padon, thought you fell off the planet, love the new tunes, let's talk about tour and recording." He read, though more from memory after reading it and rereading it a hundred times today. "They are offering me my dream." And he let the phrase hang in the air.

Quiet suffocates the party. A hushed whisper from the back of the room rang like a shot in the dark. Silence fell like a death knell.

"So, you're leaving," Maggie's voice was flat, accusatory, a statement not a question.

'Maybe," he stated.

"What does that mean?" Her arms crossed just under her breasts, her fingers digging into her own arms. "You got what you wanted — what you've been chasing your entire life. What is there to think about? Take your songs and go!" The intensity of her muted words shouted their hurt. "What is there to maybe about?" Her eyes challenged him to dispute her summation!

"It means this, if I don't leave, will you go out with me?" He did not smile. He was not joking. He stared at her.

"What?"

"You heard me, if I don't leave, will you go out with me?"

Someone dropped a pin but caught it before it could crash to the floor and break the tension and perfect quiet.

"Are you asking me out? In front of all these people?" Maggie took a step towards the stage before rocking back on her other heel. Padon couldn't tell if it was because she was going to say yes or strangle him.

"You catch on quick," a smile spread across his lips.

"Let me get this straight — the thing you've hoped for, prayed would happen for years is being given to you on a silver platter, but you'll throw it aside if I go out with you?" She is incredulous and not believing a thing he says at this point.

"Succinct and true." His stance was casual, but his look challenged.

"Why?"

"I've truly waited and wanted for few things in my life. Some I've come close to; some I never could even imagine. Most were no more than childish hopes. I guess I never really knew what I wanted — what I truly was waiting for. I think I waited for you. But, see, when I finally came across you, I had nothing to give, nothing to offer. All I ever had was the road and another stage, another place to run to while I ran from the last one. I was a broke-down-never-was, of a musician who was trying to die without a pot to piss in before he did.

"And here, I was just a guy, found by the side of the road dead. Like an old couch, I was refuse. I had to find my worth. To me, to you, to this town.

"I didn't like me, and I didn't like where I was at. To give that up and to stay here and try to win you would have been cheap, easy. I wasn't giving anything up, I wasn't invested. I was hiding. I was looking for a place to fade, to dissolve. That was what I offered.

"I had to have something, something I wanted bad, Something I had chased and finally held. Something I could taste, to say to you: you are worth giving that up for. I'm not asking for anything more than a chance. A date. A real date, and we'll take it from there. But if you'll give me that chance, I stay and work for you. I will work for you in all ways and earn you. If you don't want me after that, I will leave you alone." He made his case, stated his intentions in front of the whole damn town. His cards were on the table and he was naked to the world.

Her posture loosened, and she grinned, "Well, you sure know how to woo a girl," she muttered just loud enough.

"Well?" Said just about everybody in the bar.

"I'm not the easiest person in the world to get along with, you know," she began, and the crowd moaned.

"Jesus," someone muttered and another shushed.

"What if..." she began again.

"Then we'll deal with what if when we get to it," he took a step towards her. And she towards him.

It was an embrace a lifetime in the making, for both of them. She earned this as much as he, though he didn't know that, but he would. They both stood on the precipice of the skyscraper and held each other from falling off. Lips met, and the world began to spin, the cosmos to move and the universe to breathe. The cheering was loud and raucous. The hugs and slaps on the back convivial. And the warmest came from Doctor Caldwell and Ms. Jackson.

He took the stage once more and begged for quiet. "We didn't get married, it's just a date," he called to boisterous laughter, but the joy overflowed. He motioned for Wally to join him once again on the stage. "You got a bow?" asked Padon quietly. Wally nodded. "This is kind of a classical piece, in a way," Padon warned.

"Julliard, '85." Wally pointed at himself.

The room settled and Padon began to play his masterpiece.

ABOUT THE AUTHOR

After a life on the road performing as a singer/songwriter and Comedian, releasing eight music albums, three comedy CD's and a DVD, I have turned my creative energies to one of my great loves; reading. I have loved to read since I was very young and discovered a long time ago, I was never bored, lonely or without marvelous entertainment as long as I had a book. I have written and published three books, American Stories, in 2017, Z, my father's biography, in 2018, and Carrie Come To Me Smiling, also in 2018. For the record I am 65 years old, have been married to my love for 34 years, have two grown, wonderful daughters and a Bearded Collie, Greta. Enjoy life, travel, exploring. I have performed in 49 states, Canada, Ireland and beyond. I love to write music, comedy and stories. Slainte!

Made in the USA
Middletown, DE
11 April 2023

28560152R00149